THE DUKE I CAME FOR

The Ashton Park Series
Book Four

Abigail Bridges

ARE YOU SIGNED UP FOR DRAGONBLADE'S BLOG?

You'll get the latest news and information on exclusive giveaways, exclusive excerpts, coming releases, sales, free books, cover reveals and more.

Check out our complete list of authors, too!

No spam, no junk. That's a promise!

Sign Up Here

www.dragonbladepublishing.com

Dearest Reader;

Thank you for your support of a small press. At Dragonblade Publishing, we strive to bring you the highest quality Historical Romance from some of the best authors in the business. Without your support, there is no 'us', so we sincerely hope you adore these stories and find some new favorite authors along the way.

Happy Reading!

CEO, Dragonblade Publishing

Additional Dragonblade books by Author Abigail Bridges

The Ashton Park Series
To Stop a Scoundrel (Book 1)
A Rogue Like You (Book 2)
Nothing But a Rake (Book 3)
The Duke I Came For (Book 4)
By the Rosemary Tree (Novella)

The Lyon's Den Series
Into the Lyon of Fire

Dedication

To my writing tribe
Jamie C., Bonnie, Jack, and all my encouragers. You continue to
make this journey possible.

PART ONE

Timmons Manor

CHAPTER ONE

Friday, 9 September 1825
Timmons Manor
Litton, Skipton, Yorkshire
Half-past noon

L ADY ELIZABETH AMINTA Emalyn Ashton stood in front of the austere granite structure awaiting an answer to her second rather boisterous round of knocking. Behind her, the team of four that had pulled the Ashton ducal carriage from London over the past twenty days stomped restlessly, tossing their heads. Beth understood how they felt. She too could use a refreshing beverage and a pleasant place to rest.

At her side, her maid Kendall also stirred. "Are we certain, my lady, this is the correct location?"

Beth pushed down her own doubts. Her sister-in-law Rose had given her quite detailed instructions on how to reach the home of her aunt. Lady Sophia Timmons, the sister of Rose's father, the Earl of Huntingdale, lived a rather secluded life in a country house in the dales of Yorkshire, but Beth and her coachman had reviewed the instructions on each of the past twenty days, as well as inquiring at the homes and inns where they stayed along the way. She was more than certain they had arrived at the right destination. "The sign at the end of the road did say 'Timmons Manor.'"

"A rather tawdry sign."

Which had hung from only one chain, the left side drooping precariously. It matched the general atmosphere of the house. The double wooden doors in front of them appeared sturdy, but paint peeled away in strips, and streaks of rust cascaded down from the ancient knocker. Overall, the house appeared rather abandoned.

Beth took a deep breath and reached to knock again, only to have the door open a mere five inches. The wary blue eyes that appeared in that opening were not quite four feet off the ground.

"Who're ya?" The voice, thin and reedy, had an ostentatious tone for such a tiny person.

Beth cleared her throat. "I am Lady Elizabeth Ashton. I am here to see Lady Sophia Timmons."

"Don' believe ya. Aunt Sophie don' see nobody."

"Mattie!" The high-pitched screech came from deep within the house.

The door slammed and the sound of running footsteps faded behind it. Beth looked at Kendall, her eyes wide. "What was that all about?"

The door jerked open wide, causing Beth to step back, bumping into Kendall, both of them stumbling to stay upright. This time Beth stared up . . . and up . . . at a man in a simple black and white livery. He seemed to match the house, with his graying hair and frayed seams. Rail thin, he towered over Beth, who was not a small woman, having inherited her father's height and broad, Scandinavian frame. Her eyes narrowed as she peered up at him, and he straightened his shoulders.

"Lady Elizabeth Ashton?"

"I am."

He gave a curt nod. "Please come in. I will give your servants directions to the back entrance."

Beth hesitated as he moved out of the door frame. She glanced at Kendall, whose eyes still held doubt, but she nodded.

Beth stepped into the entrance hall as the man gave Kendall and the coachmen their instructions. Unlike the outside of the manor, the two-story space was well-kept and spotless. Black and white tile, in a mosaic pattern of a bygone era, covered the floor. Windows of leaded glass over and beside the door let in pleasant streams of sunlight, as did the entrance to what appeared to be a lush garden at the back of the manor. Two doors stood in parallel positions to either side, with a sturdy but plain stairway in front of her, just in front of the garden doors. To either side of the staircase, archways opened on to twin corridors.

The front door shut, and the man moved around Beth to face her. He gestured to the first door on the right. "Please wait in Sophie—Lady Sophia's—receiving room. She will join you in a moment."

"Thank you." Beth moved into the room. As with the entrance hall, this room spoke of wealth and welcome, although it was small, barely large enough for the sparse furnishings. A low ceiling with its wooden beams spoke of the manor's age. Sunlight also illuminated this room, casting bright rays over a settee and two cabriolet armchairs clustered around a narrow, low table. Their blue and cream upholstery matched the pale blue of the walls and plush cushions on the settee, giving the room a warm, feminine feel. An overstuffed wingback and accent table sat near the window. A prodigious stack of books on the table seemed to totter a bit, even though nothing around them moved, and Beth found the effect somewhat mesmerizing.

"Oh, my dear, do sit down! You must be exhausted from your journey."

Beth started, pivoting to face the voice, which belonged to a woman whose appearance fascinated Beth almost as much as that stack of books. While Rose had not described Lady Sophia Timmons in detail, Beth had expected her to be like most of the elderly aunts she had known over the past eighteen years—frail, gray, and somewhat rumpled.

Instead Lady Sophia Timmons stood ramrod straight and

almost as tall as Beth. Her face held only a few faint lines around her brown eyes, although her black hair—which was caught up in a neat braid that trailed down her back—held a few shimmers of gray. Her frame, lithe and taut, looked quite elegant in a simple dark green muslin day gown. Sturdy leather day boots encased her feet. She gestured again for Beth to sit.

"I know you must be famished. Have you had luncheon? I have asked Notley to add you and your servants to our tables for luncheon."

Beth shook her head as she perched on the edge of a settee. "We have not. Thank you."

"We luncheon precisely at one o'clock, so you will not have time to change. I hope you do not mind."

Beth shook her head again, still trying to find her sea legs. "I appreciate it, as will my servants. I am grateful you have invited me to stay."

"Not at all. The more the merrier."

What did that mean?

"Will your coachmen be staying long?"

Beth swallowed. "Overnight, if that's permissible. They could return to the village—"

"Nonsense. My groom will find them space. They plan to leave tomorrow?"

"Yes. It is quite the journey."

"Oh, I have made it several times. But I can think of dozens of things I would prefer to do than visit London." She smiled. "And you will probably discover that I would not fit in well any longer with all the balls and soirees. And I do apologize for the unorthodox welcome. We were not expecting you until tomorrow. We do not receive many visitors anymore."

Beth straightened. "I apologize if we have inconvenienced you. We were not sure what the roads would be like. As it turned out, it has been so hot, they were all packed as stone. We made the journey a little faster than expected."

"Not at all, my dear. Your bedchamber has been ready for

two days, as has the one for your maid."

A movement in the doorway caught Beth's eye, and she leaned slightly to the right, trying to spot what had caused a shift in the light.

Without looking behind her, Lady Sophia spoke firmly. "Come in, Mattie. It is impolite to lurk like a prowling wolf."

Beth glanced from her hostess to the small child that emerged from behind a settee. Mattie pressed against the arm of Lady Sophia's chair, and the older woman placed a hand on the child's back. Unruly golden curls framed the child's face, and those wide blue eyes remained wary.

"Mattie, this is Lady Elizabeth Ashton. She is from London. She will be staying with us for a few weeks."

The child gave Lady Sophia a sharp look. "Like the others? She don' look like she—"

"Lady Elizabeth, this is Mattie. She and her mother are guests of the household, recently arrived as well."

Others? The questions were gathering in droves in Beth's head. "We have met. Hello, again, Mattie."

Lady Sophia gave a low chuckle. "We have been trying to train her not to answer the door, but the lessons have obviously not taken hold as of yet."

Beth peered at the child. "I am sure she will learn quickly, clever girl that she is. She would not want to put Mr. Notley off his job, surely."

Those blue eyes widened.

Lady Sophia urged Mattie toward the door. "That is quite enough excitement for the moment. Run tell the others we will have guests for luncheon."

Mattie seemed to vanish from the room.

"Lady Sophia—"

"Please. Call me Sophie. Almost everyone in the house does. We are quite informal here." She paused, studying Beth. "I do hope you were not expecting the typical Society protocol to be adhered to while you were here."

Beth let out a long exhale. "Precisely the opposite, in fact. Society protocol has left my entire family in agony this season, and I was hoping to get as far away from it as possible."

Sophie nodded. "Ah, yes. Your young marquess. Whom Rose explained set you aside not because you did not suit him but because of your brother. Do I have that correct?"

Beth winced but forced a smile. "You do. My brother Robert has become embroiled in a scandal featuring a gambling hell and brothel, which has shadowed the entire family. I am convinced my mother and father can sort it all out, but the beau monde can react rather quickly, given the least hint of scandal. The marquess and I were not betrothed, but we had an understanding and would have been within a week or so when the scandal broke. The marquess wanted to continue, but his father would not have it."

"Being a duke with a high standing in the *ton*."

Beth nodded. "I liked Ludlow—the marquess—but I did not realize he had so little spine."

Sophie snorted a laugh. "Men seldom do when their family name and fortune is on the line. They will side with propriety every time, no matter who is hurt as a result. I am sorry you had to endure that, although I am thrilled you have a plan to persevere."

Beth smiled. "I am influenced by my mother in that. She is one of the most determined women I have ever met."

"How is she doing?"

"Then you have heard—"

"We are not that far removed from London. It only feels like it at times. I know your mother has been seriously ill."

Beth's stomach tightened, as it usually did when she thought about her mother's condition. "She collapsed from a hemorrhagic apoplexy two months ago. When I left, she was improving, but the doctor said it will be a hard recovery."

Sophie nodded. "It will be. Did you know my brother— Rose's father—had suffered from the same?"

"Rose told us. It's given us a lot of hope that Lord Hunting-dale is doing so well."

"He is, but it was a long struggle back to full health."

Notley appeared in the doorway, clearing his throat.

"Ah. That will be luncheon." She leaned a little closer to Beth. "Although you will find that the locals call our mid-day meal dinner. 'Luncheon' is something the nobility uses. Very high and mighty. Do not let it confuse you, as that will point you out as a foreigner." Sophie stood, grinning. "A Londoner."

Beth returned the smile as she removed her bonnet and gloves and left them on the settee. "I will try to remember."

She followed Sophie through the entrance hall and down the corridor that branched left. Wood-paneled with little decoration on the walls, the area remained dimly lit. They passed a room that appeared to be a study or office, then one opposite it that looked like a parlor. Two more doors were closed as was one at the end of the corridor. Sophie pushed open the end door to a blaze of light, and Beth blinked as her eyes adjusted. Then she stopped, staring as six pairs of stern expressions greeted her. Around the formal dining table, six women sat, silent, their glares almost malevolent. Five seats remained empty—one at the head of the table and the chairs to the immediate left and right, and two others near the other end. Sophie took the seat at the head and gestured to the one on her left.

As Beth sat, Sophie motioned to a maid standing near a side-board with a spread of trays and plates of food. She and two other maids began serving tea and the first course to those at the table.

Where are the footmen? Beth glanced back at the door, but Notley had also vanished.

"My friends, this is Lady Elizabeth Ashton. She will be staying with us for a few weeks. She is the sister-in-law and a dear friend of my niece, Lady Rose Tim—" Sophie caught herself. "Lady Newbury. Formerly Lady Rose Timmons. Lady Elizabeth—"

"Please. Just Beth."

Sophie gave her a quick smile. "Beth, these ladies are also my guests."

A sniff sounded from the far end of the table, and a woman with bright red curls stiffened in her chair. "So who the devil did you piss off?"

RICHARD CHRISTOPHER CAUDALE, Eighth Duke of Kirkstone, pushed through the heavy wooden door of The Queen's Arms pub in Litton, feeling far more like a bucket of bull's piss than the member of the nobility he was. Weariness clutched every muscle, every bone, and he longed for rest and refreshment. After being doused in a rainstorm two days before, a low fever had set in and a chill shivered through him as he ducked to pass under the door's header, then straightened and cast a glance around the cozy room. Kit enjoyed a good pub, and the blending scents of ale, venison, lamb, bread, and spices felt like a welcoming embrace.

"Can I help ya, sir?" The man approaching had just settled trenchers of food on a nearby table. He wiped his hands on a cloth he then draped over his shoulder. His hairline sat a ways back on his head, and he was almost a foot shorter than Kit—most men were—and his woolen clothes were well-made if rumpled and frayed.

"Are you the proprietor?"

The man put his arms akimbo, elbows out. "Yes, sir, I'm the owner."

Kit glanced around again. Several of the patrons had turned in his direction, their expressions suspicious. Not unusual in a country pub, and Kit knew he would not be given the automatic deference his title usually brought, especially not here—or with the way he looked. "Sir, I need a room for the night and a bath. Food for me and a stall and fodder for my horse. Rations for my travel. Can you accommodate me?"

"We can. Have you coin?"

Kit shrugged a pack from his shoulder, one of only two he still traveled with after four months of searching for his sister through every small town in the north of England. The other was draped over his horse's rump. "How much?"

The proprietor's eyes narrowed as he looked Kit from the chapeau on his head to the muddy boots on his feet. His clothes were filthy and he smelled to high heaven, but his clothes—the black woolen trousers, topcoat, and overcoat—were finely made and tailored to his broad frame. Expensive.

"For everything? A guinea."

Kit pulled the money from the pack. "Plus six shillings tomorrow for whoever takes good care of my horse."

The man took the money. His focus still on Kit, he bellowed, "Johnny!"

A thin lad appeared in a door near the entrance. "Ya, da?"

The owner nodded at Kit. "Take care of this man's horse. Out front."

The boy darted out the front door behind Kit, vanishing in an instant.

"He'll do ya good. He's good with the animals. Which do ya want first? The food or the bath?" His nose wrinkled.

Kit chuckled. "I need the food more than I need the bath, if you can believe."

"I can. You look like you been on the road a spell."

"Four months. I am depleted, in every way possible."

The owner put out his hand. "I'm Keales. Sam Keales."

Kit shook the man's hand. "I know a pawnbroker in London named Keales."

The owner grinned. "Cousin. Notorious in our family."

Kit nodded, smiling. "I have no doubt."

Keales gestured to a nearby table. "Have a preference on fare?"

"Whatever is ready the fastest." Kit sat on a bench beside the table and dropped his pack on the floor, tucking it behind his knees and stepping on one of the straps for safety. He knew every customer in the pub had seen him draw the money from it, and he was taking no chances. He'd been in more than a few brawls over money before he had gained the wisdom to disguise his rank.

Just a small part of the hell the last four months had been. The first two weeks, he had traveled with his valet Colby, a small carriage, and two trunks. He had returned home, his search fruitless, setting out again with Colby and three horses—one for their gear. He soon discovered, however, that Mary's circuitous route had not been from her confusion but for anyone who tried to follow her. He had tracked the clues she had left as far north as Carlisle and as far south as Manchester. Dead ends abounded, frustrating Kit to the point of constant rage. As his search ranged wider and into more gritty locales, he had sent his valet and the packhorse home. His title mattered less to those he encountered than the coin in his pack, so he used that to his advantage, paying sources only to find out his sister, who had absconded with a substantial amount of money, had come before him.

Acquiring information had become a bidder's war, some of which he had lost; all of which had led him here, to this cozy pub in a hamlet not sixty miles from his home in the Kirkstone Pass. Kit's exhaustion, fever, and barely tamped-down fury ran bone deep, and he had already decided that if his current information did not pan out, he would turn home and officially disown his sister, cutting all ties and leaving her to whatever fate Mary had chosen.

All because he and his mother had refused to let her marry the local vicar.

A vicar! A man almost three times her age, when she had not even had her first season. She would have debuted in the spring. The trousseau had been ordered, the town house rented, servants acquired. Mary and their mother would have traveled south at the first sign of a decent thaw, before the roads turned to spring slush. Instead, she had dug in, professed love for a widower who had obviously taken advantage of her youth, and refused to give ground.

What a waste!

"Here ya go, sir." Keales slid a trencher in front of Kit. The aroma of the venison pie wafted up, making his senses sing. Along with the two pies, the trencher held a hunk of fragrant cheese, slices of fresh black bread, and two pears. Keales set a stein of ale next to it.

Kit inhaled deeply. "A feast for a weary soul."

Keales grinned. "I will tell my wife you said so." He knocked twice on the table. "When you need more ale . . ."

Kit gave a nod, then addressed the food with relish. He had not eaten in more than a day, being out of travel rations and preferring to push on to this inn over restocking. The pies filled him with a spreading warmth, as did the ale. The cheese was lush on his tongue, pairing well with the black bread and pears. He gradually grew sated, his fury tamping down a bit farther.

Two days ago, he had met a tinker near a crossroads to the north who had more information than the man realized and more need for money and rum than integrity. Kit had put together several pieces of his sister's puzzling disappearance. That she had spread misinformation through friends to put searchers off her path. That she had been told about a "house of women" where she could find sanctuary. That such a house was hidden deep in the Yorkshire Dales, perhaps even a country estate of some kind. Gentry, or even possibly belonging to the aristocracy.

When asked about local landowners, the tinker, plied with almost a full pint of rum, waved him off. "Tain't many round heres. Maybe one or two. Mostly tenant farmers. Owners all down in London somewheres." After thinking a moment, he took a pull on a foul-smelling pipe and whispered, "'Cept the crazy one. Woman. Lady Sophia . . . something. Up near Litton. Between the fells. I tried to take my wares out there, years ago, but one of the farmers set the dogs on me. Never went back."

"Litton."

He had puffed out that nasty smoke. "Talk to the pub owner. Queen's Arms. He'll know. If not him, then the innkeep down in Arncliffe."

Draining his stein, Kit got Keales' attention. "One more."

Keales nodded and brought over a pitcher to refill the ale.

"Mind if I ask you for some information?"

Keales paused, turning the pitcher upright and focusing on Kit's face. "Depends on the information."

"I am in search of a woman, Lady Sophia. Do you know where I might find her?"

Keales froze. Everyone else in the pub, however, did not. They all turned to him, and from a chair near the fireplace, a man stood. A man who had the bearing and appearance of the front end of an ox. "Whacha be wantin' with Lady Sophie?"

A woman sitting near the man snagged his elbow. "Hush, Hugh. Sit down!"

Kit glanced at Hugh, the woman, then back to Keales, who still glowered at him. *Interesting.* Kit sniffed. "I owe the lady money. I only wish to repay her."

Keales did not relent. "Your bath is waiting upstairs. Second door, left. I suggest you take it. Stay there. And plan to leave early tomorrow."

"The lady—"

"No one by that name around here."

With that, Keales turned and left, taking any good will toward Kit with him. Hugh sat, glaring, as did several other patrons.

Kit drained his ale. He shivered, then picked up his pack and headed for the stairs. He had definitely come to the right place.

CHAPTER TWO

Friday, 9 September 1825
Timmons Manor
One in the afternoon

BETH BLINKED. ONLY her brothers had ever been so bold with her. She glanced at Sophie, who remained still and quiet as the maid placed a small plate of fruit and cheese in front of her. "I—"

She stopped as her own serving plate clicked into place.

"Our fare," murmured Sophie, "is as our manners."

Beth bit her lower lip against a laugh. She took a deep breath and straightened her shoulders. "At times, it feels as if I pissed off the entire beau monde."

Several of the women snickered, hiding their giggles behind their palms as their expressions relaxed.

The redhead did not relent. "How so? Are you ruined?"

One woman gasped and stared. "Lydia!"

Beth met Lydia's eyes. "At least for this season. But not in the way you might think. My family has become embroiled in more than one scandal. Although none of it had anything to do with me, the man—a marquess—who intended to marry me has set me aside. Anyone set aside by a duke's clan because of scandal is untouchable. I would have been a pariah had I stayed, even though I was not involved in any of the events. I preferred other options."

"So you ran away." Lydia was determined.

"I did. I asked. Sophie offered. I preferred spending time with sheep over dealing with snide comments at every corner in London. As my father told me, retreat is not always a defeat. Sometimes it is the better option in order to recover and redirect." When everyone remained silent a moment, Beth asked, "Why are you here?"

All eyes shifted to Sophie, who popped a piece of cheese in her mouth. She chewed and swallowed, her gaze slipping from one woman to the next, finally settling on Beth. "Everyone is here, including me, for the same reasons as you. We wish to be away. From prying eyes and snipping voices. From the press of family and friends to be something we are not. Did Rose not mention why I have been in Yorkshire for so long?"

Beth shook her head.

Sophie leaned back in her chair. "As I mentioned, I do not fit the *ton's* ideal of how a woman should be, in Society or in the home. My parents presented me with tutors and governesses, and my brother Edmund did everything he could. But as you will see, I have all the grace of a deer on ice—even my modiste despaired of teaching me anything about fashion. I had a season, of course, which was a disaster. When my father won this ancient manor house in a game of whist, I begged to be made its caretaker. It had been abandoned for decades and was quite the ruined pile. Before I could tumble into scandal—and I was most certainly headed that way over marriage to a noble of their choosing—they let me come here. I have been here ever since, rebuilding from the inside out."

Beth suddenly understood the appearance of the place— Sophie had focused on its heart first.

Sophie cut a slice of pear into smaller pieces. "I suspect that it was my nature that enabled Edmund to view Rose's more unusual proclivities with some kindness."

Beth nodded. "He has been quite supportive of her, with a few stumbles."

"We all stumble sooner or later, do we not, my friends."

Most of the women nodded. Lydia hesitated and decided to focus on her food instead.

Sophie took a sip of tea, then surveyed the room again. "Beth, allow me to introduce my friends. To your left, Bertie, Mary, and Lydia. The empty chairs are for Charlotte and Esther who are ill today, then Amelia and Priscilla." She nodded at the chair to her right. "This one is for—"

"Sophie! Notley, where are my darlings?" The bright alto voice echoed from the corridor. "Oh, of course, they are at dinner. What a wretch I am!" Rapid footsteps—like the beat of a wooden drum—sounded on the floor as a woman swept into the room, the skirt of her indigo riding habit swirling around her like waves on the beach. Tall and broad but well-formed, her presence dominated the room—as did the dog that followed her in. Gray and brown with a rough, shaggy coat, it was the largest dog Beth had ever seen, its head almost reaching the woman's waist.

She snapped her fingers and pointed to a corner of the room, and the dog dropped down, panting. She then untied the ribbons of a leather bonnet with a flourish, removing it and draping it over the back of the chair. Her black and silver hair was caught up in a tight chignon, and her dark eyes flashed as she bent to kiss Sophie on the cheek. "I do apologize for being late. It is a beautiful day for a ride, although beastly hot. I am sure I am soaked right through to my—" She straightened and froze a moment, her gaze lighting on Beth. "Oh, my! And who is this who has joined us?"

Sophie grinned. "Daphne, this is Beth. Beth, my friend Daphne."

"She's a lady," muttered Bertie.

Daphne pulled out the chair and dropped into it. "Oh?"

"Lady Elizabeth Ashton."

Sophie's soft words still seemed to hit Daphne abruptly. She leaned back and peered at Beth. "Oh, yes, I remember you were to arrive soon. Escaping that scandal, are we?"

Beth sighed. "Yes."

Daphne grinned. "Do not despair, my girl. We do get newspapers up here, although I suspect I am the only one who reads them. Your brother had quite the tumble, did he not?" She paused as the maid filled her teacup. "Thank you, Lois." She added milk, then sipped. "Well, if you wish to abandon the *ton* and refresh yourself as well as your reputation, you have chosen well. Timmons Manor is a haven for all sorts of women who wish—"

"Daphne, shall we respite in peace?" The words from Sophie were both caution and redirection.

"Hm? Of course." Daphne accepted her fruit and cheese with a smile, then glanced around the table. "I did not mean to disturb dinner." She tossed a piece of cheese at the dog, which caught it with a snap, and turned to Beth. "I love to ride. It invigorates me. Sometimes perhaps too much. Do you ride?"

Beth still felt a bit wobbly with all of this, and she took advantage of the pause given for the first course dishes to be replaced with plates of sliced beef, potatoes, and what appeared to be pickled beets. Platters of bread and plum cakes were set in the middle of the table.

Sophie touched her hand. "I did warn you. Even the way we serve is different here. We find it easier for Cook to prepare the plates, then have Lois and the other maids bring them up. Even supper is served this way. We do not stand on formality as much as practicality."

"I think you will find you will not only become accustomed to it, you will like it." Daphne slipped a bite of pear into her mouth, then one to the dog.

Beth glanced at the maids, who worked silently. "There are no footmen?"

Lydia huffed. "Absolutely not. We do not need—"

"Traditional footmen are difficult to find in an area this remote." Sophie shot a scowl at Lydia. "The local men are all farmers, tradesmen, with no interest in service. We hire mostly women, and when they are well trained, we provide references if they wish to search for a position in a larger house or one with more of a social life. The only men on the property are Notley, our groom Mr. Mead, and our gardener Mr. Hervey."

"Preferably so," muttered Lydia, which earned her another dark glance from Sophie.

Daphne set aside her fruit and accepted the meat plate from Lois. "So. Do you ride?"

The beef and potatoes were quite tasty, and Beth realized exactly how hungry she was. She took another bite before answering. "I do. I have a rather well-trained mount, Bella, but I had to leave her behind."

"Excellent! I would love a riding partner. Sophie does not ride—"

"I ride. I simply do not care for it."

"—and we have several horses trained for female riders. So they won't spook from a woman's habit. Did you bring one with you?"

Beth shook her head. "Mostly the essentials." She nodded at Sophie. "Rose told me not to expect parties or soirees."

"Ha!" Daphne reached for bread. "Right she was. You can borrow one of mine. Does your maid alter? I assume you brought a maid?"

"I did. Kendall. And she's quite good."

"We are about the same height, but I think you are more slender. A sash or two should make it work. I have reached that age where good food lingers much longer on the waist and bu—"

"Daphne."

"Hips." She leaned toward Sophie. "I promise I was going to say hips."

"Of course you were."

The woman next to Lydia snickered, then covered her mouth. Lydia glared.

"After pudding we can go to my room and pick one out." Daphne glanced at Sophie. "Which room is she in?"

"The Tulip Room."

Daphne brightened. "Right next to me. And I will give you a tour of the house and grounds. It is larger than it looks from the front and can be confusing."

"Daphne."

"Well, we would not want her getting lost, now would we?"

Sophie stilled. "No." Then she straightened and smiled at Beth. "Do not allow Daphne to overwhelm you. I know you must be exhausted from your journey."

Beth already felt a little overwhelmed, which probably *was* her exhaustion. She had maneuvered through most of the London season with aplomb until Ludlow had turned his back. And she had a certain familiarity with country estates. Such a place should not be all that confusing. Still . . . "I am grateful. Thank you. I know it will take a few days to settle in." She smiled at Daphne. "I appreciate the help."

Beth also found she was glad Lois appeared through a servants' door at the end of the room bearing a tray of raspberry tarts. Everyone turned their focus onto the puddings instead of her. As they scooped into the tarts, Beth felt a touch of relief. She was tired, bone weary. The days in the carriage had felt endless, and she questioned more than once this decision to travel so far from home just to evade a scandal, which might have passed by the time she had arrived at Timmons Manor. Even her mother—one of the world's most impatient people—had cautioned her, but the days that passed waiting for Sophie's response had been equally unsettling and disturbing.

Her family did not need her, including her mother, which had made Beth feel more excluded than ever. It had become abundantly clear that she was now aimless as well as useless, with nothing left of the season for her—no invitations, no new gowns, no callers. Beth felt as if she had spent a lifetime preparing for her debut, only to have everything evaporate overnight. One stroll in the park with Michael had made it all too obvious Beth had become a pariah. Even her friends had stopped visiting or sending messages. And there was only so much reading or needlework she could tolerate to fill her days.

She needed . . . *something* . . . to focus on.

Daphne wiped a smudge of raspberry from her lips and stood. "Come with me?"

Beth followed, expecting Daphne to do most of the talking, and the lady did not disappoint. The dog trotted along beside them, and Beth gave it a wary glance. But as soon as the dining room door shut, Beth heard an explosion of questions, and Daphne paused, chuckling, her hand reaching down to scratch the dog's head. "They were dying of curiosity, but they dared not ask anything with you in the room. I am certain they will quiz Sophie on every detail she knows."

"Since news of my brother's scandal broke, I suspect my life has been fodder for many conversations. I have tried to ignore them, but it is somewhat like wandering into a beehive and pretending the bees do not exist. Or sting."

Daphne's grin broadened. "A good approach, however. A bee swarm can be quite useful, when treated in the right way."

"Speaking of stings"—Beth gestured at the dog—"I assume he does not . . ."

"Boru? Not unless you threaten us." Her eyes gazed at the dog with tenderness as she scratched behind his ears. The dog responded with a gaze of pure adoration. "He's a lovey. Irish wolfhound. Gentle but a great hunter. He goes with me when I ride but is not much for conversation." She continued walking. "I do have to ask. Why Timmons Manor instead of your own family's country estate?"

Beth fell into step beside her. "Ashton Park is less than a half-day's carriage ride from London. And in another month, my mother will begin preparations for the annual Christmas house party. I wanted to get much farther away from the beau monde, and Rose has spoken so kindly about her aunt, I thought I might find a place here. In truth, I am at a loss. My life had been focused on my first season and marriage. I am not entirely sure what I am to do."

"Being at Timmons Manor will definitely be a different experience." Daphne gestured to the two closed doors. "These rooms are kept closed. One is a parlor that is rarely used. The other is storage for our staff." They continued down the corridor. "This one is Sophie's study and library. She spends much of her day here. The room across is a common area for our guests to gather, to read, to play games, or do needlework. Socialize. They all have private bedchambers on the third floor, and we ask you to respect that privacy. There is nothing else on the third floor except an old classroom that has been empty for the past twenty years. I believe the housekeeper uses it to store linens and old clothes, so they do not have to traipse up to the attics."

Beth frowned. "Since I am a guest, would not my bedchamber be on the third floor?"

Daphne shook her head. "There are none available. The Tulip Room is on the second floor with Sophie's and mine. There is an adjacent dressing room and small bedchamber that your maid will use. There are two more bedchambers on that floor, but they have been empty for some time."

Daphne paused at the foot of the stairs and pointed to the doors on the entrance hall. "You've seen our main receiving room. Across from it is a formal parlor intended for more official meetings with guests. Sophie primarily uses it to meet with the vicar, who comes by about once a month, or the doctor, who occasionally drops by. They are both in Arncliffe, which is about three miles south. The closest church is St. Oswald's there."

"I think we passed through on the way."

"Sweet little village. We get most of our supplies there as Litton is too small for many shops. Although we sometimes make an outing of it and go all the way to Skipton." Daphne pointed down the other corridor. "The two doors on the right are the manor library. You are welcome to borrow any book you choose, but there is a ledger to sign when you take one out. It is also a comfortable place to write letters, if you wish. There is an escritoire with foolscap, ink, quills, and wax. Our bedchambers are smaller than most of those in the city." She paused. "Across— I'll show you that room on another day. It's best seen rather than described." She pointed up the stairs. "Up we go!"

Beth lifted her hem and followed Daphne, who trotted up the stairs in an almost childlike manner, and Beth hurried to catch her near the top. Her exhaustion had worn down both her energy and her mind. She felt foggy, barely taking in the information Daphne spelled out as she strode forward, pointing out the rooms. "Sophie's. Mine. Rose Room, empty. Lily Room, empty"—these were across the corridor—"and they are almost identical to the Tulip Room. Servants' stair at the end." She stopped in front of one door and pushed it open. "This is yours."

"Oh!" Across the room, Kendall started in surprise. She stood in front of a trunk, and many of Beth's clothes were spread across the bed.

"Kendall, I presume?" Daphne asked.

Beth grinned. "Yes."

The maid's eyes widened as she spotted the hound, and she halted.

Daphne saw the fear and turned to her dog. "Boru. Down." She pointed at the doorway and Boru stretched out on the floor.

Beth turned her attention to the room itself. As Daphne had warned, it was significantly smaller than her bedchamber at Ashton House in London, but it held all the essential necessities for a lady's existence—a lovely four-poster bed draped with blue and gold covers and pillows with a matching bench at the end, a dressing table, a chest of drawers, a washstand with an elegant porcelain pitcher and basin, and a screen in one corner than no doubt hid a chamber pot. The walls, a blue so pale it was almost white, were painted instead of covered in wallpaper. An open area separated the bed from a small fireplace with a polished marble mantle, on which sat an ormolu clock, ticking softly, and a small wingback nearby. Small signs of wealth blended with practicality in a room that was clean and light.

A vase of red and yellow tulips sat atop the chest of drawers, and Beth blinked. "Tulips?"

Daphne grinned. "I promise to explain all later."

Her mother would have loved it.

So did Beth. "This is delightful."

Daphne seemed to glow. "Excellent. Now, we can let Kendall proceed. Come next door and we will choose a riding kit for you."

Beth followed her into the next room. This bedchamber, unlike the Tulip Room, had a darker ambiance, decorated primarily in deep browns and golds, but held the same furnishings. Daphne opened a door near the fireplace that lead Beth into a spacious dressing room filled with shelves, racks, two modiste's fitting forms, and an upholstered bench near a door on the other side of the room.

Beth stared at the door a moment, realizing abruptly that Sophie and Daphne occupied the rooms that would have been used by the master and mistress of the house. When she turned to Daphne the woman was watching her with bemusement in her eyes.

"It is a matter of convenience. Unlike you, we do not have maids. So we help each other."

"But what if you were to marry?"

Daphne shrugged one shoulder. "Then I would move to another room and we would both employ maids." She turned back to the shelves, searching them for a few moments, then pulling out two stacks of ruby red wool and handing them to Beth. "These should do." She paused. "I think you should rest this afternoon. You are beginning to look quite drained. Supper is at seven, and Lois leaves fruit and pastries out until late, should you desire something later in the evening. We will ride in the morning after breakfast. Which is at nine. It will be cooler then. I think this wretchedly hot summer is finally cooling off."

"I . . . I think that is a better plan."

"Excellent. Then I will see you for supper."

With surprising efficiency and gentleness, Daphne herded Beth back to her room and closed the door. Beth looked at Kendall for a surprised moment as the sounds of Daphne's heels and Boru's toenails faded down the stairs. "Was your afternoon as extraordinary as mine?"

Kendall slipped some of Beth's small clothes into a drawer in the tall chest and slid it shut. "I have no doubt."

Beth laid the riding kit on the bed and slowly told Kendall her experience at luncheon . . . dinner. Kendall explained how her afternoon had been somewhat similar—odd habits and a subtle secrecy—ending in one question. "What is going on in this house?"

Beth sank down on the bed. "I do not know. But I suspect we are going to have the most interesting autumn."

Saturday, 10 September 1825
St. Oswald's Church, Arncliffe
Half-past nine in the morning

KIT GLOWERED AT the vicar. The man moved around the small kitchen with all the efficiency and speed of a garden slug. Bald except for twin tufts of white hair over his ears, the man's stooped shoulders and shuffled steps told Kit that Mr. Alred would not be the vicar much longer so Kit tried to swallow his frustration. He had barely slept at The Queen's Arms, partially from the noise—which he suspected was intentional—and partially from the fever that had kept him shivering through the early morning hours and had led to a crushing headache. Keales had awakened him early, insisting Kit be on his way and providing neither breakfast nor rations for traveling.

His stomach growled and the pain in his head crept down his

neck. He ignored both sensations. "The owner at the Arncliffe inn said you knew everyone and everything in the county."

The old man nodded and set two cups of tea on the kitchen table with a clatter. "I do. I do. But Mr. Godwin has only been here a few years. Married the previous owner's daughter during one of her jaunts to Leeds. Many people in Arncliffe could tell you the same as I can. But I am pleased to hear that some folks in this village still think of me as the arbiter of history. Milk?" He pushed a small pitcher toward Kit.

Kit did not take milk in his tea, but after one sip, he winced at the dark and exceptionally bitter brew and reached for the pitcher.

The vicar gave him a sly grin. "I always brewed by sight, I am afraid, and that is dimming rapidly." He sipped his own—and grimaced. "Obviously." He held out his hand, and Kit slid the pitcher toward his host. "Now, what are your questions and why are you asking them?"

Kit straightened. After his encounter with Keales, he had decided a less direct approach might be in order. "I have been searching for my sister. She disappeared four months ago. She is quite young, so at first we thought she had been abducted, which was horror enough for my mother. But it became apparent my sister had simply fled the—simply fled. As happens with some young women, she can be both innocent and foolish, and her mother and I are mortified that she will be ruined by this. I must find her. I have tracked her through much of the north, and my last clue was that she had found refuge in this area with a woman named Sophia."

The vicar pursed his lips, peering into his cup, then he squinted up at Kit. "You do not look like a noble, but you most certainly sound like one. Eton?"

Kit hesitated. "Harrow."

Nodding slowly, the vicar moved several books on the far end of the table until he located a pair of spectacles. He perched them on his nose and adjusted the frames over his ears. He made another examination of Kit. "Who is your family?"

Kit sighed in resignation. "Kirkstone."

The bowed shoulders straightened a bit as the vicar's eyes widened. "Across Windemere from Wray?" Kit nodded and the vicar's voice dropped in volume. "Are you kin to the duke?"

Kit felt the gravel in his voice. "I am the duke."

Mr. Alred's smile crossed his face slowly, a twinkle forming in the rheumy blue eyes. "I have served tea to a duke? What will the ladies around here think?"

"Probably that you imagined the entire encounter, mistaking a vagrant for nobility."

The barked laugh startled Kit but made him smile as the vicar wagged a finger. "You are an unusual one, I will say that. And young. Most of the nobles I have met over my years were not so young or handsome. How long have you been duke?"

"Almost a year."

Mr. Alred paused. "I remember now. I heard about your father's—I am sorry—it must be hard to lose a man so young. But you are now a duke. Why did you not send an army of servants to find your sister?"

Leaning back in his chair, Kit released a long breath. "Because I did not want to humiliate her. And I am one of the reasons she left. It is my responsibility to return her to her family."

"Why did she leave?"

"Because she wanted to marry someone my mother and I did not want her to wed. She is too young, and we thought the match foolish and her foolish to want it. I tried to be her duke instead of her brother, and I did not realize how headstrong she truly was." Kit ran one finger around the rim of his cup.

"Or how much like her brother?"

The finger paused. "Perhaps."

"And if I told you she had found a place of safety, refuge? She is in no danger and may even return home on her own, in her own time. Would you allow her to stay?"

Kit's eyes met the old man's, suddenly realizing that a great deal rested on his answer. An answer, an honest one, and not his desire to throttle the old man in order to make him talk. He shuddered with another chill and took a sip from his cup, which helped—but not much. "My mother and I are not monsters. We do not plan to lock her away in a far tower like some damsel in one of Mrs. Radcliffe's novels. But Lady Mary has been tenderly sheltered, far away from the vagaries of even a city, much less the broader world. She is not yet eighteen and has no idea of the cruelty to be found beyond our walls. She is young and needs the guidance a mother—her family—can give her. No matter how safe she is, Lady Mary needs to return to the security of her family. Now."

"Would you allow her to marry this man she claims to love?"

Kit shifted in the hard chair, his frustration returning. "Not immediately. I will not declare we cannot be convinced to that outcome but running away is not the way to do so. He is almost fifty, and he has wooed her unfairly—and certainly not honestly. A great number of amends will need to be attended to." Kit felt no need to tell the Reverend Alred that the man was also one of his fellow vicars.

The man studied him closer a few moments, then gave a brief nod, almost as if to himself. "This lady you seek lives at Timmons Manor. It is a secluded estate beyond Litton to the north. It overlooks the River Skirfare but cannot be seen from the river or the lane that passes by its entrance." The vicar paused. "But I must warn you, Your Grace, that you are heading into unknown territory. The ladies who live there do not entertain visitors. And they may seem docile, but do not be fooled. They will not take kindly to your appearance at their door."

Kit's brows furrowed. "You are not saying they are dangerous?"

He sipped his tea, grimaced, and pushed it aside. "Not in the way you may be thinking. But hear me. If your sister is there, it is precisely because she does not want to be found. In truth, I would wager to say that no one who lives in that house wishes to be found."

CHAPTER THREE

Saturday, 10 September 1825
Timmons Manor
Half-past nine in the morning

Beth laughed. The sound dissipated in the wind that flew past her, but she had not laughed—a true laugh that she felt to her core—in weeks. Galloping alongside her, Daphne's face lit with a similar joy. In the distance, Boru raced along a hilltop, his long strides covering an astonishing amount of ground. The three of them had cleared two low free-stone fences in their ride, scattering a flock of sheep, and Beth had not been filled with such exhilaration since her season had begun in April. Memories of riding with her three brothers at the Ashton Park estate flooded her as she leaned forward over her mount. The air surged around her, whipping a few strands of blond hair that had worked loose from her bonnet about her face and neck, and the mane of her dappled gray Dales pony swept back to sting her face.

"Hold!" Daphne called.

Beth rose up, urging the horse to slow to a canter, looking over at Daphne, who nodded ahead of them.

"The river. We can go no farther." With a shift of reins and gentle stroke of her riding crop, Daphne slowed her mount—a lovely black Arabian—to a trot. She pointed up to a rise on their west. "Fountain Fell. We will climb there a ways so you can see the full estate, then head back." She grinned. "Unlike yesterday I do prefer to wash up between rides and meals."

Beth laughed again. "So yesterday was unusual for us all?"

"Oh, most definitely. From stem to stern, as a sailor might say."

Beth took a moment to catch her breath, looking around. Located between two steeply sloping fells, the dale where Timmons Manor lay was one of the most beautiful settings Beth had ever seen. The rolling meadows, many divided into squares by the low free-stone fences, held sheep, cows, and late summer crops. The River Skirfare, a shallow fast-moving stream, framed the area with white-tinged ripples and reflected light. Tree lines crisscrossed the fields, their tall canopies creating ever-moving shade.

"It is so beautiful here."

Daphne's mount shifted, and she patted its neck. "Paradise. She pointed her crop toward the fell. "Let me show you more."

Beth urged her horse—which had the sweet name of Grace—into a walk, and they headed across two fields and up the north side of Fountain Fell, Boru at their side. As much as their earlier gallop had exhilarated her, Beth found a deep pleasure in the slow climb, the feel of Grace's muscles bunching and stretching, the soundness of the animal beneath her. A few hundred yards up, Daphne paused and turned her Arabian, and Beth followed suit. And her breath caught.

Daphne grinned. "As I said. Paradise."

Below them the estate spread out over the dale, lush and serene beneath a cerulean sky. Cottony clouds scudded across the blue, casting undulating shadows over the land. The main house faced what must have been elegant grounds at one time, but now grew wild with flowers, hedges, tress, and overgrown paths, its wild beauty secluding the house from the lane that passed in front of the property.

Behind the house, however, was a garden that rivaled the

finest royal gardens Beth had ever seen. Hidden behind tall hedges it was accessed only by one gate in the hedgerow and a small conservatory at the back of the house—the one she had noticed when she first arrived. Pristine, pruned, and planned, the garden's flowers blanketed the area with a riot of color. Statues in the Greek style dotted the serpentine pathways, and iron benches beneath vine-covered trellises provided spots of respite. At the rear of the garden, a glass house nestled against the hedges, its partially fogged glass walls and ceiling gleaming.

On the outside of the tall hedges, the stables and other out-buildings seemed well kept but ordinary. It was as if a jeweled crown had been set in the midst of a plain green blanket.

"Who—?"

"Mr. Hervey. And Sophie, of course. She is the real architect of that beauty. Our guests are welcome to roam the paths. Or even help, if you would like. The glass house you see is the source of your tulips and other flowers, herbs and vegetables through the winter. Although I will admit we eat an extraordinary number of potatoes during the cold months."

"Do any of the others—?"

"Mary. Bertie has, on occasion, but she prefers the animals. She has been with us for a while and has taken to visiting the tenants with flowers from the garden, along with eggs and the occasional slab of gammon." She pointed to the northwest. "We have six tenant farms on the property. Two tend to the sheep and goats, one to the pigs, one to the cows. They all grow crops, which they share with us as rental payments. Two of the crofts are vacant. The previous tenants died, and we have not been able to find new ones. The sheep and cows are currently grazing those lands to keep the grass tended but the cottages are unoccupied."

Beth peered at her. "Do you act as the land manager?"

Daphne smiled. "I help. But mostly Sophie. She prefers staying close to the house, so I pay the visits and make inquiries."

Beth paused. She had many more questions, but it was the most anyone had said to her about the estate since she had arrived, and she felt she should not press for more now. Except for one curiosity that would not relent . . .

Supper the night before had been similar to dinner, with even more silence from the other end of the table. Beth had chosen not to socialize with the group afterward, begging off for exhaustion. But her night had been restless, and she had been awakened twice by what she thought was . . .

"Daphne?"

"Hm?"

"Last night, I thought I heard someone crying."

Daphne remained silent a few moments. "We do have cats in the house."

Beth waited. It had not been a cat.

Daphne's horse stomped a foot, and she quieted it with a few long strokes. "Beth, like you, women come to Timmons House for a variety of reasons. We do not seek them out. They find us, and we welcome them in. But they are a varied group. Tempers sometimes clash. They can be wary when someone new arrives. Sometimes they mourn. Most of all, they need rest, healing, support . . . and privacy. Do you understand?"

"So let them come to me?"

"Yes. They will. Give them time. Come to the back parlor after supper. Let them know you."

Beth nodded. "You know this is against everything I have been taught about interacting with others. Privacy always, and you never let anyone get close."

"I know. That was my training as well, since that way lies scandal." Daphne adjusted her leg over the sidesaddle pommel. "Believe me, I know." She scowled, looking past Beth toward the main house. "Who—?"

Beth turned. A man on a large black horse had halted in front of the house. He dismounted and stepped up to the door. Even from this distance, they heard the pounding he laid upon the wood.

"New guest?"

"No." Daphne's face darkened. "And certainly not one of that kind." She tightened her hold on her reins, and with one touch of her crop, the Arabian bolted, flying down the side of the fell, Boru along with them.

Beth did likewise, clinging to Grace as the horse almost dislodged her in the sudden dash down the slope. The Arabian was significantly faster, however, and Beth realized Daphne had held back in their earlier ride. The Dales gray was sure-footed but moved with more caution. By the time Beth reached the front of the house, Daphne was already inside, and sharp bellows and barks reached her through the open door. Beth halted next to the stranger's horse and dismounted, glancing at the black.

She stopped her brows furrowing, staring at the animal, which stood at least two hands taller than the gray. "I know you," she muttered. She reached out a hand and touched the animal's tautly muscled neck, her mind flipping through where she could possibly have seen such a magnificent horse before.

The park. But who—

"I will see her immediately!" A dark voice echoed from inside.

Beth's gut clenched. She knew that voice as well.

"You have no right here! I demand you leave. Now!"

Sophie. Beth rushed inside but stopped only a few feet inside. Before her, Sophie and Daphne stood resolutely at the foot of the staircase, facing down a man. Boru growled, a deep, ominous sound, his shoulder pressing against Daphne's thigh with her hand curled in the fur of his neck.

The man rivaled Beth's father in height, allowing him to loom over the two women. His long, unkempt blond hair clumped in long sweat-soaked clusters and curled over his collar. "I have tracked her for four months." His deep voice held both grief and gravel. "I know she is here! All roads lead here!"

"And I tell you there is no one by that name here. You must leave!" Sophie's fists clenched at her sides.

The man took a step toward them, and Daphne raised her riding crop in front of her, pointing it at him. "You will come no farther, sir, or I will release my dog!" Boru barked.

Beth felt as if her chest would collapse. She knew that voice, that stance, that hair. Although the last time she had seen him, it had been near a beverage table at a ball, disappointment in his blue eyes as she had explained that she had chosen another man as her final suitor. And felt a wrench in her own heart as she realized in that moment the foolish choice she had made.

"Your Grace?"

All sound stopped, and the three people in front of her froze. A roaring grew in Beth's ears as Daphne and Sophie shifted their eyes to her. The man stiffened but did not turn.

Beth took another step forward, the word pinched. "Kirkstone?"

Sophie gasped, raising a hand to her mouth.

The man slowly turned, his eyes narrow as he peered at her.

Something was wrong, and Beth moved closer. The normal stolid and handsome Duke of Kirkstone looked as if he had been slammed into a wall. Sweat beaded his face, and the fiery red blotches in his cheeks emphasized the unnatural shine in his blue eyes. His broad shoulders were stooped, his black clothes loose on his tall frame and covered with dust. With a rumpled pack slung over his shoulder, he looked far more the vagrant than the man she knew he was.

His barely audible words sounded as if he were chewing cotton. "What are you doing here?"

Beth stepped a bit closer, feeling the heat that radiated from him. "I might ask you the same."

He swayed. "My sister. They have my sister."

"We do not!" Daphne stepped in front of Sophie.

He nodded, still facing Beth. "They do. I know they—" He blinked, looking confused, then his eyes rolled upward, fluttering, and his knees gave way. He slumped to the ground, his head hitting the marble tiles with a sickening thump.

The three women stared at him, silent, for several minutes, then Sophie looked up at Beth. "You know him."

Beth nodded.

"You called him 'Your Grace, Kirkstone.' Are you saying this . . . creature . . . is the Duke of Kirkstone?"

Beth chewed her lower lip. "Yes. I met him earlier this season. He . . . he courted me. His father died last year." She took a deep breath. "Should we not do something?"

Daphne let out a low growl. "I suggest we drape him on his horse and send him on his way."

Sophie's scowl deepened. "Daphne. Do you wish to bring the entire force of the aristocracy to our door? No one can know he is here."

Beth had to ask. "Is his sister here?"

Sophie pursed her lips. "Yes. But I promise you she does not want to see him. She left her home with good reason. And we will protect her."

"And him?" Beth looked over Kirkstone again. "He is obviously quite ill."

Sophie exchanged looks with Daphne again.

Daphne shook her head. "A stall in the stable."

"Sometimes I forget you were ever aristocracy. We cannot let a duke die in our stable." Sophie sighed. "Summon Notley and Hervey. Send Mr. Mead for Dr. Thornton. We will move the duke into one of the empty bedchambers on the second floor—"

Daphne growled.

"Only until he is well. As long as he is"—she gestured toward the prone form—"like this, he is no threat. Once he is well, we will engage Mr. Keales and Hugh to evict him. Until then you tell the women what is going on."

"And his sister?" Daphne's voice held a barely contained rage.

"Warn her. Assure her we will take precautions and make provisions for her."

"This is not a wise idea, Sophie."

"No. But it is what we have to do." She looked at Beth. "And you, my girl, will tell me all you know about this man."

⟫⟩⟩⟩⟩⟨⟨⟨⟨⟪

THE VOICES RETURNED. Vague. Distant. Garbled. Kit thought they must have appeared out of his fever, but they seemed oddly real. Some harsher than others. Male. Female. He groaned as he felt his body being lifted, hauled. His head throbbed and he shuddered, pain racking through him as hands turned and shifted him, undressing him, slowly lowering him into a softness that embraced every joint, every muscle. Something wet and cool touched his lips, and a slightly bitter and oily liquid passed his lips. He swallowed, then coughed, a deep, racking noise, like rocks being ground into dust.

A soft hand touched his cheek. A familiar voice whispered, "Rest. The doctor will be here soon."

"Mary?" Kit did not recognize his own voice. Grit in cotton.

After a pause, the voice spoke again. "No. She is not here. Rest."

Kit tried to fight back to consciousness, but the struggle remained too great. The moist coolness of a cloth passed across his forehead, then the darkness closed in again.

⟫⟩⟩⟩⟩⟨⟨⟨⟨⟪

BETH DROPPED INTO a chair in front of Sophie's desk, uncaring about her posture as the events of the morning cascaded over her. Her hostess peered at her over the top of small round spectacles. "Well?"

Beth glanced behind her as Daphne entered and closed the door of the study. She took up a position just behind Sophie, arms crossed, Boru at attention beside her. They both looked—and Beth felt—as if she had betrayed them simply by recognizing Kirkstone.

She took a deep breath. "It is somewhat complicated."

Sophie's mouth jerked. "I will take notes."

Beth fought a smile. Now was not the time. Instead she swallowed and sat straighter. "I made my debut in April. Despite how well my mother had prepared me, it was all rather overwhelming."

"We remember," murmured Sophie.

Beth hesitated, looking from one woman to the other, realizing for the first time that both women had been presented, had had a debut season in London.

One side of Daphne's mouth curled in a half-smile. "We are not that old."

Mortified, Beth raised a hand in protest. "I did not mean—I just did not know—" She looked at Daphne. "Who *are* you?"

Sophie took off her spectacles and rubbed her nose, then looked over her shoulder at her friend. "Your choice."

Daphne hesitated, then gave a quick nod. "My father was, and my brother *is* the Duke of Embleton."

Beth stiffened. "Your brother is Matthew Rydell?"

Daphne gave a quick nod.

"My brother Michael is conducting business with him."

Sophie fingered the earpiece on her spectacles. "The English aristocracy. Always tumbling over each other in one way or another."

"As just happened in our entrance hall," Daphne muttered.

"Go on, Beth."

Beth shifted to the edge of the chair and took a deep breath. "You have not seen it in me yet, but I have always been somewhat . . . outspoken. Mother warned me this would be a detriment where men were concerned."

Daphne snorted but said nothing.

"My brothers encouraged it. My brother Robert even taught me to box, if you can believe it. My mother was . . . not pleased . . . she felt it would not help me. I only realized later that my brothers were trying to protect me. And mother was correct about most of the men I met. The moment I was no longer demure and soft spoken, they fled. Except for three, who seemed to enjoy my humor, and the fact that I could talk about some-thing other than fashion and food. Eventually, I settled on the Marquess of Aldermaston."

"He with no spine," mumbled Sophie.

Beth did smile this time. "Yes, but I did not see it early in the season."

"And the others?"

"One chose another. The third"—she looked from Sophie to Daphne—"disappeared abruptly. My pride told me that he did not take the rejection well and did not want to be seen in Society. Now I know . . ." She looked down at her hands.

"He left to search for his sister."

Beth nodded. "He may be angry at you if he thinks you are hiding his sister, but he will despise me." She looked up again. "His sister is named Mary. Is she the same one—?"

"Yes."

"The one who helps in the garden?"

Sophie's eyebrows arched and she glanced at Daphne, who nodded.

"She has been quiet at meals."

"She knows her speech would give her away. Regal but quite Yorkshire."

Beth shifted. "I have a suggestion."

Sophie nodded.

"Let me take care of him. If you wish to protect Lady Mary, then he should see no one in the household other than the people he already has. The three of us and staff. I can ensure he does not harass the maids for information or ask questions that would catch the others off-guard. It will also undergird your insistence that she is not here."

Sophie shifted a stack of papers on her desk. "I am not sure that is wise."

"One of the reasons I came up here is because there are only so many hours a day I can spend reading or stitching before I lose my sanity, and in London, I was confined. I need to be doing something. Preferably something helpful. And in truth, he is far more likely to believe me if I insist Lady Mary is not here than either of you. He knows I am a stranger here. Why would I lie?"

Sophie and Daphne exchanged glances again. Finally Sophie sighed. "I wish to hear from you every day on his condition. And he must leave as soon as he is able."

"Without a doubt."

"Just one thing." Daphne stepped closer to her. "Remember that you are, indeed, still a stranger here. Do not give us a reason to distrust you either."

Beth stood. "I will not."

A rap sounded on the door. "Enter," Sophie called.

Notley opened the door. "The doctor has arrived."

"Take him up." She nodded at Beth. "Go with them." She looked at Notley. "If the doctor protests her presence, send him to me."

Notley gave a quick bow, then held the door open for Beth, who hoped the twinge in her stomach did not become more violent. It would not do for her to be sick as well.

The doctor—a man who appeared just as Beth expected a country physician to look, with his simple black linen clothes, spectacles, and bald spot at the crown of his head—arched one eyebrow at Notley's instruction but did not protest beyond a muttered "Good God, Sophie" as he started up the stairs. Beth followed and waited at the foot of the bed while the doctor examined Kirkstone, who was still unconscious. Notley hovered next to the open door.

The doctor listened to Kirkstone's lungs with an odd tube-like instrument Beth had never seen before, then thumped Kirkstone's chest and pressed on his neck and armpits. "What has been done so far?" the doctor asked.

Beth cleared her throat. "Cool cloths and a small dose of laudanum."

The doctor straightened and peered at her over the spectacles. "There is no need for that unless he is in pain. It depresses the breathing. It appears to be a fever, with the possibility of pneumonia, but we cannot know more until he is awake. Continue with the cool cloths on his face and keep his head and chest elevated." The doctor stood and began to repack his bag. "I will send over a mixture, a tisane, which will help, once he is awake enough to drink. Boil it with ginger and honey to make a strong tea. Two to three times a day, if he can tolerate it. And ask your cook to prepare an onion poultice. Also twice a day. If his head hurts, and I suspect it will given the knot on the side of it, soak a cloth in vinegar and place it on his forehead."

"No bloodletting?" asked Notley.

Beth stared at the butler, horrified. The doctor merely shrugged. "Not yet. The latest medical journals are casting doubt on its efficacy. But still a possibility if he does not improve in a few days."

Beth bit her lip.

The doctor removed his spectacles and tucked them into a pocket. "You will be caring for him?"

She nodded.

"Hm. Baths will also help. Cool if he can tolerate it. Warm if not. Do not overheat him. I will be back on Monday to check on him."

"Yes, sir." Beth stood and followed the two men downstairs. As the front door closed, Notley looked down at her, expectation in his eyes. She stood a little straighter. "Has the duke's horse been cared for?"

Notley nodded. "Yes, my lady."

Beth tilted her head. "She is Sophie. I am Beth."

Notley actually smiled. "Old habits, I'm afraid, my—Beth."

"I suspect the only person in this household who would expect that is upstairs unconscious."

"No doubt."

"Can you ask Cook about the poultice?"

He nodded. "I will."

"I will tell Sophie and Daphne what the doctor said, then I

need to get with Kendall. Can you also ask Mrs. Trew to meet me upstairs in thirty minutes? If I am to care for him, I need to make some preparations."

"I am heading downstairs now."

"Thank you, Notley."

The butler paused, his eyes kind. "You are most welcome."

Beth felt flushed as she returned to Sophie's study to report what the doctor had said. Sophie and Daphne listened closely, then Daphne murmured, "I will ask Bertie," and strode from the room.

Beth watched her go. "Bertie?"

Sophie nodded. "Bertie has been visiting the tenants. One of the women is a midwife, who has quite an extensive knowledge of herbs and such. She will probably know what mixture the doctor is referring to and if she can supplement it." She leaned back in her chair. "Are you quite sure about this, Beth?"

Beth rocked up on her toes. "I am. I think I can help him. I have watched all that Rose did for my mother after her collapse, and I helped her as well. I helped when my brother Thomas was shot earlier this year and when my brother Michael had a serious fever several years ago." Beth paused.

"And?"

"I suppose this sounds awful, but I am rather engaged with the idea of having something vital to do."

Sophie smiled. "Why do you think I help these women who come to us? And why I do all this"—she gestured around the office—"rather than hiring it done. Yes, it is more frugal to do it myself, but it also gives me a sense of belonging. Of helping. I felt completely useless in London."

"Life amidst the beau monde is rather limiting for women."

"Indeed it is. Here I am content." She picked up her spectacles and replaced them. "So get on with your caring for the duke. But do let us know the moment he tries to stir from his bed."

Sophie resisted the urge to curtsy. "Yes, ma'am." She headed back up the stairs, her mind already making a list of all that needed to be done.

CHAPTER FOUR

Sunday, 11 September 1825
Timmons Manor
Half-past two in the afternoon

THE VOICES RETURNED. Whispers seemed to circle his head any moment that Kit awoke, more distinct now, but he was never quite sure if they were around his head—or inside it. These sounded similar to the ones before, only this time one of them was . . . smaller.

"Is he really sick?"

"Yes, he is."

"Is he going to die?"

"We hope not. We will know more tomorrow when the doctor comes back."

"Is he going to have a baby?"

A choking sound followed. "Erm . . . ah . . . no. Only ladies have babies."

"Oh. That's why Mummy is sick. A baby. They say she might die."

"Oh." Silence. "I am sorry."

"It's why I'm here, but I don't want her to die. Aunt Sophie and Aunt Daphne are nice, but I miss Mummy. She is upstairs but too sick to play. Would you play with me?"

"As soon as this gentleman gets well. I will play all you want."

"Mattie!"

This whispered hiss, harsher than the others, made Kit's head ache. He moaned, and a flurry of activity rustled around him. A cool cloth bathed his face and neck.

"Your Grace?" This whisper was soft and feminine. And definitely outside of his head.

Kit wanted to wake up, but the fog encasing his mind resisted. His chest felt like an anvil rested on it, and his body wanted to cough but could not quite make that happen. After a moment, an odd warmth settled on his chest and the smell of stew tickled his nostrils.

Stew?

Confusion layered onto the fog. His mouth, which had been bone dry, began to water and he swallowed.

He felt a slight pressure on his lower lip.

"It's only a spoon of water. You need to drink, if you can."

The water filled his mouth, cool and cleansing. He swallowed again and blinked, then moaned against the light in the room.

"Keep your eyes closed a while longer. You must rest. Another sip."

The spoon pushed against his lip, and Kit accepted the water.

"Good. I am going to offer you something else. A tea. Medicinal. It is to help with the fever. It will be bittersweet."

It was indeed, and Kit almost gagged as he swallowed. "Nasty." The barely audible word sounded like a bull's snort.

"I believe it is a universal rule that medicine must taste like soot."

Kit let his eyelids lift, squinting despite the dim light of the room. But the beauty before him made him think that he still dreamed, still wandered through tangled delusions. A sweet, slim face framed by reddish gold curls caught up in a green cap. The pale blue in her eyes looked almost gray in the low light, and her expression, tender and kind, made him want to reach for her. It was a familiar face, one he remembered—not that he remembered much at the moment—but could not place with a name.

She lifted the spoon again. "You need to drink as much of this as you can before you sleep again. It will help with the fever. Help you rest."

"Yes." It was as much as he could manage. He took several sips of the tea, then sighed, unsure he could drink any more.

Everything hurt—every muscle, every joint—and although he was conscious, the miasma lingered. Awareness had flitted in and out, like a faulty gas lamp. The darkness brought dreams— endless spurts of running. Of grasping for something just out of his reach. Of falling, endlessly, never to land. Dreams of sinking in a vast expanse of water, his chest tightening from the pressure usually led to a waking jerk and fits of gagging or coughing. Any sense of time passing had evaporated—along with any sense of where he was. And—often—of where he had been.

He remembered his visit with the vicar, but what the man had told him came and went in sketchy memories. He remem- bered falling—in reality—at least twice, once from his horse. Little else. His head ached, a deep throbbing, every time he awoke, however briefly. His body had quivered as chills came and went, alternating with a deep, penetrating heat.

He paused and she waited until he was ready for more. Kit swallowed several more sips of the bittersweet tea, which she spooned to him in small amounts. He tried to reach for the cup, but his hand fell limply at his side.

"The doctor said your exhaustion was thorough." Her voice remained soft, feathery. "Which weakened you for the fever. It has not broken yet, but I am glad to see you awake."

"You know me."

"I do." She paused. "The fever is clouding your mind. Years ago, my brother had one so great he could not remember his own name. It will pass when the fever does."

Kit swallowed more tea. "Where am I?"

Another hesitation. "Timmons Manor, near Litton."

He mulled this information over. Nothing.

"Why do I smell stew?"

She gave a soft laugh. "You smell onions. There is an onion poultice on your chest."

He looked down. Sure enough, a bundle of moist cloth rested above his sternum. The source of the aroma.

"Does it make you hungry?"

He considered the question. "No."

"Good. You should not eat yet. But Cook is preparing a bone broth for when you are stronger." She observed him quietly. "I think you have had enough for now. Rest."

She bathed his face and neck again with the cool cloth. As she did, Kit slid back into his netherworld, letting the darkness settle over him yet again.

⇥⟫⟪⇤

BETH WATCHED AS Kirkstone drifted away. He had roused several times yesterday and overnight, which he obviously did not remember. She had explained about the tea at least four times, spooning it into him anytime he could tolerate it, yet he still seemed surprised by the taste. When he had had the breath to speak, his words rambled.

He breathed somewhat easier now than he had through the night, but an ominous rattle still sounded deep in his chest, and the heat of his body filled her with a growing concern. His skin, gray and blotchy, felt clammy to the touch. She had told Mattie that he would not die, but Beth could not promise herself that. She tried to take comfort in the fact that years ago her brother Michael had experienced just such a fever after one of his midnight rides in the snow. His fever and congestion had lasted more than a week, but he had recovered, with no lasting effects. Although she was four years younger—just fourteen at the time—Beth had helped her mother and their housekeeper nurse Michael through it.

A light touch on her shoulder got her attention, and she looked up into Sophie's eyes. Motioning for her to follow, Sophie stepped out into the corridor and turned to Beth, arms crossed. "Beth, you must rest. You have been with him all night."

"I slept some."

"In the chair at his side. That is not resting."

"But—"

"I am serious. Ring for Kendall. Wash. Eat. Put on your night rail and sleep for a few hours."

"It is the middle of the afternoon!"

"All the better because there are other people awake who can care for him. I will make sure you are awake in time for supper."

"But—"

"If you make yourself ill, then you will not be able to care for him at all."

Beth glanced back at the door. "I am rather tired."

"Then listen to the wisdom of an old woman."

Beth grinned. "You are not old."

"Older. Definitely wiser."

"That I will concede."

Sophie smiled. "Good. I will send a tray up to your bedchamber." When Beth hesitated, Sophie pointed at the door of the Tulip Room. "Now."

Beth relented. With one glance back at the door of the Rose Room, she retreated into her own bedchamber and rang for Kendall. She sank down on the bench at the end of the bed, her weariness washing over her. She did need to rest. Sleep—a deep one—might even ease the memories that had plagued her through the dark hours, when nothing she did seemed to bring him rest.

Memories of spring balls, when every eligible man in the *ton* seemed to come her way. Memories of afternoon conversations and laughter over tea. After her presentation to the queen, she had been inundated with invitations to balls, musicales, soirees, and teas. At each ball, her dance card filled quickly—young and old, widowers and rogues, all ranks and titles. Her brothers had tried to watch out for the more nefarious ones, but Beth, enthralled by the attention, relied mostly on her mother for guidance. Together they had winnowed the number to a select few, then to three. She had encouraged them, accepted their calls, their gifts.

One of the three had been Richard Christian Caudale, the newly invested Eighth Duke of Kirkstone. Her father had embraced him. Her mother reminded her that of all the potential suitors, he had the loftiest rank, one equal to her father. Beth had found him charming, entertaining, and intelligent. And unlike many of the others, at seven and twenty he was less than ten years older than she was.

But Kirkstone—his family seat—lay in the far north of England, almost to the Scottish border. As much as she had enjoyed his company, Beth—captured by the festivities of the season—could not imagine spending months on end in an isolated and snow-covered dale. She had settled on a different man, a marquess, who she believed cared for her and would make a good marriage.

How things had changed in a few short weeks.

After a soft tap on the door, Kendall entered carrying a large pitcher of warm water, followed by a young maid with a tray of victuals—cold beef, fruit, cheese, and bread. Kendall set the water on the washstand and gestured for the maid to put the tray on the stool of the dressing table. The maid left, and Kendall turned, letting out a long sigh. "You do look worn to a frazzle, my lady. What shall we do first?"

"I want to wash. I feel gritty. I suspect I will nibble on the food as we go."

With a nod, Kendall began, and Beth found comfort in letting her maid take care of her. She had not realized exactly the toll her vigil had taken until she realized she had no energy to eat more than a few bites. Once clean, she slid between the covers of her bed and let sleep take her as Kendall closed the curtains on her windows and quietly eased from the room.

She awoke again to the gentle touch of Kendall's hand on her shoulder. "I am sorry, my lady. Lady Sophia has requested you join the others for . . . supper."

Beth pushed the covers down and sat up. "I thought everyone in the house called her Sophie."

Kendall's lips pursed a moment. "I . . . cannot. I have tried."

Beth smiled. "I am afraid it is ingrained in us. I still stumble over it. How late am I?"

"She sent me up in time. I have pulled one of your day gowns, since no one dresses appropriately either."

Beth swallowed a laugh. Kendall had always been more proper than anyone else in the Ashton household. "If we stay too long, I shall have to find a modiste to prepare some simple frocks. More practical than anything I currently own."

"Let us hope it does not come to that."

Dressed and coiffed, Beth padded downstairs to the dining room. As usual, the others were already seated and waiting. Gathering in the drawing room until everyone was downstairs and the food was ready seemed to be another custom the household had set aside. And, as before, they peered at her in silence as she took her place next to Sophie and across from Daphne. Curled in his corner, Boru released a long sigh and placed his head upon his paws.

As she settled, Beth realized that a third chair remained empty, the one between Bertie and Lydia. She leaned closer to Sophie. "Where is Mary?"

Bertie brightened. "She has gone to stay with the mi—"

"Mary," Sophie interrupted, "has temporarily moved to another household. She will return shortly." She gestured to Lois, who began to serve the first course with the help of two other maids. Soup this time, a clear broth with bits of beef and potato.

Chagrinned, Bertie fell silent, sipping timidly at her soup. No one else spoke for a few moments, then Lydia laid her spoon aside with a clank. "If no one else is going to ask, I am." She focused on Beth. "Who is he, what is wrong with him, and what is he doing here? And why are *you* taking care of him?"

Beth looked at Sophie, a twinge of confusion in her gut. "You have not told them?"

Sophie hesitated a moment, long enough that Daphne answered instead. "We only know what he demanded before he collapsed. You seem to know a great deal more, so it should come from you."

"Ah."

"So?" Lydia's tone demanded an answer.

Beth dabbed her mouth with her serviette and shifted in her chair to face the women more directly. "He is the Duke of Kirkstone and his family seat is north of here."

Alarm filled all their faces, but Sophie held up her hand. "Please listen."

Beth went on. "A few weeks ago, his sister disappeared from their home. He has been trying to find her ever since. He has tracked her here, but in his travels he has become quite ill. He had only just arrived here when he collapsed. He has been told that his sister is not here, but he does not believe that."

She glanced at Sophie, who nodded.

Lydia understood immediately, glancing at the empty chair. "It's Mary. Does he know—"

"We do not know how much information he has." Sophie spoke evenly. "At this time, we only know that Mary does not wish to return to her family home. We have offered her sanctuary, and that has not changed."

"And I am the one caring for him because I asked to. I know him. I met him earlier this year. He does not remember who I am yet, but he will, and he already knew I was here. It is best if he is unaware of the others in the household, which would only add to his curiosity and conviction that his sister could be here. I have a family connection with Sophie, which provides a plausible reason for my presence beyond my need to be away from London."

"What happens when he gets well?" Lydia crossed her arms,

hugging herself, and Beth realized she was as fearful as she was defiant.

What are their stories? Why are they here?

Sophie motioned for Lois to take away the soup bowls. "He will be told, again, that his sister is not here, and he will be asked to leave. If he refuses, we will . . . ask for help in making sure he abandons his search on these premises." Sophie's tone held a tension Beth had not heard before, and Boru growled.

"Calm," Daphne whispered, and Beth was not sure if she was referring to the dog or to Sophie.

Plates bearing tidbits of roast lamb and cabbage were distributed. They were a tasty treat, but Beth still had little appetite and nibbled at the meal as she looked at each of the women in the room. Except for Daphne and Sophie, they all seemed to be around her own age—definitely less than twenty. Bertie, who had seemed pleased by Mary's move, now looked wan; she drank from her water glass in repeated gulps. Lydia's eyes had turned haunted, afraid. Amelia tried to eat, but chewed slowly, as if reluctant to swallow. Priscilla did not even pretend, staring at the wall opposite.

Whatever joy she had seen in these women when she had arrived had dissipated, as if it had never existed.

Because of Kirkstone.

What was going on in this house?

Whatever it was, it had given these women a place, a sense of security. Joy.

Beth pushed her chair back and looked at Sophie. "If you will excuse me, I should get back to the patient. The faster he is gone, the better."

Sophie nodded and she stood. As she reached the door, a quiet voice called her name.

She turned. Lydia cleared her throat. "Thank you."

Beth took a deep breath. "I promise you, I will do all I can to keep him away from everyone." She turned and left, her thoughts tumbling over themselves. *Why did I promise that? What did I even mean by it?* As she trotted up the stairs, she was not certain, but clearly she had made a decision about where her loyalties lay.

And they were not with the man whom Beth had once thought of as a possible husband. Whatever was happening in this house felt more important than that. She prayed she was correct.

CHAPTER FIVE

Monday, 12 September 1825
Timmons Manor
Half-past two in the morning

THE FIRE ROSE up, devouring him. The searing heat penetrated every muscle, every bone. Kit screamed, fighting the flames, twisting and flailing at them. His muscles spasmed from the agony, bunching and shooting hot spears of pain into his torso. Sweat boiled off him, drenching his hair, his clothes, but provided no cooling against the unbearable heat.

The scorching fire grabbed at him, clenching around arms and legs, pulling, stretching, lifting as Kit continued to writhe, fighting against the pain.

Then, in visions that crashed over him in rolling waves, fire gave way to water. An ocean, vast and endless, consumed him, pulling him down. His chest tightened as the water pressed around him. It drove the fire deeper as he sank, and he bucked, coughing, his body racking with the violent paroxysms. Water and phlegm seemed to burst from his mouth and nose, pouring forth.

He tried to scream, but the fluids blocked the noise as they erupted from him.

Then, abruptly, the fire was quenched. The coughing ceased.

He floated, weightless, in the gently rocking waves. After what felt like an eternity, the waves buoyed him up on land, soft sand. They rolled him back and forth. Then stillness.

Darkness.

Monday, 12 September 1825
Timmons Manor
Half-past six in the morning

BETH SAT IN an armchair next to Kirkstone's bed, slumped against the back, her legs stretched out before her. Exhaustion of a kind she had never known consumed her, from heels to hair. Her muscles felt limp, drained of all strength and energy.

The past four hours had been excruciating, terrifying . . . and yet exhilarating in a way nothing in her life ever had been. Not even being presented before the queen had filled her with such . . . satisfaction was not the correct word, but Beth's brain felt fogged and muggy.

Near half-past two, Kirkstone had screamed in his sleep, his body writhing and jerking, the heat of his fever radiating off him in waves. Terrified, Beth had awakened Kendall, Daphne, and Sophie, all of whom looked as if they knew both what was happening and what to do about it. Daphne threw an extra covering over Kirkstone and lay down on him, trying to keep his flailing from injuring him or those around him. The others woke the three men and the maids, and in minutes a bathtub appeared in the room along with the first buckets of lukewarm water.

Using the sheets, the men lifted Kirkstone and lowered him into the water. Kendall and one of the maids soaked cloths in vinegar and wrapped his head. He fought everything for long minutes, then without warning, he bucked, raising up, his body seizing with coughs. Daphne grabbed another sheet, bunching it, and caught the fluids that surged from his nose and mouth. At first they seemed almost solid, greenish, with tinges of red. Then yellow. Finally, clear.

Then, gradually he began to calm, his body easing down into the tub.

Watching him, Sophie had ordered Beth, Kendall, and the maids out of the room. When Beth had protested, Sophie told her to clean up and dry off, since she would be with him most of the day. Sophie's tone left no room for argument.

When Beth had returned, Kirkstone had been returned to his bed, clean and dry, his head and chest propped on a fresh stack of pillows. The tub had disappeared, along with the soiled linens—and Kirkstone's clothes. The covers were draped high on his chest, but he was obviously naked beneath.

He still slept, but his color had returned to an even tone, his skin dry. And the ominous rattle in his chest was gone.

Perhaps he would live after all.

Perhaps.

The door behind her opened and Sophie entered, bearing a small tray with a cup of tea and a plate of cheese, bread, and pears. She set it on the bench at the foot of Kirkstone's bed. "You should try to eat."

Beth hesitated, then nodded. "He seems better, but he still does not wake up."

Sophie put a hand on her shoulder. "His fever broke, but he remains ill. His body is taking the rest it needs. So should you."

"I want to be here when he awakes."

"Why?"

After another pause, Beth whispered. "I am not sure."

Sophie knelt in front of the chair and reached for Beth's hand. "What happened between the two of you earlier this year? Beyond what you have told us."

Beth leaned forward, lowering her voice. "My debut went better than expected. A lot of men called on me, mostly because of my dowry and my father's title. Winnowing out the fortune-hunters and rogues took a bit of work. My mother and brothers helped. We had chosen three men for my father to investigate." She nodded toward the bed. "He was one of the three, and in the beginning, my preferred choice."

"In the beginning?"

"I . . . we . . . liked each other. A great deal. I enjoyed his companionship, his manner, his mind." She paused, her gaze lingering on Kirkstone's face, now shadowed with stubble as well as pain, as she remembered how much she had welcomed his visits, their dances. "I . . . I almost chose him."

"Why did you not?"

She looked down at Sophie. "I did not want to live in the Lake District."

Sophie pressed her lips together, but her eyes gleamed with humor. "You were young."

"And a fool."

"Not necessarily so. The entire nature of the Marriage Mart is to display people at their best. It does not always allow for an accurate assessment of someone's character. And decisions are often made for reasons that later seem foolish. His behavior here was not the most genteel."

"No. But it does speak of his dedication to his family."

"You think now you should have chosen him?"

Closing her eyes for a second, Beth pursed her lips. "I do not know. He could have reacted the same as Aldermaston to our scandal. And he did bolt from London in pursuit of his sister. I might not have had the chance."

"What will you do when he improves? This must surely test your earlier promise to us."

"It will." Beth shifted. "But I will stand by my word. I do, however, want to ask him one question."

"What is that?"

Beth shook her head. "I have not decided yet how to ask it. But I believe it will make him question his determination to carry his sister back home, no matter what she wants."

Sophie stood. "Then I wish you luck with that. Because if he becomes the beast he was when he first arrived, his quest will be all for naught anyway. The only way she leaves here is how and when she wishes it. Not before." She nodded toward the tray. "Eat, child. Before you are as weak as he is. The doctor should be here soon."

Sophie closed the door quietly behind her, and Beth stood and went to the tray. As expected, the tea had grown lukewarm, but the cheese was pungent and delicious, the pears sweet and delicate. The food did feel satisfying as it settled in her stomach, warming her. But her weariness claimed her again, and she picked up the bread and returned to the chair. She broke off a few morsels, chewing them slowly, hoping the fog in her brain would lift.

"You were wrong."

She froze, staring as Kirkstone's blue eyes slipped open.

"You would have had a chance."

CHAPTER SIX

Monday, 12 September 1825
Timmons Manor
Half-past seven in the morning

KIT WATCHED LADY Elizabeth Ashton closely as she absorbed what he had said. She sat perfectly still, a bit of bread halfway to her mouth. Her lips, parted to accept the bread, were unusually pale, almost as if she were ill herself. In truth, her entire appearance seemed far removed from the exquisite and glittering diamond he remembered dancing with earlier in the summer. That woman had been witty and joyous, her blond curls with their tempting red highlights caught up in the latest styles and adorned with feathers and jewels. Her gowns had sparkled, displaying her tall, elegant frame in the latest fashions. She had captivated all the *ton*, even the women.

This woman, however, looked far more like a bedraggled maid than a bedazzled aristocrat, with her hair bound by a blue scarf and wearing a rumpled muslin day gown. Purple shadows circled her eyes and shaded her cheeks. She had lost weight and seemed frail.

The woman he remembered, however, could never *be* frail. And if the words of the woman who had left were any indication, she had been caring for him, which he doubted was a task for a weakling.

Lady Elizabeth lowered her hand to her lap and swallowed hard. "How do you feel?"

He tried to clear his throat but only succeeded in making his voice grate harder. "As if I have been dragged several miles behind a runaway carriage."

"That well? I suspect that's an improvement over the last two days."

Ah. That was the Lady Elizabeth he remembered. "Then it is probably fortunate I do not remember the last two days." And, indeed, he did not. He released a long breath as his body sagged against the pillows.

"Most definitely." She paused. "What *do* you remember?"

"I remember talking to a vicar about a woman I was searching for—" A dry cough erupted from him, and he pushed up.

Instantly, Lady Elizabeth was beside him, her arm around his bare shoulders, helping him to sit, bracing his back with a solid press of her palm, which felt warm and firm. Two more hard coughs followed, then they eased, and he tried to swallow the phlegm he felt in the back of his throat, an action that felt like a knife slid down his gullet.

And with a start, Kit realized he was naked beneath the covers, which had dropped away from his chest. With a jerk, he covered his chest.

Lady Elizabeth turned away. "Let me get you some water." She headed for a nearby table as he settled back against the propped pillows and tucked the covers back into place. She returned with a small cup.

He took it and downed the water quickly. It felt astonishingly refreshing—manna from heaven—and he gestured for more. She brought over a pitcher, refilling the cup. When he could speak again, he looked her over, then down at his own bed. "If anyone in London saw this, you would be ruined."

She scowled. "We are not in London, are we? Besides, I am already ruined. This would be insult to injury. Meaningless."

He handed her the cup and pressed his head against the pillows, snuggling the covers a bit tighter beneath his armpits. He could barely believe how little will he had. "Whatever do you mean?" A horrid thought came to him then. "Aldermaston! Did he—"

"No!" She held up a hand. "Do not exert—No. I mean, he is the reason—but not how you think." She sat back in the chair, cradling the cup in her hands. "My brother—"

"Lord Newbury?"

"No. Robert. Thomas had his own problems—"

"I heard he had been injured."

"Yes, but, no, Robert was caught up in a scandal—"

"When?"

"You were already gone." She paused. "I thought because I had rejected your suit."

Kit thought about this a moment. "No. I got word that"— understanding seeped into his brain—"Aldermaston set you aside because of Lord Robert?"

She nodded.

"That was rather gutless of him."

A smile flitted across her face. "I do not blame him. Most of the aristocracy turned on me. I am sure that my parents will find some rectitude in it—they always do—but my season was over. No invitations, no calls." She looked down at her hands. "To be truthful, that did not concern me as much as my boredom." Her smile held a sadness in it. "I am afraid I have a great capacity to become a nuisance."

Kit swallowed hard, but his words still sounded harsh. "You thought northern England would be more entertaining?"

She gave a low laugh. "I thought I would be less of a problem for my family. With me gone, whatever my parents had planned for my brothers would go much smoother. I thought if I could get far enough away, I would not be a constant reminder . . ." As her voice trailed off, she straightened and stood. "Would you like more water?"

"I would like to know where my sister is."

She glanced at him, her lips a thin line, then replaced the cup on the table. "She is not here."

"I am certain she is. I heard the two of you discussing her."

Lady Elizabeth's lips pursed as she turned back to him, and she crossed her arms. "You cannot be sure of what you heard."

Annoyance fired in his gut. He swallowed hard, trying to clear his throat. "I may be ill but it has not affected my hearing. She called me a beast—"

"You acted like one. Arriving without invitation. Barging in. Demanding—"

"'The only way she leaves here is how and when she wishes it. Not before.' That is what she said. That implies—"

"A duke, a genuine duke would never treat ladies—"

"Ladies! They are kidnappers! Are you part of this scheme, Lady Elizabeth? To keep a young girl from her family?" He tried to push up on one elbow, but fatigue dragged at him, pushing his annoyance into anger.

"She is not a young girl. And no one is keeping her here. That is what Lady Sophia meant. Lady Mary is free to come and go as she pleases. She is not a prisoner. And she does not want to see you."

"I want to hear that from her."

"You do realize the stupidity of that statement."

"I will never believe it otherwise."

"So you want to browbeat her into changing her mind?"

"I am her brother. Her duke! I will—" A cough erupted from his chest, taking his breath. Then another.

"Oh, bloody hell!" Lady Elizabeth grabbed a cloth from the end of the bed and held it beneath his chin as another cough shook him, producing a choking flow of phlegm. "Spit it out, you fool!" She pushed him from behind again, and he bowed over her hand, clearing his mouth.

As the spasms ceased he took the cloth from her and blew his nose, wiping his mouth. She fetched more water and offered the cup. Kit took it, gratefully, and drank. She took it from him and set it aside, then helped him shift up higher on the pillows before settling back in her chair.

"Obviously," she said, her words soft, "you are not up for a heated discussion as of yet."

"A heated—"

"You will never heal if you do not rest."

He glared at her.

She let out a long sigh. "Lady Mary was here. She is no longer. They asked if she wanted to see you and she refused. She has moved to another location. I do not know where."

Kit swallowed, testing his voice, trying to control his temper. "But they do."

"I assume so. I do not know."

"Then I wish to see them."

She pushed an errant curl away from her face. "I will tell them." She stood. "You should drink more of the tisane the doctor sent over." She stepped to the head of the bed and tugged on the bell pull. Within a few moments, a maid appeared at the door, and Lady Elizabeth requested hot water and that the tray on the bench be removed.

He waited for the girl to leave, trying to take deep breaths, hoping to calm his irritation. "Lady Elizabe—"

"Beth."

He stared at her. "I beg your pardon."

Her smile was slight and sweet. "It is the nature of this house. Everyone here seems to have wanted to escape the protocols and dictates of the *ton*. We use our Christian names. Beth. Sophie."

"So manners are not called for either?"

She gave a soft laugh. "Of course they are. But not all conventions of the beau monde are manners. Some are simply that. Conventions. I am sure you have chafed under a few of them."

His eyes narrowed as he considered this. "Perhaps. Probably no more than anyone else being brought up in the confines of the aristocracy."

She held her hand out, palm up. "Precisely. Although women are more constricted than men."

"Oh, I do not see that."

"So if a duchess rejected you in marriage, you would be ruined? A pariah and outcast from your peers?"

"I—well—" He stopped.

"Wise choice," she muttered.

At a tap on the door, Beth stood. "Enter."

Three people entered the room, and Beth straightened, a solider snapping to attention. The maid had brought a pot of hot water, and Beth motioned for her to put it on the same side table. She did and scurried out. Two men had also entered with her—a tall man in a butler's livery, who stood to one side of the now open door, and a quick stepping man in the clothes of a shop-keeper or mill owner, carrying a doctor's bag.

Beth moved to the foot of the bed, waiting.

"Ah," the man said. "You are awake. I am Dr. Thornton. How do you feel?"

Kit considered repeating his earlier answer but decided it might be too flippant for the doctor. "I suspect better than I was the last time you saw me."

"Indeed. You are conscious, which is a vast improvement." He looked at Beth. "Tell me what has happened in the last forty-eight hours."

As Beth described the events of the past two days, Kit stared at her, mortified and astonished. He had never been that ill in his life, and when her descriptions became unreal to him, he glanced at the doctor—who remained impassive—and the butler—who merely nodded.

As she concluded, the doctor turned back to Kit. "All right, let me listen." And with that, he withdrew a tube from his bag with shallow cups on either end. "Lie still," he said, then pressed the larger of the two cups to Kit's chest and the smaller one to his ear. As he listened, he occasionally murmured to himself, especially as he moved the cup from one area to another, then asked Kit to sit up, and listened at his back. He eventually returned the tube to his bag, then pressed on Kit's neck and shoulders, ignoring the scowls Kit gave him.

What in the world is this man doing?

Finally, the doctor eased Kit back against the pillows and sat in the chair that Beth had vacated. He glanced at her again. "How often has he been getting the potion?"

"Anytime he was awake. Two to three times a day. I was about to brew a new batch."

Thornton looked back at Kit. "You are much improved, but you were in bad shape." He gave Beth a quick glance. "In truth, I was not sure you would make it through the first night. And I can tell you are still weak."

"I am not certain I could get out of bed."

"Probably not. And not a good idea."

"What illness do I have?"

"Pneumonia, which prompted an exceptionally ferocious fever. Your lungs have a build-up of fluid, probably from the extreme conditions you recently experienced. You seem to be past the most dangerous hours, but this is not a mild cold from which you can recover quickly. If you push too hard too soon, you could easily suffer a relapse." He addressed Beth. "Continue the potion and onion as well as camphor poultices—rotate them—and as much water as he can tolerate." Turning to Kit again, he said, "You need nutrition but not much. You will need at least another week in this bed. Cough as much as you can, but if you begin to feel severe pain in the chest, have them send for me. I expect some of the coughing will be extreme, and it will be easy to snap a rib." He stood and closed his bag. "I will speak with Sophie before I leave."

The doctor followed Notley out. The door closed and the room fell silent. After a moment, Beth moved toward the side table and began brewing the medicinal tea. Kit watched her move through the preparation with a neat efficiency, realizing that side table held much more than fresh water. There were three cups and two teapots, along with two canisters, a bottle of amber liquid, spoons, picks, and a stack of clean white cloths.

"You really put me in a bathtub?"

A smile flickered. "Why do you think you are without clothes?"

"If I were healthier, I am sure I could suggest several reasons for that."

Her cheeks pinked and the spoon she had been using to dip—something—from a canister into a pot clattered.

Kit smiled. This, too, was the woman he remembered, who could be outspoken and straightforward but unexpectedly shy when it came to suggestions of romance. She had been in a household with three strong-willed brothers and had held her own in conversations about the world around them, all the while maintaining a surprisingly in-depth innocence. He knew from speaking with Aldermaston—they had compared their respective suits of her over brandy at White's—this was one reason the marquess had found her so alluring.

That—and her substantial dowry. Aldermaston had confided that he needed the dowry to bolster his father's estate.

Kit had not. In truth, he had found the dowry somewhat off-putting, as it drew men to her whose intentions were less than honorable, and he questioned the wisdom of her father in placing such a bounty on her head. Yet he suspected those men, if they could see her current state—bedraggled, behaving more like a nurse or a maid—would rapidly lose interest.

Kit, instead, found himself oddly charmed.

"Who was the little girl?"

The spoon clattered again, and Beth paused before adding hot water to the pot. She replaced the lid on both pot and canister, then turned. "Her name is Mattie."

"So I gathered."

"I do not know much about her. That was only the second time I have seen her."

"But she lives here?"

"A guest here, along with her mother. Apparently. There are quite a few people in this household, but I do not know who is a permanent resident and who is a guest."

"Like my sister."

"I know her to be a guest. Or she *was* a guest."

"But she is no longer."

Beth picked up the teapot and swished it around a bit. Then she added honey to a teacup. "She left shortly after you arrived. Because you arrived." She turned, hands on hips. "It seems to me that would be enough indication that she does not wish to see you."

Kit considered this. "Unless she was forced to leave."

"Why would they make her leave after offering her sanctuary? And her reluctance to see you should also be indicated by her leaving her home in the first place."

"Because I—" Kit stopped. *Because as duke I could bring the force of the law down on this house.* And although the question as to whether Lady Sophia would insist Mary leave because of that might be in doubt, the fact that Mary would leave because of it was not. After all, he had not been surprised to hear she had fled from her own home. His last battle with her had been . . . fierce.

"Because you . . . what?"

Kit felt his body sink a bit deeper into the pillows as he fell silent. Beth turned away to continue preparing the tea.

"Why do you hate me!" Fury flashed in Mary's brown eyes.

"I do not—"

"You do. You and mother both! You hate everything about me. Who I am. What I want. You control everything!"

"I am the duke! And your brother. You are a young lady of the aristocracy. You must—"

"I must! I must do that and I must do this! Go there and do this. Talk to this man but not that one. Do not want anything for yourself. Everything is about this estate. Taking care of the future. What about me? You don't care about me at all!"

Kit watched Beth for a few moments, her movements efficient and precise as she finished the tea. Her skirts cupped the slender curves of her hips, tucking in neatly at her waist. The rudimentary gown laced at the back and seemed without a distinct design or fashion. Perhaps she had borrowed it during her vigil. He had not been able to touch her during his suit, much less hold her, and Kit felt the sudden urge to do to both.

"Why Aldermaston?"

She stilled but did not turn. "I beg your pardon."

"Why him over the others? You had the entire *ton* at your feet." *Why not me?*

She poured the tisane into the cup and brought it to him without a saucer.

He curled his fingers around the porcelain, relishing the warmth. "If I remember, this is bitter."

"I added more honey since you are awake. It will help soothe your throat."

"It *is* painful."

"You do sound as if you have swallowed a bag of rocks."

He sipped the tea and grimaced. Still bitter but with an arching sweetness that did, in truth, feel quite good slipping down his throat. Its warmth spread as well, easing across his chest and into his shoulders. He took another swallow, then another. "Please tell me."

She paused, then sat in the chair. "I thought we were well suited."

"But you might have been well suited with any number of men who paid call." *Including me.*

Beth crossed her arms. "Why does it matter?"

If he gave a little . . . "I am trying to understand Mary. I do not. And it is quite frustrating to try to deal with a situation you do not understand."

She frowned. "You do not know why she left?"

"No. I assumed it was because we would not let her marry a man quite unsuited for her, that she would see reason when she realized how much we wanted her back home. But she has done a masterful job of avoiding discovery." He drank more tea.

"Does she love him?"

"She claimed to. But if that were the case, I would have thought they would have gone together. Eloped to Gretna Green or some such nonsense. Which is the first place I searched for her. But she left alone." He gestured weakly toward the north. "He is still there and claims he has no idea why she left."

"Does he deny he cares for her?"

"He says not, but he may have been lying. I was . . . quite angry."

A smile flitted across her face. "I suspect that was a terrifying sight. Who is he?"

"Our vicar."

"So you object to her marrying a vicar?"

"Yes. No! Not a vicar. *That* vicar. And the way they conducted themselves. I do not trust him. They hid this from us. He is almost fifty. He has a daughter older than Mary and two sons, one in business in Manchester and one in the army."

"And you wish someone better for her."

"Of course I do! She is an aristocrat. She is beautiful, clever, funny—when we are not fighting. One of the reasons I went to London this season was to look for prospects for her."

Beth's eyebrows arched. "And not for yourself?"

"Also myself. I had hoped to find a woman wise and clever, someone who could help Mary in her season next year. Someone who could help her understand the ways of the *ton* as I cannot, being a man."

Beth chewed her lower lip. "But someone more for your sister than yourself."

Kit hesitated. This felt a bit like a trap, but he was not entirely sure why. He swallowed another sip of tea, then drained the cup. "Family is everything."

Beth studied him, then nodded, almost as if to herself. "And that is why I chose Aldermaston."

"How do you mean?"

"His father is a duke—"

I am a duke.

"And he is a powerful voice in Parliament and with the magistrates. He is training his son to follow his path, and people already acknowledge the presence of the marquess at events. He is friends with my brothers. He understands the obligations of being a high-ranking member of the aristocracy, and the joining of our families would produce a powerful dynasty. My dowry would have provided needed capital for his estate, and the merger of our families would create a most powerful business enterprise as well as a political one."

"Did you like him?"

"He was pleasant to be with and we could discuss topics of the day without tripping over each other."

"And if he had fallen to his knees and declared his eternal love?"

Beth grinned. "I would have laughed. He is not a poet and we were not a love match."

Kit looked at the empty cup, his hands relaxing. "Your parents have one of the legendary love matches of the beau monde. You did not want this for yourself?"

"The primary word in that being 'legendary.' They were fortunate but out of the ordinary. I could not desire something so few people ever find. It would be foolish."

And yet I thought Mary foolish for claiming to have found one. Kit blinked, his eyelids feeling heavy. His muscles seemed to sag. "So you chose based on what you thought best for your family."

"Of course." She appeared to lean a little closer, but his vision had blurred. "That, and I had little desire to move to the Lake District, despite Mr. Woodsworth's poetry."

"Ah, the romantic advantage of geography." He let out a long breath, weariness dragging him deeper. "But you should see the view from our garden."

Beth stood and pulled the covers higher up on his chest and shoulders. She lifted the cup from his loosening fingers. "Perhaps I will someday."

CHAPTER SEVEN

Monday, 12 September 1825
Timmons Manor
Quarter of eleven in the morning

BETH WATCHED KIRKSTONE drift off to sleep, a bit unsettled by her reaction to him during this conversation. While he had been unconscious or almost so, as ill or more so than her mother or brothers had been, she had responded to him as she would have a strange child—distant and reserved. As a doctor would to a patient.

But over the past half-hour, Beth had been reminded of how she had felt about him as a man, a potential suitor. Her hands on his bare skin, the feel of the muscles in his back, had sent an unfamiliar shock through her, a fiery heat that had resonated through her chest and down her body, to the point that she had almost jerked away. Only his raucous coughing had reminded her how much he still needed her as a nurse.

She took a shuddering breath. This was dangerous. She had never responded to Aldermaston this way. Their relationship had been civil, agreeable, and built on a growing friendship. His touch—what little there had been of it—had been calm and reassuring. Aldermaston had been an intelligent, decent man who always treated her with respect, even as he had apologetically set her aside.

Kirkstone, who had also treated her with respect, had a raw-ness about him—even during their brief times on the dance floor—that had terrified Beth. Aldermaston embraced his world with a placid acceptance, satisfied with his position and his responsibilities. Kirkstone had seemed to grab his world with both hands, shaking it to see what he could stir from its depths. Aldermaston had talked politics, theater, and fashion. Kirkstone had regaled her with tales of wild rides over the dales, his love of dogs and hunting, and his affection for his home estate. He had accepted the necessity of spending time in London when Parliament was in session, but he had craved returning to the district of his heart.

Of his passion.

It was not just geography that had made Beth step away. She had seen what passion had done to her brothers. It had driven Michael into the gutter and Robert into scandal. It had gotten Thomas shot and almost killed.

Aldermaston had been by far the safer choice. Wise. Com-fortable.

Beth swallowed hard, realizing that she had slowly reached her hand toward Kirkstone, as if to stroke his shoulder.

His bare shoulder.

A longing. A desire to touch him again surged through her. To feel that heat, that strength beneath her palm.

She clenched her fist and stepped away. From what she had seen of the tisane's effects over the past two days, he would be asleep for a while. He remained ill, but not dangerously so. She could let him sleep without a guardian, since his weakness would keep him confined to the bed for a few more days. She desperate-ly wanted a bath, but even more so needed to speak with Sophie.

She needed to be away from this man.

Beth opened the door and eased from the room, pulling the door closed. When she turned, she started to find one of the younger maids standing behind her. "Oh!"

The girl gave a quick curtsy. "Is everything all right?"

Beth blinked at her. "Yes. He is sleeping. Why are you here?"

The girl's cheeks pinked. "Miss Daphne, ma'am. She has asked us to keep watch in case you needed anything."

"You mean, in case I called for help as opposed to ringing for a servant."

The girl chewed her lip. "Yes. She does not . . ."

"She does not trust the gentleman."

The maid shook her head. "No."

Beth took a deep breath. "He is sleeping for the moment, so I think we are all safe for a while. Could you find Kendall and help her arrange for a bath in my bedchamber? Also ask Cook to send up a camphor poultice for this afternoon. I need to see Lady . . . I need to see Sophie." Beth wondered if she would ever be able to surrender the protocol training of the *ton*.

Probably not.

The girl gave another quick curtsy and dashed toward the back stairs. Beth turned toward the front ones and made her way to Sophie's study, where the head of this peculiar household was once again bent low over a stack of correspondence, her spectacles perched on the tip of her nose.

Beth tapped lightly on the door, and Sophie looked up. She smiled and motioned for Beth to sit in a chair at the front of her desk. She removed the spectacles and leaned back in her chair, her fingers entwining around the frame of the spectacles. "How is he doing?"

Beth sank into the chair, her weariness pulling at every muscle. "Did you speak with the doctor?"

"I did. But I wish to hear your assessment as well."

"He is definitely much improved, but still remarkably weak. After the doctor left, he had two coughing spells and needed help dealing with them."

Sophie's eyes narrowed. "What type of help?"

"Support. He could push up, but could not sustain the position. His coughs are also still quite . . . productive. I gave him more of the tisane, which let him fall back asleep. He is alone for now, but I doubt he will stir for several hours, unless it is to cough. I have asked for Cook to send up a camphor poultice this afternoon."

"How long was he awake before you gave him the potion?"

"From just after you left the room until a few minutes ago."

"But not awake or well enough to leave his bed."

Beth thought again of the way his body had sagged after the coughing spasms. "No. He is far too weak even to use a chamber pot. It will be several more days before he can move about. The doctor thought it might be a week or more."

Sophie's lips pursed. "So he told me. But he assured me that Kirkstone would be spending more hours awake than asleep from this point. It may be time for you to relinquish your care of him to one of the maids."

Beth considered it. It would be much easier for her. But something else tugged at her, as if something still needed to be resolved between her and Kirkstone. "I would like to continue for another day or two."

"Why?"

"He is no danger to me in his condition. And you do not have the staff to add nursing to their duties."

"I could bring in extra help from the village."

Beth looked down at her hands. Her fingers clutched each other, tense and fidgety. The way they always had when she had tried to lie to her mother. It was the way the duchess had always known Beth had been hiding some truth. Beth gave a half smile.

"What is it?" Sophie asked.

Looking up, Beth straightened her shoulders. "Why is Mary here?"

Sophie's eyebrows arched. "I beg your pardon?"

"Kirkstone told me about her. Told me they had fought over a man Mary thought she loved, but instead of eloping to Gretna Green, Mary had left alone, something that horrified her mother and terrified her brother. Kirkstone thought it was because of this man, but now he is unsure. She wandered a bit before coming here, but this house seems to have been her destination from the beginning. He's curious and hurt and quite determined to speak with her—"

"I cannot allow—"

"I told him he could not. That she did not want to see him and was no longer in residence. He seems to have accepted that, but he is still angry as well as hurt. But his explanation raised more questions than answers. Why would she come here? Specifically here? Is she a friend of someone here?"

Sophie hesitated, her eyes on her correspondence. Finally, she set her spectacles aside and stood. "Come with me."

Beth followed Sophie, and they left the first floor, climbing to the third. As they reached the top, Sophie turned. "I know that Daphne told you not to come to this floor, as this is where our other guests reside. That much is true. But she also told you that there was nothing else here but storage, which is not true. I do ask that for the next bit you do not speak. You may ask questions when we return downstairs. For now, only listen. Do you agree?"

Beth's curiosity had never been so piqued, not even when her brother Michael had refused her access to the stables at Ashton Park when she was fourteen. He had blocked her path for hours, until Thomas had brought forth a newborn foal—they had not wanted her to witness the birth—and presented it to her, the beauty that had grown into her beloved Bella. "I agree," she whispered.

Sophie led off again, passing several doors until she came to one at the far end, near the servants' stairs. She gave two soft raps on the door, then pushed it open. Beth followed her inside, and stopped dead, her breath frozen in a constricted chest.

Four women stared back at them. Lydia, her red curls muted by the dim light of the room, sat in a rocker, an infant curled against her chest. Esther also sat in a rocker cuddling a baby, her green eyes wide with fear as she looked at Beth. Amelia walked near the back wall, an infant on her shoulder. Near one of the five cribs in the room, an unfamiliar woman lowered a much smaller baby down to the mattress, a look of alarm clouding her face.

Sophie held out her hand, a gesture of patience, and spoke, her words calm and soft. "It is time." She rested her other hand on Beth's arm. "This is our nursery. Lydia gave birth about three months ago, Amelia and Esther almost four. Bertie and Priscilla have yet to give birth. This is our nurse, Mrs. Seton, and the tiny one is Charlotte's son, born last week just before you arrived. Charlotte is still quite ill—the doctor and midwife both think it is too soon to leave her bed. She has only been able to nurse the child a few times, so we have a wet nurse in the village who is helping her. Charlotte is Mattie's mother as well."

Beth's lips parted in shock, but she could not have spoken, even if allowed to. The details of what she saw tumbled over in her head like knotted strings.

Lydia stood, handing her child to Mrs. Seton before turning with ire on Sophie. "What are you doing?" Her words were a sharp hiss. "She is one of *them*. She will betray us just as *they* did!"

They? Who are they? Beth opened her mouth to ask, then remembered her promise. She pressed her lips together.

"And reveal that she has been living among us?" Sophie asked, a light gleam in her eyes. "I do not think so."

Understanding and relief crossed Lydia's face. "She would be ruined."

Beth bit her lower lip. *I am already ruined.*

Sophie nodded. "And we all know too well how tenuous the position of any woman in Society."

Lydia scoured Beth head to toe with a milk-curdling glare. "You will be silent?"

Beth nodded once.

The young woman looked at Sophie again. "And him?"

"He is too ill to be aware of anything untoward at the moment. When he is well enough, we will move him to The Queen's Arms until he can travel. The doctor will care for him there. I have already made the arrangements with Mr. Keales."

Lydia looked somewhat mollified, but her eyes remained narrow. "And my situation?"

Sophie hesitated but met Lydia's steady gaze. "I have sent a second letter. If there is no response in an appropriate amount of time, we will have to consider another option."

Lydia's words became a tight hiss again. "I will not send her to an orphanage!"

Sophie touched Lydia's shoulder. "Of course not, my girl. We would never even allow that as an option."

Lydia swallowed hard, but her face relaxed. She nodded, and Sophie turned, guiding Beth back to the door.

Beth followed Sophie in silence as they descended back to the first floor, her mind spinning as she tried to fully grasp what she had seen and heard. All the young women living in the house had either recently given birth or were about to. They had apparently sought this house as a refuge, and Sophie and Daphne had opened it to them. Obviously none were married, abandoned by the men who had created the problems for them. No wonder no footmen or other male servants worked in the house, except for Notley.

Beth now had even more questions than before, but one of the outstanding ones had already been answered.

Lady Mary Caudale was with child.

Monday, 12 September 1825
Timmons Manor
Four in the afternoon

KIT SHIVERED, A chill shuddering through him, and his hands clawed for the covers as he tried to rise up, blinking sleepily.

Warm hands pushed at his shoulders, then his arms. "Shh. Do not fight it. The chills will come and go for a bit."

Beth's sweet voice. He relaxed, closing his eyes, letting his head rest against the pillows.

An odd and heavy weight disappeared from his chest, then the covers were pulled higher, slender fingers tucking them around his shoulders, slipping his arms beneath them. A different weight settled over him as an additional blanket spread over the bed. An odd pungent odor reached his nostrils and he almost sneezed.

He swallowed instead. His throat was not as painful but still raw. He felt a spoon press his lower lip.

"It's water. Try to sip a bit."

He let the water roll around in his mouth before swallowing. "What day is it?"

"Still Monday. You have only slept a few hours this time. Sip."

He did. "What is that stench?"

"The part that is not you is from a camphor poultice. For your breathing. I removed it. Sip."

He swallowed. "I hope it worked. And that I will not need it again."

She gave a low laugh. "Are you hungry?"

Kit considered the question. His body still ached, his chest heavy, his muscles weak. But a hollow emptiness had opened in his belly. "I believe so."

"This is good. I will ring for some of the bone broth Cook has been simmering for you."

He heard the rustle of soft skirts—not the rough muslin she had worn earlier, something more . . . genteel. He blinked, then forced his eyes open.

The room remained dim with only a few strands of sunlight streaming through gaps in the curtains. Beth stood near the head of the bed, her hands releasing the bell pull. Her earlier gown had been replaced with a deep blue silken day gown. The scarf gone, her light curls had been bound up in a neat chignon, topped with a small blue cotton cap.

"You changed gowns." His voice rasped.

"I felt the chances of you covering me with phlegm and spittle had lessened."

He smiled. "Let us both hope you are correct."

A maid opened the door and poked her head inside. Beth gave instructions for the broth and an onion poultice. The girl vanished, and Beth settled in the chair near the bed, her movements far more *ton* debutante than nursemaid. "When the broth arrives, you will need to sit up to drink it. I will ask the maid to help me adjust the pillows. Will that be all right?"

He nodded. "By chance could I have a shirt?"

Beth grinned. "Yes. Your clothes have been cleaned. Both your travel packs have been stored in the dressing room. Although I do not think the maids here would be scandalized by a shirtless man."

"It is far more that I am uncomfortable being shirtless in front of a strange maid."

Her smile widened. "Surely you are not so modest as that."

Kit peered at her. "A duke cannot be modest?"

"A duke who is dressed by another man most of the time?"

"A professional valet who has known that duke more than a decade. It is quite different."

"So your valet worked for your father?"

Kit paused at how quickly she had deduced that. "He did. Loyalty is valued among my family."

Beth fell silent, then she stood and walked toward a narrow door on the far side of the room. She returned with his linen shirt, which had obviously been whitened as well as washed. It had turned a dingy yellow in his travels but now almost sparkled. She handed it to him. "If you can get it over your head and arms, I will help you straighten it down the back." Then she turned her back on him, waiting.

The shirt was soft as well as clean, and it smelled of pine and fresh air. He gathered the fabric and slipped it over his head, fumbling a bit as he found the sleeves and inserted his arms. He situated it the best he could, making sure the V opening was over his sternum and the front pulled down as far as he could manage.

"All right."

She turned and slid her arm behind his shoulders. Together they managed to push him forward enough for Beth to pull smooth the cloth over his back. The shirt, long enough to be tucked into his breeches, bunched a bit over his hips, but he felt infinitely more decent as Beth helped him settle again.

"Thank you."

"You are welcome." She sat down again.

"Are you the only one in this house who can care for me?"

Her eyes narrowed. "Do you wish someone else to care for you?"

He shifted in the bed. "Do you not find it odd that a lady of the beau monde is playing nursemaid?"

"This is a peculiar house."

"So I have gathered."

Beth looked down at her hands. "May I ask you a question?"

"Of course."

After another hesitation she looked up at him. "Why would you want Lady Mary to return to a place she feels unhappy and unloved?"

Kit felt the weight of the question in his gut, and his anger at Mary, his fear for her, bubbled up again, threatening to choke him. His words emerged on a tight rasp. "She is not unloved. She is cherished!"

Beth did not relent. "But what of her own feelings? If she feels unloved, there must be a reason."

Kit felt the heat in his head, which began to throb. "Because she is a child! Foolish and full of unrealistic notions about life. She would not listen to her mother. She does not listen to me."

"Yet you think you can persuade her to return?"

"Yes. And the law says she must. She is under my rule."

"Ah. I know that would persuade me that I am cherished."

Kit glowered at her. "She must listen to reason."

"Why? You just said she is a child. Do many children in your acquaintance behave according to reason?"

Kit tried to sit up, but his muscles would not cooperate. "Why are you doing this? You know what is required of a lady in Society, even if no one else here does. If word spreads of Mary's behavior, her chances for a good marriage will be destroyed. And the longer she is without supervision, the more likely she will find herself in danger—real danger. Not just that of the *ton's* gossip but physical harm. She is too young—too innocent—to be alone!" Frustrated, he collapsed back against the pillows.

Beth fell silent, watching him, her voice falling in volume and pitch. "You said she is not unloved. Do *you* love her?"

Kit fought for a breath. "Of course I love her. What an asinine—"

"Not as a duke. Not as her 'ruler.' As her brother. Do you love her?"

Kit stilled, her meaning finally penetrating his protests. "What are you asking?"

"I want to know if all this fury is about her defiance of you as duke. Are you trying to control her? Or save her?"

"Is there a difference?"

Beth let out a long breath. "Yes. Without a doubt."

The bedchamber door opened as a light tapping sounded from the other side. The maid entered, carrying a tray, followed by a tall woman with gray and silver hair—and an Irish wolfhound. Beth stood and moved to the foot of the bed, just as she had when the doctor had entered.

The woman looked from him to Beth. "Did I interrupt?"

"No," Beth muttered. "We were just discussing the vagaries of the beau monde."

The woman's dark brown eyes narrowed. "Hm. A topic that could take years."

Kit's attention turned to the wolfhound, who had begun to snuffle at the blankets near his feet. His gamekeeper kept two wolfhounds, amongst a half dozen other dogs, and Kit knew the breed well. He lay still, allowing the animal to sniff his feet. After several deep snuffles, the dog sneezed.

As the woman grinned, Kit pulled his hand free of the covers and held it out to the dog, palm down.

"Easy, Boru," the woman muttered as the dog moved toward his hand.

As expected, Boru—what a perfect name!—sniffed his hand, then nuzzled it, pushing his head beneath it. Kit scratched between his ears, and Boru let out a snort.

"At least the dog likes me," Kit murmured.

The woman gave a low chuckle. "Not unexpected. Boru likes everyone, unless they are an immediate threat to his family."

Kit looked up at her. "You think I am a threat."

"Indubitably." She crossed her arms. "I am Daphne. We met briefly in the entrance hall before you decided to make it into a bed."

Kit raked through his memory, then shook his head. "My apologies, but I do not remember."

Daphne's eyes narrowed farther and she looked up at Beth, who shifted her weight. "He claims not to remember anything after he left Shipton to head north."

"Hm."

Kit swallowed hard. "I do remember being told I would find my sister here."

"But you have now been told she is not here."

"Not here any longer."

"Do you believe that?"

Kit glanced at Beth, whose face remained remarkably impassive. "I do."

"Good." Daphne moved closer to the bed, her hand resting on Boru's head. The dog gazed up at his mistress, pure affection on his face. "Let me be clear about how things will proceed from here. We will continue to care for you until you are able to leave the bed and move a few steps about the room. You will not, however, ever leave this room without being escorted by me. Once you are able to walk more than a few steps, you will be moved to The Queen's Arms, where Mr. Keales will oversee you until you are strong enough to leave Litton and return home."

"Mr. Keales does not exactly care for me."

A smile flitted across Daphne's face then vanished. "So he has indicated. But he has agreed to this plan out of loyalty to Sophie."

"I wish to see my sister."

"Your wishes are irrelevant. You are the intruder here. Mary has been informed of your presence and has no desire to speak with you."

Kit felt his ire stirring again. "Then she is being irrational. I have done nothing to her. We had a row. That should not be sufficient reason for her to abandon the people who love her."

Daphne stilled. "A row?"

Kit's fist clenched. "Yes! About that bloody fool she wanted to marry—who now claims he does not know what she is talking about. She said she loved him, but he says he only saw her as another parishioner. I do not know if he is lying or she is. And I cannot know without speaking with her."

Daphne studied him. "Who is he?"

"Our vicar. The man is three times her age and widowed less than a year. He has a daughter older than Mary. All I want is the chance to tell her I talked to him. To explain what I have done to help her."

"To persuade her to return home."

"Of course."

"And if she refuses to go?"

Kit's head throbbed. "Then let her tell me."

Abruptly, Daphne pivoted and marched from the room, Boru at her heels. With a quick glance at Kit, Beth followed, closing the door behind them.

Chapter Eight

Monday, 12 September 1825
Timmons Manor
Half past four in the afternoon

BETH SCURRIED TO keep up with Daphne and Boru as the older woman headed for the stairs. "Daphne! Please wait!"

At the top of the steps, Daphne halted and looked back, her face hard. "He does not know, does he? Just as you told Sophie."

Beth stared at Daphne, annoyance drilling into her gut. This had been a test, a trial to see if Beth had been truthful with Sophie, following the visit to the nursery. After they had returned to Sophie's office, Beth had quizzed her about the other women, where they had come from, and why they—like Mary—had sought out Timmons Manor. Sophie confirmed that Mary Caudale was with child—and that for more than twenty years Timmons Manor had been a haven for young women who had been seduced by the unsavory men in their lives. They had maintained their privacy primarily through seclusion—and because the people of Litton had adopted and protected them.

In turn, Sophie had inquired about everything Beth and Kirkstone had discussed since he had awakened. Most of all, Sophie had wanted to know if Kirkstone knew about his sister's condition. Now she told Daphne the same thing she had said to

Sophie.

"No, from what he has said so far about Mary, he does not."

Daphne crossed her arms tightly across her abdomen. "You believe what he said to be the truth."

"I do."

"Then that damned vicar is lying, and Kirkstone believed him."

"Since he does not know about Mary's condition, what evidence would he have not to?"

"He could simply believe his own flesh and blood."

"He is a man, speaking with a trusted clergyman. I am not sure my own brothers would have believed me, if they did not have all the details. And Mary could have confided in him."

"I certainly cannot say I would trust that man with such information, if he were my brother."

Beth chewed her lower lip.

"And you would not have either, would you?"

Beth shook her head.

Daphne uncrossed her arms, and some of the hardness eased from her expression. "I agree with Sophie. I think it is time you spent less time in his presence."

"I think . . . I think I can ease his determination."

"I do not see how."

Beth straightened her shoulders. "To be truthful, I am not sure how I can do it either. I simply believe I can."

"Without telling him about Mary? That should be her decision."

"Yes."

"Hm." Daphne turned and headed down the stairs, but stopped a few steps down, looking up at Beth. "I will talk to Sophie. I do think you should rotate with others on the staff, but not leave him entirely." She held up one finger. "On one condition. You get more rest. That gray pony needs more time with you in the saddle."

Beth smiled. "Agreed."

Daphne gave one sharp nod and continued down the stairs. Beth returned to the Rose Room to find Kirkstone propped up on a mound of pillows, an earthen bowl on a tray across his lap. With his left hand, he slowly lifted a spoon of broth to his lips, his hand quivering slightly. He sipped, then returned the spoon to the bowl.

Beth turned to the maid, eyebrows raised. The maid, who was tidying the table holding most of the medical supplies, gave her a slight smile and a shrugged one shoulder.

"Meg," Kirkstone said, his voice still a low gravel, "is stronger than she appears to be."

Beth bit her lower lip to keep from laughing. Meg's cheeks pinked and she turned back to the table.

"So I see." Beth moved to the side of the bed. "I hope she is not also responsible for the new flush in your cheeks."

Kirkstone's eyes widened, mock innocence covering his face. "Absolutely not. The broth is hot."

"Hm." Beth suddenly understood the usefulness of Daphne's almost universal response.

A smile twisted his mouth as he lifted the spoon again, his hand trembling a bit more than before.

"The broth will give you more strength."

"Provided I do not spill it all over the bed." He did make it to his mouth with all the liquid, but his eyes narrowed, and he lowered the spoon to the bowl, then his arm to the bed.

"Why not try drinking it from the bowl? You could hold it with both hands. It might be more stable."

He glowered at her. "I am not an animal."

Beth gave a light shrug. "No, but you like to resolve problems. Otherwise you would not have undertaken a quest to find your sister, even if it led you to this. What would you suggest?"

Kirkstone looked down at the bowl. "Perhaps a cup—"

Beth scooped the bowl off the tray. Meg emptied a cup holding the medicinal tea into the pot and dipped a serving from the bowl into the cup. Beth returned to the bed and placed it on the tray in his lap. He managed better, but Beth could see it continued to be an effort of will to get it to his mouth. She itched to simply take over and feed him, but in this moment, that felt like the wrong solution.

She went back to Meg and asked her to bring up some stale bread and fresh tea. As the girl scurried out, Beth returned to the chair.

"I think you should wait." Her quiet words got his attention.

He set down the cup, his face a raw mask of frustration. "I have to improve."

"You are. I do not think you realize exactly how sick you have been. The doctor was surprised that you were awake, much less sitting up. Less than twenty-four hours ago, you were so feverish you were delirious. You have not eaten in three days. A weaker man would still be flat on his back."

Before he could respond, Meg entered with a plate of sliced bread and a pot of hot water. She gave Beth the bread and returned to the side table with the water, where she began to make a fresh pot of tea. Beth broke the slices of the bread in half and put the plate on his tray. "Dip a piece in the broth. You need the broth for strength, but the bread should be light enough for you to handle. Small bits of bread, lots of broth." She reached for one of the ever-present white cloths and draped it over his chest. "It will drip, but let's not worry about that for now."

It worked. Kirkstone was able to dip the bread, let it soak, then lift it to his mouth with no signs of weakness. After consuming several pieces, he let out a sigh. "I never realized eating like a child could be so heavenly." He paused and looked at her. "How did you think of this?"

She smiled. "I was the younger sister of three stubborn, rambunctious boys. They always teased me, daring me to do exactly what they did."

His eyes narrowed. "I hear an exceptionally bad result coming in this tale."

Beth nodded, chuckling at the memory. "My brother Michael

was especially gifted with horses. I followed him over the fields at Ashton Park, including over an unexpectedly high hedge."

"How old were you?"

"Nine. Michael was thirteen and home from his first year at Eton. He returned cocky and a bit belligerent. I was a defiant child, insisting I could do what he could."

"What happened?"

Beth held up both arms. "Left wrist and right arm broken. I could not feed myself for two months, and even after my arms were released from their prisons, they were weak."

He looked down at the tray. "Bread and broth."

"My salvation." She lowered her arms and studied her hands in her lap. "You know they do not trust you."

He ate more bread. "Expected."

"You tell a different story than Mary has told."

Kirkstone adjusted the cloth covering his chest. "Also expected."

"And a vastly different one than the vicar told you. Do you believe him?"

He had picked up a piece of bread but set it back on the tray. "You think I should not?"

"I suspect it will require several versions of the story to gain one truth."

"You think he is lying."

"Perhaps. I do think any man confronted by an angry duke of your size and belligerence will develop a sudden capacity for deception."

His mouth tightened but a slight gleam appeared in his eyes. "You think he was lying."

"I am currently not in a position to believe anyone's tale."

"Have you ever considered a political career?"

Beth blinked, slightly confused. *Why would he ask—*

"Because you have a politician's capacity for dodging an answer to a perfectly reasonable question."

"Arse."

A barked laugh burst from Kirkstone, immediately followed by a spasmed cough. Beth leaped to her feet, motioning for Meg, and grabbed the tray. The maid, at her side in a mere second, took the tray, and Beth pushed Kirkstone forward. Several coughs wracked his body, and Beth lifted the white cloth to his mouth. Beth spoke to Meg over her shoulder. "Make more of the tisane."

Kirkstone spit into the cloth, then gulped air into his lungs as he calmed.

With her arm still supporting him, Beth helped him lie back against the pillows. "Obviously, laughter should not be on your agenda for a few days."

He nodded and took the cloth, wiping his mouth again.

As he settled, Beth turned and took a cup from Meg. "Have Cook prepare another camphor poultice." As the maid left again, Beth helped Kirkstone take a few sips of the bitter potion.

"It is still nasty," he whispered.

"And it will still help you rest. You are better. You are not well."

She offered and he took another sip, swallowing slowly. "Will you please answer my question?"

Beth hesitated, knowing that an honest answer could possibly reveal too much. But she would not lie to him. "Yes. I think he is lying."

"Why? What do you know?"

"Did you and Mary have a cordial relationship when you were children?"

He gave one slow nod. "I thought so. I was older, but we still shared similar family events and experiences. We hunted together as she became old enough. She has traveled with my mother and me to London numerous times. I believed she was anticipating her debut season with some joy. It was postponed due to our father's death. My mother would not travel during her mourning."

"Was Mary close to her father?"

Kirkstone gave her a sharp look. "Why would that be important?" Beth waited, and he finally answered. "Yes."

"So her father dies and her brother bolts for London, for investiture and Parliament. Did she go with you?"

"We thought it best if she remained at home. She was upset, naturally. Grieving."

"Did your mother remain with her?"

He paused again, his eyes narrowing. "No. She came with me for the investiture, but as she was still in mourning, she returned as soon as the ceremony concluded."

"But she was engrossed in her own mourning. So Mary sought comfort elsewhere."

His gaze sharpened again, his words grating with anger. "She would not dare! Nor would he! What you are suggesting is impossible."

"Yet I believe a younger sister will not usually defy her older brother without reason. Speaking from my own experience, of course. I argue and fume at my brothers, but I would not truly defy them without an act of Parliament. Or something similarly drastic."

Kirkstone opened his mouth to speak but shut it, shaking his head. His eyes turned downward, his gaze distant. After several moments of silence, Beth moved closer. "You should drink more." She offered the cup, but he refused.

"I would prefer you leave now."

Beth tried to ignore the stab of pain his comment caused in her chest. Instead she stood. "Meg will bring another camphor poultice. It will help you breathe as you rest."

He gave no response, and Beth eased from the room and into her own, just before the first tears stung her eyes. She should not care—she had declined his suit, seeing no future for them. He should mean nothing to her. Neither should Mary or any of the others in this house. She had come north to escape drama, scandal, conflict—and had managed to land in the middle of one bigger than she could have imagined. She should not care.

But she did.

KIT FELT HORRID—AND not because of the pressure in his chest or the pungent odor of camphor.

He had sent Beth away. Told her to leave. For three days she had stayed by his side, nurtured him, nursed him through a fever that easily could have killed him. She had behaved in a way he had never known any woman of the *ton* to do—he could not even imagine his own mother tending to him the ways Beth had done. Those sweet blue-gray eyes had peered at him as she had never done on the dance floor in London, with kindness and concern.

And he had sent her away because she had dared suggest he could be wrong about his sister. That somehow *he* might be at fault for Mary leaving, that *his* behavior had caused her to seek out this strange house run by women.

A daring, inappropriate, and outrageous thought.

Kit also feared that Beth could be right.

As the tisane and poultice began weaving their effects on his body, his mind swirled through a hundred memories of Mary over the past year. Her inconsolable grief at their father's death, at first even denying he was gone. The hours she had spent abed, refusing to eat or even move. When she finally emerged, she spent almost every day with her Dales pony, walking the fells and vales near their home. She had told Kit that her wanderings had led her to the vicarage, to seek counsel with a man she had fallen in love with—a love she claimed he returned, but that he had later denied experiencing. When Kit and his mother had gone to London for the investiture, Mary had refused to go, and they returned to find a bedraggled, unwashed girl prone to crying fits and temper tantrums.

Had he and his mother truly failed Mary?

Kit felt a cough building in the back of his throat and pushed higher on the pillows. Meg came to his side as he coughed twice—raw but productive bursts—and plumped the pillows before he leaned back. She offered him more tea, but he asked for water instead, and she brought him a small cup.

As he handed it back to her, he cleared his throat. "How long has Lady Eliz—Beth—been in this house?"

Meg closed both hands around the cup. "She arrived the day before you did."

His eyebrows arched as that detail registered. "Only one day?"

"Yes, Your Grace."

He smiled at the young girl. "I thought you did not use titles in this house."

Her cheeks pinked. "We do not, but I was uncertain what else to call you."

"I can understand. It would seem to be difficult to break such training."

"It does take time." She gave a quick curtsy and returned to a chair near the table with the supplies. Unlike Beth, Meg did not seem to want to linger near his bedside.

Beth. He had longed to call her that down in London, after hearing it from her brothers. But that would have been impossible, completely inappropriate among Society, or even in the privacy of the Ashton House receiving room, where he had paid his calls on her. "Beth" suited her, so much more than "Lady Elizabeth," with its formal recall of an earlier, austere queen. Especially as she had sat near his bed, her hair held back by a rough scarf, her long braid trailing down her back, a light flush on her cheeks.

His loins tightened and Kit's mouth twisted at the feeling— his physical illness had obviously abated somewhat even as the trials in his mind and heart worsened. He shifted in the bed, using the covers to disguise his body's response to the image of Beth next to his bed, her softness and wit engaging him. With any other woman, he would have thought she wanted more than his recovery.

But Lady Elizabeth Ashton had rejected his attempts to court her, in favor of an older, mature, and calm-natured marquess. Kit knew Aldermaston from encounters at balls and at White's. The man had been a peacemaker, a voice of reason in the most heated of debates. A man of protocol who had stood next to his father, in agreement with all that duke's opinions.

Yet a man who could not stand on his own, who could not defy his father when trouble arose. A man who had turned his back on Beth when scandal reared its face.

The rotter.

She deserved better.

But was he any better? A man who may have driven his own sister into an untenable situation, allowing a young girl in his care and protection to take a dangerous and unsustainable path?

The emotion that drilled into Kit in that moment was pure frustration. Frustration that he had no answers and no way to get them. *Damnation!*

Any arousal he had felt vanished, and Kit tried to push up, to swing his legs out of bed. One leg slid off, but as his body lurched forward, his head spun, and he began to topple sideways, panic surging through him as he fell. The camphor poultice hit the floor with a soft plop, and his head seemed to follow it.

Then he stopped, Meg's body under his, shoving him up and back. "Your Grace! What are you doing?" Her frantic words matched the pale expression and wide eyes. "You cannot do this!"

Kit collapsed back against the pillows, a wave of exhaustion searing through him. His muscles were weaker than he had anticipated. "Apparently." The word, a harsh rasp, rode out on a long exhale. He allowed the young maid to help him push back up on the pillows, repositioning him in the reclining pose that had been his since he had been awake. Probably before, given the soreness in his hips and rear.

Meg tucked the covers around him as he caught his breath, grateful that his attempt had not resulted in another coughing spasm. As she replaced the camphor poultice, he nodded his thanks. "Meg?"

"Yes, Your Grace?"

"That woman who was here. Not Beth, the other one."

"Sophie? Daphne?"

"The one who owns this house. Sophie?" At Meg's nod, he continued. "I want to see her. As soon as possible."

CHAPTER NINE

Tuesday, 13 September 1825
Timmons Manor
Seven in the morning

"**B**ETH! WAIT!"

She did not, urging Grace into a gallop, their path circling the base of Fountain Fell, into the vale beyond, northwest and away from the river. Beth had no illusions that her sturdy gray could outrun Daphne's Arabian, but neither did she want to stop. She needed this, the rush of the wind, the feel of Grace's muscles beneath her, the sting of the long mane as it trailed back and flicked against her cheeks. The exhilaration of it filled ever fiber, making her feel as if her body were singing, crying out from the effort.

A series of rolling meadows opened up before her, and Beth urged Grace on, leaning low over the horse's neck. With a glorious rush, they cleared a low stone fence, the pony's hooves landing with certainty and elegance. She heard Daphne's Arabian clear the fence behind her, then felt the presence of the sleek horse move up beside her. She glanced over to see Daphne's wide grin and dark eyes. The Arabian pulled ahead, one length, then two. At three lengths, Daphne straightened in the saddle and moved in front of Grace, forcing both horses to slow.

Beth relented, sitting up and easing Grace into a canter, then a trot, as Daphne moved back beside her.

Daphne's breath came in quick gasps. "What the devil are you doing out so early?"

Beth slowed Grace to a walk, reclaiming her own slowed breathing. "I could not sleep."

"Ah. Were the babies keeping you awake? Two of them had a rough night."

Beth shook her head. "No. It was not the babies." She turned her gaze over the meadows. From the rise where they walked, she could see three of the tenancies, demarked by fences and clusters of small buildings. The grasses surrounding them had begun to fade to an autumn hue, the interspersed trees tinged with the first golds and reds of the season. Beyond them, a fourth crofter's cottage stood atop another rise, the grass around it unkempt, its outbuildings shabby and needing repairs.

"Kirkstone?" Daphne's softer question held a note of concern.

Beth hesitated, then gave one nod. "And Mary."

"And why did this brother and sister pair disturb your slumber?"

Beth glanced at the older woman, then down at Grace. She was not sure she wanted to put voice to her feelings—not even to herself. That she had spent much of the night trying to escape those feelings—and the way they had crimped and crumbled at the sound of his voice when he ordered her from his room—had left her mind blurry and spinning. Thus for the need for the gallop across the fields to clear her head and make her blood rush.

"I—I—" She stopped and took a deep breath. "After you and I spoke yesterday, I confronted him. I suggested that he had misjudged his sister and believed the wrong details, including what his beloved vicar had told him." She shifted in her saddle. "And he asked me to leave."

"Hm."

"I spoke without truly knowing Mary or the situation myself. And—" Beth looked out over the meadows again. "I am beginning to think I may have been wrong as well."

"About the vicar? Or about choosing Aldermaston over Kirkstone?"

Beth sighed. "The latter."

They fell silent, and Beth relished the moment, taking comfort in the early morning sun on her back and the first smells of autumn in the air. She knew that after she returned, after a wash and breakfast, she would be exhausted, but in this moment, she felt as if she had reclaimed something lost in Kirkstone's words. *I would prefer you leave now.*

Her purpose in being here. "May I see Mary?"

Daphne stroked the Arabian's neck. "Why?"

"I wish to know her story."

Another pause. "You will not try to persuade her?"

Beth fought a surge of excitement at the possibility of seeing Mary. "No."

Glancing behind her, Daphne urged the Arabian into a trot and motioned for Beth to follow. She did, and they rode without speaking, the only sounds around them the creaks and jangles of the horses' tack and the warbling of birds in the tree line. They headed for the first tenancy, and Daphne slowed as they approached the cottage. Beth did likewise until they both halted. They slid from their saddles as a man emerged from an outbuilding near the cottage. He looked to be in his forties, with a shock of red hair and ruddy cheeks. He wore thick woolen clothes, knee-high work boots, and a flat cap. A flock of sheep huddled on the far side of the building, milling about and bumping into each other, their late summer coats of wool a light beige of mud and lanolin.

The man touched the flat cap on his head. "Daphne."

"Bowlin." She pointed at the cottage door with her crop, and the man nodded, although his eyes narrowed as he examined Beth head to toe.

She wondered if he realized she wore one of Daphne's riding habits. Or if he was just wary of a stranger, even with Daphne by her side.

Daphne rapped twice on the door, then opened it and entered. Beth crossed the threshold and stopped just inside the door. The cottage was spacious, clean, and brightly lit from the morning sun's rays flowing through two windows. The wooden floor had been swept clear, and a cozy fire burned on the hearth. An area to their left held a table with six chairs, cabinets, and shelves lined with dishes, pots, and food. To their right, two low beds were pushed against the walls, and in the open area were two armchairs, a rocker, and several low stools. Through a door at the rear, Beth could see two more beds and a washstand. A welcoming scent of warm bread, spices, and fried meat hung in the air, and a pot hanging on a rod in the fireplace gave off a deliciously fragrant aroma of cabbage, potatoes, lamb, and onions.

Two young girls played near the hearth, while an older girl stirred the pot. A woman stood near the larger table with a cloth in her hand—a bowl of water and dishes near her revealing what they had interrupted—and on the far side of the room, Mary sat in the rocker, a basket of sewing balanced on her knees in front of a stomach swollen and heavy with child.

They all stared at Beth. In the growing silence, Beth looked to Daphne, who merely waited.

"What is *she* doing here?" Mary's caustic demand broke the spell.

It seemed to be what Daphne had been waiting for, but she addressed the woman, not Mary, in her usual brusque manner. "Ruth, may I present Lady Elizabeth Ashton, who is a guest at Timmons Manor. Beth, this is Ruth Atkinson. The Atkinsons have farmed this plot for seven generations, since Timmons Manor was constructed."

Beth nodded at the woman. "Mrs. Atkinson."

"My lady."

Daphne strode toward Mary, stopping a few feet away. "As to why she is here, that would be because of you. She asked to see you."

Mary scowled. "I don't see why. She will only go back and tell him where I am."

Beth moved closer. "I will not. I have promised him nothing. But I have heard his story, and I would very much like to hear yours."

Mary's lips pursed. "What concern is it of yours?"

"None. And you obviously do not have to tell me anything. But your brother courted me this past season, and I felt he was a good man. I know this situation grieves him to the core, and I would like to understand what caused such a chasm to open in your family."

Mary gave a low, dry laugh. "So you are merely nosy, wishing to gather gossip of my ruination to take back to the wagging tongues of the *ton*."

Beth grimaced. "You may have missed the discussion where I have come to Timmons Manor to escape my own scandal. Do you truly think I would flee back to London merely to spread more?"

"You would, if it would deflect from your own."

"You obviously do not know how the beau monde works, my girl," Daphne muttered. When Mary shot her a sour look, Daphne shrugged. "She would have to admit how she came by the information."

The girl's brows furrowed as she looked from Daphne to Beth, and Daphne sighed. "Timmons Manor is not exactly a house of ill-repute, Mary, but we have operated as a haven for more than twenty years. Beth may have come to us in all innocence, but I assure you rumors have swirled about the place for years. The younger members of the *ton* may be unaware, except for those who have sought our aid—but the dragons would definitely know who we are. It would not be only your reputation to be sullied."

Before Mary could absorb this, Beth gestured toward her stomach. "The vicar?"

Mary's eyes shot wide. "How did you—"

"When is the child due?"

"Within the month," said Ruth, who dried her hands and moved to stand next to Mary. She stroked the girl's hair with affection. "We have had a few moments of alarm already."

"Ruth is our midwife." Daphne tapped her crop against her leg. "It is why we moved Mary here. We could not send her where Ruth could not get to her quickly when the time came."

Beth counted the months backward. "So February? When they were in London for his investiture?"

Mary set her basket aside and crossed her arms. "Yes."

"Solace," Daphne muttered, "arrives in many forms. Not always wise ones."

Beth took another step closer. "You loved him. He listened to you, comforted your grief. Shared his wisdom. He said he would take care of you. Love you." She ignored the glance Daphne and Ruth gave each other and squatted in front of Mary. "No matter what happened, he would always be at your side."

Mary's expression softened, and her eyes gleamed with tears. "How did you—"

"Rose Timmons," Beth whispered. "Sophie's niece. You know of her?"

Mary nodded, one tear slipping free. "She helps women avoid scoundrels."

"She is my sister-in-law. Married my brother two months ago. We have talked for hours. She warned me what men would say to get close to me, to persuade me to be alone with them. So did my mother. How the men would say it, as if I were the only woman in their world. Close, familiar, caring."

Mary nodded, her lips trembling.

"And each and every word a lie."

The wail burst from Mary like the call of a banshee. Beth threw her arms around Mary and hugged her close. To her side, Beth saw Ruth gather her daughters and send them scurrying outside. Daphne stood, a stern statue, as Mary clung to Beth, who stroked her back as a great wave of sorrow rolled from the young woman. The wail eased into gulping sobs of grief.

With no wonder. Beth whispered, keeping her words as gentle as possible as Mary's tears soaked her shoulder. "You have been through so much. Your father. Your brother and mother leaving. Then this. But you found this haven. You are not alone. You will never again be alone."

The sobs continued. Ruth pulled one of the armchairs closer and stroked Mary's hair again. "Sweet child, she is right. You are not alone. We will be with you."

When Mary finally caught her breath, she gasped. "He will hate me."

Beth knew she no longer meant the vicar. She shook her head. "I have been talking with him. Right now he is terrified, confused, and hurt. That has made him angry. He does not know why you fled. And he only has the vicar's story. Not yours. He sees only your defiance. He thinks you have betrayed him and your mother and want to bring ruin to the family. And he does not understand why. It is why he has struggled to find you."

A few more sniffles, and Mary pushed back. Ruth handed her a small white cloth, and Mary wiped her face and blew her nose. "What did the vicar tell him?"

"That there was no affair. That it was your imagination."

Mary looked askance at her, then down at her stomach. "I certainly did not imagine this!"

Beth gave a short laugh, which made Mary half-smile. "But Kirkstone does not know about"—she pointed at the baby—"this." She paused. "Does he?"

Mary hesitated, then shook her head. "I left as soon as I knew for certain."

"He thinks you are rebellious but not a liar. He believed you when you said you were in love with the vicar."

Blinking, Mary pursed her lips a second. "He did?"

Beth nodded. "When they discovered you were missing, he did not check the vicarage first. He headed straight for Gretna

Green, thinking you had eloped with the man. He only spoke with the vicar after he could not find you. It was never about whether or not you were speaking the truth but that they felt you deserved a better match than an ancient and corrupt vicar. And he has tracked you all over the north of England."

Concern crossed Mary's face. "Is that why he is sick?"

"It is."

"I just do not know if I can—"

"If I may be a bit mercenary," Beth whispered, "there is no better time to tell him than now. He is too weak to get out of bed and can barely speak. Even if he is angry, rage would exhaust him. You could see him, then return here. He still would not know where you are."

Mary looked up at Daphne, who nodded once, then squeezed Beth's hand. "All right."

Ruth leaned a bit closer. "But she cannot ride a horse, not now."

"Of course not." Daphne tapped her crop again. "I will send Mead with a wagon. Ruth, you come with her. We will pile it full of pillows, and we will have you both back here before dusk. Beth, you stay here for now. We will return shortly." With that she strode from the room.

Beth kept her gaze on Mary as the young woman's face cascaded through a dozen emotions. "Now. Tell me what you intend to say to him."

Tuesday, 13 September 1825
Timmons Manor
Ten in the morning

KIT WATCHED LADY Sophia Timmons watch him.

After he had requested a meeting with her, Kit had fallen asleep before she arrived in his room. The tisane and the camphor poultice had done their job, and for the first time since he had arrived at Timmons Manor, he slept through the night without restlessness or coughing spasms—and alone. Meg had returned earlier that morning with coffee—actual black coffee—and a breakfast of broth and bread.

Kit now sat straighter in the bed than in recent days, and he felt both the weariness and the heaviness in his chest easing. He felt grimy, however, and his jaw itched from the four-day growth of beard that had sprouted on his face. Definitely no longer the elegant duke he had prided himself on being earlier in the year, when he had peacocked around the Society events, far too proud of his rank and appearance. Now he was sure he bore more resemblance to a Covent Garden beggar than an aristocrat. Probably smelled more like one as well.

But a lot of things had changed in a very short period of time. And as the morning had worn on, he had time to think, to process what Beth had said to him, to prepare for what he hoped would be the next step in this drama.

Lady Sophia now waited, her eyes studying him, her expression stern.

Kit cleared his throat, knowing his voice remained raspy, although some of the soreness had lifted. "Lady Sophia—"

"Sophie."

He paused. He would never get used to this. But when in Rome . . . "Sophie. I would like to see my sister"—he held up one hand—"not to harangue her or demand she return home. I have spoken with Lady Eliz—Beth—at great length, and I realize that you are housing her out of sympathy because of what she had told you. But I do not know what she has said that would cause you to take such a drastic action—"

"Drastic—"

"As to separate and seclude her from her family." He gestured at his bed. "I am obviously not in any condition to take any action at this point, but I would like to understand her actions as well as yours. I wish to know what she told you."

Sophie remained silent. Kit did not know if he had ever seen anyone sit as still as Sophie Timmons did in the next few moments. Nothing moved, not even her eyes. He waited. He had rehearsed those last two sentences in his mind for hours, polishing and trimming them, knowing he needed to be clear, succinct—and without the anger and frustration of his earlier demands, which had put this woman in a rage herself.

Sophie blinked, then her gaze ranged over him, head to toe. Her lips thinned, then she straightened in the chair. "You and I are at an impasse, sir, facing each other from two sides of a conflict. Two perspectives. Two . . . truths."

"And I wish to know my sister's. If Beth is correct, there have been serious misunderstandings on both sides."

"So you do not realize what it is *you* have done to send your sister seeking the help of others?"

"I do not. Although I now realize some things I have *not* done that I should have."

Sophie's eyes narrowed. "What is it that you have *not* done?"

A hiccupped cough burst out of him, and Kit swallowed a bit of phlegm that suddenly appeared in the back of his throat. *Damn this sickness!* "When our father died, I was thrust into a role I was not entirely prepared for. My father had shown me how to run an estate, manage our business affairs, but not how to manage my family. As her brother, I saw Mary as loving and independent. Despite our age difference, we had shared a lot of our childhood together until I went off to school, and when I came home for holidays, she followed me about, pestering me about my school mates. She was my younger sister, able to care for herself and others and understanding of her place in our family and Society. I failed to see her as a duke should—as her protector and guardian—as my father had been. Someone who should have been guiding her as she became a young woman in Society."

"You turned your back on her."

It felt like a slap, but a deserved one. "I became focused on my own role in Society. As a representative of my family instead of the head of it."

"And Beth helped you see this?"

"In part. I have also had a great deal of time to think, lying here in this bed."

"And if I do not believe you?"

The frustration of the last four months flared in his gut again, and he reflexively clenched his left fist, an action that caused her gaze to dart to his hand. Her eyebrows arched, but she waited.

Kit forced his hand to open and he pressed his fingers flat on the covers. He met her gaze. "Part of my anger over the past four months is that I cannot understand why Mary left us. Why would she take such a risk to flee from the protection, safety, and love of her family. And no one will tell me. Even as a duke, I cannot force you to reveal her to me, and you can certainly bar me from your house. But I will not leave this area without knowing why my sister has done this."

A muscle jerked in Sophie's jaw. "But you realize it is her story to tell, not yours to demand."

Kit gritted his teeth. "Yes."

Sophie returned to studying him. "You have never been this ill before, have you?"

What did that have to do with—

"This helpless."

Ah. "No."

"Enlightening experience, isn't it?"

"Frustrating."

She gave a half-smile. "Remember, then, that this is how women feel when entangled in the choking protocol of Society, sir. Helpless. Told where to go and who to meet, as if we do not have brains or hearts—or dreams—of our own."

"I do not think—"

"Most men do not. They do not see women as independent of their own needs, their own dreams, their own duties to provide a legacy. We are merely extensions of their ambitions, to use as they see fit, to betray or discard as they will, no matter what harm has come to us."

The flash of insight blindsided Kit and he stared at her as the words formed in his head—impossible words, words born out a half dozen conversations and the presence of one precocious—parentless child.

"Are you saying—" He stopped, unable to put a voice to the horror he was thinking.

The door of the room swung open, and Daphne strode in, her heels thudding on the carpet. She leaned over and whispered in Sophie's ear.

Sophie paled, her eyes wide, as she stared up at the other woman. "Is that wise?"

Daphne shrugged. "It is what she wants. All Beth did was ask."

A flash of hope popped into the back of Kit's brain. *Were they talking about . . .*

Sophie stood. "Very well. Bring her." As Daphne left, Sophie turned to him. "Well, Kirkstone, it seems you will get your wish sooner than either of us expected, courtesy of your friend Lady Elizabeth."

Kit's breath caught as she stepped away from the chair. He looked at the door, where three women entered. Daphne was in front, her expression cold, her eyes fixed on him. To the left and slightly behind Daphne, Beth followed, but she seemed to be speaking low to someone to her right, someone hidden by Daphne's body. On the right, another woman walked, also seeming to support someone. Kit had never seen this woman, who seemed to be a servant of some kind.

They crossed the small room slowly, then as they neared the chair, Daphne stepped away. There, supported between Beth and the servant stood a young woman he barely recognized as his sister.

"Mary?" he whispered, his mind refusing to accept what he saw.

This woman was pale and wan, with hair that was partially

undone, stringy clumps hanging near her face. Her dress was rudimentary and too small, especially as the skirt pulled tight over a stomach swollen and full.

A chill shot through Kit and he shivered.

"Kit." Her voice, barely audible, sounded as raspy as his. "You are sick."

He stared, a flood of emotions now raging through him, a deluge that robbed him of intelligent thought—fury, sorrow, frustration—a wave that had been building for months. His lips trembled and he fought to speak. "You are with child?"

She nodded once.

His eyes burned. "The vicar?"

Another nod.

Tears flooded his eyes. "I will kill him. Lying bastard."

She bit her lower lip. "Kit—"

He had to make this right. Had to bring her home. He reached for her, his voice grating out one harsh whisper. "Mary!"

Her eyes widened as she looked at his outstretched arm. Then a raw sob burst from her, and she fell against him, collapsing onto the bed. Kit did the only thing he had the strength to do. He wrapped his arms around his sister and crushed her to his chest. The tears flooded out and down his cheeks, but he did not care.

He would do what it took to make this right, to make his family whole again. Family was everything.

CHAPTER TEN

Tuesday, 13 September 1825
Timmons Manor
Half past ten in the morning

W HEN MARY COLLAPSED against Kirkstone's chest, Beth reached out to steady her, but Sophie stopped her with a raised arm and a shake of the head. Beth hesitated, watching as he held his sister, their sobs blending, flowing, then slowly subsiding.

Daphne watched the scene a moment, then turned and left, pulling the door closed. Ruth retreated to the end of the bed, her eyes observing everything but keeping the closest watch on Mary. Beth moved quietly to the table of supplies and picked up two of the white cloths, then waited until brother and sisters raised their heads. She handed one to each of them, and Kirkstone nodded to her as he wiped his face. Mary's perch on the edge of his bed seemed precarious, and Beth and Sophie helped her into the chair, scooting it close enough that she could touch her brother without stretching.

Kirkstone shifted in the bed. "Mary, I—"

"I did not know what to do. I was a fool. And afraid." She shrugged. "Ashamed." Mary looked down at her hands, which she clutched together across her stomach. "And really angry. At you. At Mother. At him. At the world." She gave him a slight smile. "I suppose we have that in common."

"The Caudale temper," he muttered. "Mother used to claim it would be the death of all of us."

Mary grimaced and nodded at him. "It almost was."

"You were not the only one who has played the fool." He let out a long sigh. "I thought it my duty to bring you home, whether you wanted to come or not."

"I knew you would be angry. I am ruined."

A low growl sounded in Sophie's throat, but she said nothing.

Kirkstone glanced at her, then back at his sister, his face somber. "I am angry, Mary. I do love you, and I beg you to return home with me. But no matter what the reason, you have destroyed your future. If you cannot marry him—"

Mary's face crumpled. "I will not! He lied! He promised—" Mary gasped, a hiccup of a sound, then her tears flowed again. "He refused. I would have, but he—" She gasped again, this time her hand braced her stomach as she looked down at the floor.

So did Beth. A dark stain had formed around Mary's feet, darkening the carpet and soaking her slippers. "What is—"

"Daphne!" Sophie's scream startled them all. She motioned for Ruth, then slid her arm under Mary's. "We have to get you to a bed, child."

Mary's face scrunched in confusion. "What is happening?"

Ruth, at her other side, also urged her up. "Looks as if you are ready to have this baby. You have to stand up."

Mary did so, still befuddled. "Now?"

"Now!" Both women cried.

"What?" Kirkstone, paler than ever, gaped at the women and tried to push up.

Sophie pointed at him. "You. Stay! You cannot be a part of this." He started to protest, but she repeated the command, then looked at Ruth over Mary's head, as they headed for the door. "I do not think we can get her to the third floor. But the only empty one on this floor is not made up."

Beth stepped in behind them. "Use my room."

Sophie glanced at her. "This could take a long time."

"I can sleep elsewhere."

"Oh, I doubt there will be much sleep tonight."

Mary cried out, and her legs gave way. Beth grabbed her waist from behind and helped the two women hold Mary up until she found her feet again.

"I do not want to do this!" Mary's wail echoed down the corridor, as Daphne and several of the maids appeared from the servants' stairs.

"You have no choice, my girl," Ruth said. "But we will help you."

Sophie pointed at the Tulip Room, and they all flooded inside, startling Kendall, who had just emerged from the dressing room. She watched, wide-eyed, as the maids went to work, pulling back the covers, prepping the washstand, and stacking piles of thick white cloths on the bench at the end of the bed, and placing a thick pad of some kind on the bed. Mary was stripped down to her chemise as pillows were packed against the headboard, then several of the women helped her into bed.

Beth moved toward the dressing room door, standing next to Kendall, watching the efficient preparations.

"Obviously, they have done this before," Kendall muttered.

Beth gave a half-grin. "I have much to tell you."

"I am certain of that, my lady."

Another cry rose from the bed, and Mary's body jerked, contracting with a spasm of pain. Ruth stroked her hair, whispering in her ear.

Daphne gestured to Beth and Kendall. "You two. Come with me." She ushered them into the corridor, closing the bedchamber door, then turned to them, addressing Beth. "You cannot be in there."

"But—"

"No. You are unmarried, and unless I am mistaken, a virgin. There are many ways this house violates Society protocol but that is not one of them. Besides, once you see this you will never want to marry."

Kendall put her hand over her mouth, her eyes gleaming.

Beth ignored them both. "But I could help—"

"We have plenty of help. You are also a stranger to her. This . . . process . . . is difficult enough without stranger in the room. We will keep you informed, and you will be best used by taking care of Kirkstone, making sure he does not erupt from that bed on a wave of fury." She turned to Kendall. "I am going to ask that the Lily Room be made up for the two of you, just for the next day or so. You will need to move enough belongings to that room"—she pointed across the passageway. "It will be inconvenient, but this should be over within three days unless something goes horribly wrong."

"Is that what happened with Charlotte?"

Daphne froze, her lips pursed. "You have talked to Mattie." When Beth nodded, she went on. "Yes. We think . . . infection . . ." She straightened. "Now is not the time. The doctor has been sent for. Ruth will take care of Mary as she gives birth, but we will ask the doctor to check her a couple of times. I will ask he visit the duke as well. And Charlotte."

"Daphne—"

A burst of coughing, followed by a sudden thump and a string of curses, erupted from the door of the Rose Room.

"What the devil—" Daphne led the charge back into Kirkstone's bedchamber, where they found the man prone on the floor, cursing and coughing. "Damned arse." She turned to Kendall and pointed at the table of supplies. "Fetch a cloth." To Beth, she said, "Your task may be harder than you expected."

The two of them squatted next to the duke. "You have to be one of the biggest fools I have ever met. And I have eight brothers." Daphne took the cloth from Kendall and held it to his face as he coughed, his back jerking with the spasms as he braced on both elbows.

He gasped for breath. "My sister—"

"Is in the care of one of the most experienced group of women in the north of England. They have overseen dozens of births, and Ruth is a superb midwife. There is nothing you can do for Mary. Now get your arse back into bed."

Together, the three women helped Kirkstone push to his feet and stagger back to the bed. His shirt was long enough to cover his loins, but when Kendall realized he was otherwise unclothed, she turned away with a gasp. Daphne smirked at Beth as they settled the duke into bed. "I am afraid we come as a shock to most people."

"I have no doubt."

Daphne straightened, looking down at Kirkstone. "The doctor will be here later today to examine your sister. He will also visit you. Perhaps he will give all of us a better idea when you can leave this bed without toppling over on your face."

Beth bit her lip as Kirkstone's face scrunched into a reddened scowl, and his mouth opened. "Do not say it," she muttered, and his eyes shifted to her. She shrugged. "It will not help."

"Would help me," he growled.

Daphne chuckled. "I will leave him to you." She headed for the door but paused before shutting it. "We will let you know how Mary is doing."

The door closed, and Kendall looked at Beth, her back still judiciously turned toward Kirkstone. "This is what you have been dealing with for the past four days?"

"It is."

Kendall's lips thinned. "You will never be able to explain this."

Kirkstone's brows furrowed. "Explain what?"

"I am hoping I never have to."

"Explain what?"

Beth nodded toward the door. "Perhaps you should move our clothes now."

"Of course. You are all right being here alone?"

"It is obvious he is not capable of anything untoward."

"Oh, good Lord." Kirkstone's growl of disgust followed his

words. "I am not dead."

"Yet."

A flitted smile passed over Kendall's face, then she left. Beth turned on Kirkstone. "Whatever gave you the idea you could get out of bed?"

"I have been searching for my sister for four months. In less than five minutes, she is revealed to me, with child, then whisked away by a group of harridans who seem determined to bring down my household. What would you think?"

"If I had not eaten anything but bits of bread and broth for four days and been laid low with a fever and pneumonia, I might think I needed rest before trying anything so foolish."

"So you also think I am a fool for caring for my sister?"

Beth let out a long, exasperated breath. "I do not think you are a fool. But you are behaving like one. I do not care how strong you are as a man, there are some things you cannot bully into submission and one of those things is your own body when you are this ill." She dropped down into the chair next to his bed, then immediately yelped and jerked to her feet, staring down at the sodden cushion.

Kirkstone gave a harsh bark of laughter.

Beth frowned, but after a moment, the image of how she must have looked formed in her mind, and she too let out a short laugh. "Obviously, I need a new chair."

"Obviously." He scooted away from the edge of the bed. "Sit here."

Beth hesitated. "I should not."

"I am obviously incapable of anything untoward, remember? I promise not to touch you."

She fought a smile, but it eked out anyway as she perched on the side of the bed. "I wish—" She stopped, looking down at her hands.

"What?"

Chewing her lip a moment, she looked up at his eyes. "That we had known each other longer."

He gave a slow nod. "Do you believe things work out as they were meant to, no matter what we do to change them?"

She shrugged. "Sometimes. It seemed that way when Rose and Thomas came together again after so many years. Or Michael working with the horses again when he had been so close to them as a child. Why?"

"Because I would have left London, no matter what had happened between you and me. When I got my mother's frantic messages, I knew I had to go. It seemed to be the right thing at the time that you had declined my suit, no matter how disappointing it had been."

"I did not mean to disappoint you. I thought that you and the others . . ."

"Were like Aldermaston."

She nodded.

"Do you wish to know how I was not?"

Beth's throat tightened. She did. And she should not. But she could not deny that her feelings about Kirkstone had shifted over the past few days. No longer did she see him as a distant and former suitor. His illness had stripped away the proper *ton* persona, leaving before her a raw and vulnerable man. A head of household—a duke—who cared deeply for his mother and sister—his family. Just as her own father and brothers did. More than that, she had seen him delirious with fever, mumbling wildly between life-wreaking coughing fits. She had seen him sweating profusely and racked by chills. She had also seen him naked, or close to it, as she had tried to deny her appreciation of his physical beauty in light of his sickness. To no avail.

She should most definitively not want to know more.

But she did.

"Yes."

He tilted his head to one side, studying her, his eyes narrow with curiosity. "Truly?"

She whispered the word this time. "Yes."

He licked his lips.

"Would you like some water?"

He blinked. "I think so."

She brought him a cup and watched him sip cautiously, as if testing his throat. After several sips, he handed it back to her. "Thank you." He watched as she set the cup aside and returned to sit on the edge of his bed.

"You know Aldermaston needed your dowry."

She nodded. "I believe we were open about the nature of our courtship. My dowry would provide a needed bolster to his family's estate. In return, several of the businesses his father had begun to invest in would be welcome additions to my family's holdings."

"You knew he did not love you."

"I did. But neither of us desired a love match. We were well suited. We believed we would make an excellent partnership."

"And what did you see for yourself after the wedding?"

Beth paused. "I had not thought much beyond that. Children, of course, and my place in Society. Eventually I would have been a duchess, and I have seen the obligations my mother has faced over the years."

"But here you have strayed far from any attempt at social protocol."

Beth hesitated. "You will not be ill forever."

"That is not what I meant. Do you really wish to return to a life of parties and balls, stitching and books, your day broken only by tea and changing for supper?"

"I like books."

His teeth clenched, the muscle in his jaw so tight it bounced.

She relented. "I am not certain what else there could be for me."

"You do make a more than adequate nursemaid."

She grinned. "Only because it is someone I care ab—" Beth bit her lip, realizing too late what she had said. She looked down at her hands again.

He waited, then his words came on a quiet rasp. "So I am not imagining things in my fevered state."

After a brief hesitation, Beth shook her head, and Kirkstone closed his hand over hers. "Beth, I believe we can help each other through this time. You need to get beyond your family's scandals without descending into another one. I need to get my sister home and find a way to salvage her life as well as her reputation."

She looked up. "How?"

"I do not know yet. But will you help me?"

BETH STILLED, AND after a moment, Kit released her hands. In that moment, he knew how much he relied on her answer.

He *had* been a fool, driven half out of his head by the sounds of Mary's screams, to get out of bed. But every instinct he had drove him to help his sister, even as his head told him that a man had no place in the events happening across the corridor. But he had tried . . . only to find himself face down on the floor, coughing his lungs out.

A child. His sister—his beautiful, adventurous, clever sister—was delivering a child. His mind still had not quite accepted that undeniable fact, but now he understood why she believed the vicar loved her.

And Kit was going to kill him for that deception, even if the man was a clergyman. He had seduced Mary and lied to Kit. Despicable creature. Surely they would not hang a duke for seeking such revenge.

But before he could do that, he needed to gather his sister—and her child—and get away from this house. To do that, he would need help.

He waited.

Many of the women he had met since his investiture had what he referred to as "curated faces," an expression his mother found both amusing and annoying. As he had made his rounds of

Society events, he had been struck by how stoic women were, except when they were flirting with potential husbands. At that point they all appeared to be falsely cheerful, laughing in choked and feminine titters behind gloved hands at the least touch of humor, batting their eyes, and leaning close enough to give a man a view down the front of their dresses. In the first two months of the season, he had glimpsed more cleavage than he had since he left school.

But overall, their laughter never showed in their eyes, as if their practiced stoicism had become embedded in them.

Lady Elizabeth Ashton, however, was not one of those ladies. He had adored that about her from the start. Her heart, all her feelings, seemed to live on her face. As they did now, as she struggled to answer his question. Her eyebrows arched, then dropped. Her mouth twisted, scowled, and pursed. Her eyes widened, then narrowed, and she looked from her hands to his face to the window on the wall beyond his bed and back to her hands.

He decided a little nudge might be in order. "You can ask me anything you wish."

"May I call you Kit?" The words blurted out of her as if breaking a dam.

Not what he had been expecting. How would she know . . . ah . . . Mary. Mary had called him that during their brief meeting. "I think I would prefer it to 'Your Grace,' especially in private."

Her mouth turned up in a sweet smile. "'Kirkstone' is beginning to feel a bit like I'm spitting out a rock."

"An image I will try to forget before my next session of Parliament."

Another scowl. "Do you miss London?"

Kit had actually not thought about London since he had left. "Not particularly. Family is more important."

She stilled again, then finally nodded. "What do you have in mind?"

A sense of relief flooded through him. "I am not sure as of

yet, but my mind is not quite back to normal." He gestured toward the spot where he had taken a sprawl. "As you have seen."

Beth nodded. "So the first step will be to rebuild your strength. And to clear your lungs. I will ask Cook if she can make the poultices more powerful—"

"A frightening thought."

"Or if Dr. Thornton has something more potent—and what he thinks you should eat or do at this point to strengthen your muscles. And perhaps instead of trying to run across the corridor, you take small steps." She peered under the bed, where Meg had stashed the covered chamber pot, then toward the screen in the corner. She opened her mouth, but Kit saw her intention clearly.

"Yes. Like trips to the corner."

Her cheeks pinked, but she nodded. "But remember that as soon as you are able to walk up and down the corridor, they will send you to the pub in town."

"Not a pleasant prospect. I met Mr. Keales on my first stop in Litton, and we took a distinct dislike to each other. Probably because I demanded to know where Sophia Timmons lived."

"Ah. My understanding is that the people of Litton are quite protective of Sophie."

"Indeed." Watching as she looked away again, her gaze out the window, he reached for her hand again. "Beth, I am not asking for you to betray any promises you have made to your friends."

"Friends."

Her barely audible whisper puzzled him, but Kit went on. "I am asking merely for your guidance. You know them better than I do, even if you have only been here a short time. Meg said you arrived just before I did."

"A day."

"They have talked to you. You have seen how this household operates." He took a deep breath, fighting a cough lingering at the back of his throat. "And you have talked to my sister."

"We are still strangers. I suspect I know you better than I know them. And I am coming to realize I did not know you well at all."

Her words made his gut clench. "Beth—"

She stood abruptly, pulling away from him, her gaze still averted. "I must go."

And she did, closing the door and leaving him alone in a stranger's bed.

CHAPTER ELEVEN

Tuesday, 13 September 1825
Timmons Manor
Noon

FIGHTING A SUDDEN feeling of being smothered, Beth fled from Kit's room, slamming the door behind her. In the passageway, Kendall struggled to pull a portmanteau across the plush carpet. Beth rushed to help her, causing her maid's eyebrow to arch. "My lady, you should not—"

A scream erupted from the Tulip Room, making both women jump, losing their grip on the portmanteau, which thudded to the floor.

"Heavens!" Beth stared at the bedchamber door.

"Expected," muttered her maid, "but not alarming."

Beth stared at her. "That is normal?"

Kendall nodded, then reached for the luggage. Beth bent to help her. When Kendall began to protest, Beth interrupted. "Hush, Kendall. Let me help. We can return to normal once we leave this house."

Kendall remained silent as they towed the portmanteau into the Lily Room, where two maids were in the process of laying the bed with fresh coverings. All four worked to settle the room without speaking, although one of the maids gave Beth a quick curtsy before they left.

"Their staff must be larger than I thought."

Kendall shook her head. "No, it is quite small for a house this size, and almost all are women. Not as many are needed for Lady Mary, now that the room has been prepared, so they are returning to their regular work." She gestured toward the newly made bed, then began to unpack. "Did you know that even Notley's room is over the stable? There are no men in the house overnight."

Beth hesitated, then let her voice drop. "Have you seen the nursery?"

Kendall's lips pursed. "No, but I have been told about it, as well as about the work of this house." She looked up at Beth. "My lady, you are risking a great deal by staying here."

Beth dropped down on the bench at the foot of the bed. "I know, although Robert had already destroyed my presence in London this season. And when Aldermaston set me aside—"

"Coward."

Beth had to smile. "Quite forward of you to speak so of an aristocrat."

"Merely falling in line with the tenor of this house."

Beth laughed. Kendall, who was only a few years younger than Beth's own mother, had been her maid for almost five years, since her courses had begun and Emalyn Ashton had desired her daughter to have more privacy and direction than she received from her governess. Kendall had been an elite lady's maid for more than twenty years, and knew the *ton* better than anyone Beth knew, even Emalyn.

"I know you will help me step back into line when the time comes." Beth glanced at the door. "Have you ever been around . . ."

Kendall stopped her unpacking. "Two, my lady. One a former mistress of mine. The other a daughter of the house."

"Were they . . . all right? One hears horror stories about childbirth."

Kendall stilled. "The daughter . . . yes. My mistress . . . well, that is how I came to be in your employ."

Beth felt a jerk of fear. "She died?"

Kendall nodded, then averted her eyes, returning to her task. "It happens, my lady. Often."

Beth found her mind wandering over her short time out in Society—only a few weeks this year—and over the number of older gentlemen who had sought her out for dances or visits. "Is this why so many gentlemen are in search of second or third wives?"

"Many times, my lady."

Beth's chest tightened. "I never realized."

Kendall took a deep breath. "That is because Society seeks to keep such information from young women. Which is a shame in some ways. Women are encouraged to embrace the benefits and joys of marriage, but it leaves them ill prepared for the dangers that come with being with a man. Many men, even honest and upstanding ones like your marquess, do not see women as independent creatures. They are a part of their household, and childbirth is merely part of the price of continuing their lineage."

"That's rather cold."

Kendall shrugged. "Truth sometimes is, my lady."

"You sound as if you approve of what Sophie and Daphne are doing."

Kendall began to load Beth's underclothes into a chest of drawers. "Not approve so much as recognizing the need and admiring them for taking the risks in doing so. The women they are helping have been preyed upon by wicked men, yet they have few options to save themselves beyond the streets. A maid who has been seduced by a son of the house will often be cast out, with few ways to feed her child beyond the workhouses and prostitution. And Lady Daphne and Lady Sophie have sacrificed their own places in London Society to help them. It is a bit of a wonder that they have not besmirched the rest of their families' reputations."

"Daphne is the sister of a duke. Sophie's brother is an earl."

Kendall nodded. "Rank always carries some privilege of protection." She looked at Beth. "The same will help you, if you do not stay here too long."

Beth hesitated. "Kirkstone has asked me to help him get Mary out of here."

Kendall closed one drawer and opened another. "As I expected."

A scowl scrunched Beth's face. "Why would you expect it?"

Her maid rested both hands on the edge of the drawer a moment, then turned to Beth. "You do not see it?"

"What?"

"I was in the room less than five minutes, and I saw it immediately."

Beth stood. "Kendall, what are you talking about?"

Her maid shook her head, her lips tightening into a slight smile. "The way he looks at you. My lady, that man is in love with you. And I suspect has been so for some time."

Beth stared at her and stepped back, her knees giving way. She dropped back to the bench as her legs grew numb, a feeling that swept up over her. She stared at the floor as her vision blurred. She shook her head slowly, but the hurt that had appeared in his eyes when she declined his suit lingered in her head. And his words—*It seemed to be the right thing at the time that you had declined my suit, no matter how disappointing it had been.*

A London season was the Marriage Mart. Suitors came and went like pastry trays at a teashop. Kendall had been correct if blunt: men did not fall in love—they were shopping for the best mate to continue their lineage, or—at worst—a dowry to bolster their income. When a young woman declined their pursuit, they simply moved to another one.

"Impossible," she whispered.

Kendall came to her side and squatted next to her. "My lady, it is not. It happens. And while it is not my place to speak of such, I feel I would be amiss if I did not say I have seen that same look in your eyes."

Beth's eyes focused again. "You believe I love him?"

"I do. Or are falling rapidly in love with him. And that makes it even more imperative that you leave this place as soon as possible. Return to London before even more damage to your reputation is done. I know your family will help you."

"My family is rather embroiled in their own troubles at the moment."

"But your parents are strong. The duke and duchess—they are the strongest people I have ever met. They will weather this."

Beth let another thought settle over her. "Do you think that is because they love each other so much? That they are so bonded?"

After chewing her lower lip for several seconds, Kendall nodded. "Indubitably."

That feeling of being smothered, of choking, returned in full force. Beth pushed to her feet. "I need to get out." But Daphne had left her in charge of Kit. "Ah." Her hands flitted about, but she could not look at Kendall. "If you see Meg . . . I have to go."

Another scream followed her down the corridor, and Beth broke into a run, rushing down the stairs as fast as she dared. At the bottom, she looked around frantically, then spotted the lush growth of the garden through the windows at the rear. She fled toward the doors, bursting out into a sunlit path and causing several birds to take flight from nearby hedges. She stopped, awed by what lay before her.

Daphne had not exaggerated about the beauty of the Timmons Manor garden. A few saplings dotted the area, and except for the serpentine paths, flowers, short wild grasses, and thick shrubs carpeted the grounds. A riot of asters and amarines lined the paths, banked by rudbeckia, coneflowers, and poker plants. Reds and yellows mingled with deep golds and purples. The last butterflies of summer and frantic bees danced from bloom to bloom. Benches appeared on the paths here and yon, and in the far corners of the garden, two ancient oaks anchored the landscape. Although it first appeared to be a chaotic cacophony of color, the garden had clearly been planned as a cluster of smaller gardens, each with its own theme of hues and blooms. Red poker plants circled shrubs while beds of tall grasses were dotted with the tiny purple blooms of autumn crocus.

Beth took a deep inhale, savoring the blended fragrances that ebbed and flowed in the late summer breezes. Despite her frantic bolt from the house, her steps now strolled as she wandered, pausing at each new area, admiring the work that had been involved into developing such a paradise. Daphne had been right about that as well.

Along with her steps, Beth's mind began to calm as well, her tumbling thoughts slowing, even while they remained entangled and scattered. Kit wished her help, but too many questions arose. He wanted to salvage Mary's reputation, but how did one even do that? Even in London, where cajoling visits could be made to the women in the *ton* who controlled such things, reputations could be ruined beyond any repair. Beth knew of far too many women who had to retire to the country or exile themselves to the continent or—God forbid—America.

Mary was having a baby. How did one hide that? A horrifying thought broke through a bit of the fog. Would he give the child away? Pretend it never happened. Find a tenant or wet nurse who would take it as their own?

Surely he could not be that cruel.

But he did seem determined.

Determined to restore his family.

Beth felt a gentle nudge at her hip and jerked sideways, catching her breath as she looked down at the deep brown eyes of Boru.

"What are you doing here, you fine boy?"

The dog pushed at her hand, and she scratched behind his ears. He gave a whuffing sigh and pressed his body against her leg, almost causing her to stumble. She looked around, spotting a bench under one of the oaks. "Let us walk over here." Beth rested her hand on his neck as they walked, and they both settled beneath the tree: Beth on the bench and Boru stretching out on the ground, his weight heavy on her feet.

Beth sighed. She knew the wisdom of Kendall's words—she should leave. Immediately. Pack what she needed for the trip and catch the next available mail coach out of Litton. She could have the rest of her things brought down later. It would put her back in the heart of her own family, and maybe hibernating at Ashton Park until the Christmas ball would not be so bad after all. Boredom was not the worst thing that can consume one's time.

But Beth could not deny how much she had relished caring for Kit, how engaged she had been by what Sophie and Daphne were doing to help these women. Just as Rose had done before marrying Thomas—and in some ways continued to do so—they helped young women who had been taken advantage of by rakes and scoundrels. It was the eternal curse of the *ton*—in a Society where women needed to marry for security—and marry young— naïve women could easily fall prey to a charming man who wanted nothing more than to ruin them for pleasure. And every season dozens of unwary women fell victim. It was hideous, and if Beth dwelled on it too much, it infuriated her.

She understood all too well why Sophie and Daphne did what they did.

After all, Beth had done nothing to deserve this scandal. She had behaved impeccably. Yet she still faced ruin because of what her brother had done, which resulted in a marquess setting her aside. No fault of her own, yet here she was.

Beth growled under her breath, and Boru raised his head, ears perking in curiosity. She almost laughed but stroked him instead. "What we humans get ourselves into, eh?"

Boru huffed again.

A scandal not of her own making but one she needed to find her own way out of. So how did one redeem a season of scandal? Options were limited. Exile and hibernation until the smoke cleared. A high-ranking marriage—if such a man dared—after which all would eventually be forgiven. One could leave Society entirely—become a shopkeeper, for instance—but that would require giving up family entirely, too. Become completely notorious—a world-acclaimed musician, perhaps—which would make one such a novelty in Society that they would embrace the curiosity, even showing her off to their friends.

Beth thought of her own limited skills with the pianoforte and knew such a path was a fantastical pipedream.

"Boru, I should have been inappropriate with Aldermaston. Then he would have to marry me."

The humor of the thought, however, gave way to another troubling question. Would Kit make Mary marry that horrid vicar? The man denied her. It would be a marriage made in misery. Again . . . would he be that cruel?

No.

While she did not know him well, the past four days had revealed more about him than the few weeks they had spent together in London. Then he had been handsome, charming, witty, and quite clever. Her father—and Rose—had found nothing untoward in his past or current behavior. He struggled to find his place in Parliament—the session had been short this year—as well as Society since his father's death, but Kit had been loyal to his family and eager to learn and embrace his role in government.

His illness, however, had laid him raw. He had mumbled in his sleep, delirious and wreaked with nightmares. He had struggled to remain polite when he wanted to bolt from his bed. Kit's own weaknesses distressed him, but he accepted—if not with complete contentment—his limitations.

Most of all he had been more concerned about his sister—and Beth—than he had his own embarrassment.

And Beth realized many men would have been mortified to show such limitation to a woman like her, a girl of the *ton*, in her first season and unused to being around men. He had been naked, or partially so, his entire illness.

Something that had befuddled Beth in the beginning, as she

had resisted the way she reacted to his physicality.

Her brothers were tall and athletic, but Aldermaston had been only slightly taller than she was. Like many of the men of the beau monde, Aldermaston had been of a fair complexion, trim and lithe, with no signs of physical activity beyond a brisk walk in the park. Kit's build more resembled her father's, he of the Nordic heritage in both stature and musculature. Kit stood almost five inches taller than she did, with shoulders that revealed his stated pleasure in working the lands and horses of his Kirkstone Pass estate. His waist was slim but his legs were taut with strength, and when he battled whatever demons brought his dreams, his muscles bunched and stretched beneath the skin of his back and hips in an uncompromising fight.

Which he had won.

So far.

Beth felt a deep warmth building in her stomach, spreading up through her as she thought about Kit's body.

Wrong. So very wrong.

She should leave. But how could she? Now? Just as he recovered? Just as he had pleaded for her help with Mary and that child. What would he do with the ch—

All thoughts stopped.

A plan. An idea, as tiny as one of the miniscule autumn crocuses, began to form in the back of her head. A glimmer. A smidgen of true madness, a touch of—

The sound of hooves on gravel reached her from beyond the garden's hedges, and Beth knew the doctor had arrived. Whatever was birthing in the back of her head would have to wait.

Beth stood and headed down the path, the big Irish wolfhound on her heels.

KIT HAD NEVER felt so alone in his life. Since Beth's abrupt departure, his room had been eerily silent. No one had stepped inside, no one had spoken, even in the corridor outside his door. Occasionally he could hear Mary's sudden but muted cries, which unnerved him, as they were usually followed by the sound of running footsteps.

But no one checked on him, even following another coughing spasm, which he had managed on his own. His fear and frustration increased with every moment that passed. Worry about Mary consumed him, even more so than when he had not known where she was. His sister was now experiencing horrible pain in an event that could destroy her life—and that was if it did not take that life.

Kit swung his legs out of bed and sat on the edge of it, his hands clutching the edge of the mattress. As before, his head spun, his vision blurring a bit. But as he sat there, it cleared and he took a deep breath. He could do this.

The door opened and Beth entered, stopping when she saw him. "Are you this foolish or merely determined?"

He snarled. "Determined. No one will tell me anything."

She approached the bed. "They will not tell me anything either. Apparently it is improper for an unmarried woman to be in the birthing room."

His lips twisted. "*Now* they are concerned with impropriety?"

She returned the smile. "I think it is me that they are concerned with. Daphne said if I saw childbirth I would never want to marry."

Kit felt nonplussed. "Is childbirth that bad?"

Beth shrugged. "I do not know. Have you ever seen one?"

"Not unless you count one of our mares foaling."

Beth bit her lip. "I do not think that would count."

"It does sound painful."

She nodded. "Although I have to admit I am more concerned about what will happen after the baby is born." She stepped a bit closer. "Do you know yet what you will do?"

"No." He closed his eyes, feeling a bit dizzy again. He felt his body sway.

Beth was immediately at his side, her hands on his shoulders, steadying him. "Kit, you need to lie back."

Kit. He liked the way his name sounded on her lips. He opened his eyes. Beth was impossibly close, her eyes wide with concern, her lips full. Warmth radiated from her, and she smelled like sunshine and flowers. "You have been outside."

"Yes. They have a garden behind the house. I went there to think."

Her eyes, so close he could see dark flecks in the gray blue, had tears brimming at the edges. *Why was she crying?* "Think about what?"

"What you asked. Mary. My own situation. What you might do."

He closed his hand around her arm, wanting to draw her closer. "Beth—"

"Are you trying to get up again?" Daphne's words held an impatient growl.

Beth stepped away, and Kit watched the doctor and Daphne enter the room.

"How's Mary?"

The doctor's eyebrows arched over his spectacles and he looked at Daphne.

"She's his sister."

"Ah." The doctor approached the bed. "Lie back. You should not be up yet."

Kit growled. "How is she?"

"As well as can be expected." The doctor motioned for Kit to move back against the pillows. "She is young and healthy and has been well cared for. The baby seems to be in a good position, and she shows no signs of trouble. For now, we just wait. You lie back."

Kit complied, and the doctor began his questions about fever and coughing fits, food, poultices, and potions. What Kit did not answer, Beth did, her voice calm and even. The doctor listened, poked, and prodded, then packed up his equipment. He addressed

Kit but looked several times at Beth.

"You too are being well cared for, which does not surprise me. Your youth and health will also help, and you are making a tremendous recovery. I pray it continues. I will send over a slightly stronger tisane for you to drink, which will help clear your lungs—yes, we want you to cough. The worst thing you can do is to let all of that rest in your chest. You should be able to tolerate more solid food but do not overdo it. No heavy, rich foods." He looked at Daphne and Beth. "Boiled eggs, broth with bread, chicken with a little salt. Coffee. He can—"

"Daphne!" Meg skidded into the open door, her eyes wide as she spotted the three of them. She focused on the doctor. "Doctor! You have to come quick!" She vanished, running down the hall toward the back staircase.

Kit felt a lurch in his gut. "Is it Mary?"

Daphne and the doctor vanished, but Beth hesitated, glancing across the hall. She looked back at him. "No. It's upstairs." Then she too disappeared, leaving his bedchamber door open.

All went silent. The still quiet felt unbearable.

Then a high wail split the air, echoing throughout the house, a sound like the legend of the banshee. It bounced off walls, sending a shiver through Kit.

He had to get out of here. He had to get Mary and leave this haunted place.

CHAPTER TWELVE

Tuesday, 13 September 1825
Timmons Manor
Half past one in the afternoon

BETH FELT NUMB staring at the tableau of grief displayed before her. She stood in the door of one of the third-floor bedchambers, watching as the doctor, white faced but calm, closed his bag yet again, his eyes somber behind the spectacles as he looked at Daphne. "I'm sorry. She was already gone."

The wail that had already filled the room and sounded down the corridor rose again as Mattie clambered up on the bed, burying her face against her mother's stomach.

Meg reached for the child. "Mattie, no—"

"Leave her be," the doctor said softly. "For a few moments at least. Let her have this."

Beth clung to the doorframe, her vision blurring with tears. Daphne, near the head of the bed, stroked the young woman's hair. Beth knew without a doubt this was Charlotte, Mattie's mother, but she looked no older than Beth did, her face clean, smooth, and now peaceful. Her dark hair flowed out over the pillows.

The other women in the house had filled every corner of the small room, which had to have been a servant's quarter at one time, with its narrow bed and sparse furnishings. A smaller bed had been pushed into one corner, its covers wrinkled, with two small dolls propped against the head of it. Sobs began growing in the midst of them all as the sorrow spread. Tears trailed down Daphne's bronzed cheeks, but she looked up, even as Beth felt a presence behind her.

Sophie pushed into the room, her steps stumbling as she headed for the bed, her words choked. "No! Oh, Charlotte!" Her knees gave way, and Daphne was beside her in an instant, her arms around Sophie as she eased her friend down to the foot of the bed. Sophie gasped out a sob, her hand running up and down Charlotte's legs beneath the blankets, as if trying to give warmth back to her frail form.

The doctor took off his spectacles and slipped them into a pocket. "She was too weak. She found you too late, I'm afraid." He took a deep breath. "I will send the undertaker from Shipton. You will need to prep—"

"We will do it." Lydia stepped forward. "We will take care of her."

He looked at the normally fiery redhead and nodded. "Good. I know you will." He put an arm on Daphne's shoulder. "You will take care of the rest."

She nodded as tears continued to flood down her face.

Mattie wailed again, and Sophie reached for her, but the girl shook her hands away. "No! You can't take her!"

"Mattie." Sophie's voice cracked, almost inaudible. "We must—"

"No!" The girl screeched again.

The other women in the room clung to each other, their grief crippling them. Daphne and Sophie looked confused, then Daphne reached for Mattie again. "Child—"

Mattie's wail strengthened.

Beth suddenly realized that none of these women had any experience with small children. Babies, yes, but children? None.

"I will take her." Beth moved to the side of the bed. When

Daphne's eyes looked dubious, Beth gave a one-shouldered shrug. "I have cousins, and I have been in charge of the children at our Christmas ball for years." She squatted down next to the bed and placed a hand on Mattie's back.

The girl jerked. "No!"

Beth leaned closer. "You knew this might happen. Remember? You told me. You knew your mother was really ill. You even told me she might die."

"I didn't mean it!" She buried her face deeper into her mother's stomach.

"I know. And I know you really missed playing with her. Missed her taking care of you."

"Yes!"

"But she cannot do that anymore. She's gone for good this time."

Mattie turned her head to look at Beth, her lips trembling. "I know. I hate it. I don't want her to go."

"I know. But she has already left, hasn't she?"

Mattie pressed her lips together.

"These ladies want to take care of her. Get her ready for her last trip. Why don't you come with me, and you can tell me about your mother. What she did to make you happy."

Mattie didn't respond, but Beth waited. After a few moments, the tension seemed to leave Mattie's muscles, even though she did not move. Beth gently lifted Mattie from the bed, and the girl went willingly, wrapping her arms and legs around Beth and pressing her face into Beth's neck.

As she headed down the stairs, Mattie shifted a little. "Are you going to be my mummy now?"

"We will have to see," Beth said, holding the girl a little tighter. But that glimmer of an idea that she had in the garden began to bloom.

Tuesday, 13 September 1825
Timmons Manor
Half past five in the afternoon

TEA HAD COME and gone, delivered to Kit's room by a round, scowl-faced woman who plopped a tray with tea and biscuits on the chair next to his bed, then left without a word. With the tray's proximity, he was able to pour a cup and nibble a biscuit, which made him feel better than he expected it to. Apparently, any sort of solid food was going to be an improvement.

Shortly after the same woman marched in, snatched the tray up, and disappeared again, Beth came in, a small child clinging to her hand and half hiding behind her skirt. Tucked in her other arm, Beth carried two books, which she placed on the end of the bed, then smiled at him.

"Your Grace, this is Mattie. She is the girl you asked about earlier."

Mattie's eyes swept upward. "He asked about me?" Without waiting for an answer, she turned back to Kit. "You asked about me?"

"I did."

"Why?"

"I heard you talking to Lady Elizabeth. You thought I was too sick to hear anything."

Her lips rounded. "Oh, that is wicked."

Beth bit her lip.

He leaned a bit toward the edge of the bed, lowering his voice. "Why do you think that is wicked?"

"Pretending to be something you are not. Mummy said that was wicked."

"Apparently, Mummy has never been in London Society," he muttered, surprised as Beth's eyes shot wide and she shook her head. *What?*

Mattie scowled. "Oh, Mummy went to London many times. That's where she met the bad people."

Beth's eyes squeezed shut.

What?

"There are bad people in London. I would have to agree with you about that."

"We came here to get away from the bad people. But it didn't work. Mummy still died."

Kit felt as if he had been punched. He looked at Beth for help. When she spoke, she looked at the ceiling a moment. "The earlier excitement," she said softly. "It was Mattie's mother, Charlotte."

"She died." Mattie announced as if she were stating they had visitors.

Kit swallowed and fumbled for words, finally whispering, "I'm sorry, Mattie."

"I know."

Beth squeezed the girl's hand. "No, Mattie, what did I tell you to say when people told you that."

Mattie squinted. "Oh." She looked up at Kit. "Thank you."

"My father died last year."

"He did?" She looked around. "Can I sit on your bed?"

Kit wondered if he would always feel this befuddled around children. "Um. Of course." He scooted over toward the middle of the bed and Mattie climbed up and sat cross-legged next to him. "How did he die? Did he have a baby too?"

Kit blinked, unsure he had heard the question correctly. Perhaps the fog of his fever had not lifted as much as he had thought.

Beth leaned over and touched the girl's shoulder. "Remember, Mattie. I told you only girls have babies."

Mattie looked up at Beth. "Oh. Yes." She looked back at Kit. "Was it a horse? Beth said that sometimes when horses don't want to be ridden, they just toss people off."

Beth gave a short cough. Or was it a laugh? "I took her to the stables."

Mattie bounced on the bed, startling Kit. "And the garden and the kitchens and the liberry. That room has a lot of books. We brought you two because Beth said you might get bored and being bored is horrible, although I don't usually get bored. There's too much to do. And I picked flowers for my mother, and then Cook gave me a biscuit after they showed me the pastry room where the biscuits are made. I guess it was because my mother died, because Cook never gives me a biscuit. Unless it's teatime. I can have biscuits at teatime, but not any other time because she says they are not good for me, that I would get too big and fat like she is."

"I think Cook brought me biscuits earlier."

Mattie bounced again, but this time Kit was prepared for it. "Really? I didn't think she ever left the kitchen. She told me cooks almost never left the kitchen, that they were"—she caught her breath and pronounced the word slowly—"ab-so-lute-ly not a maid who ran all over the house doing who knows what, so if I wished to continue running all over the house like I have been doing I should think about becoming a maid but one of the other maids said it depended on what kind of maid you were and Aunt Sophie said I would never be a maid that my mother was not a maid and she would make sure that what happened to my mother would never happen to me, and I thought she meant I would never die but now I think she meant having a baby, and if babies kill you I definitely would not want to have one. Would you? Are you ab-so-lute-ly certain he did not have a baby?"

In that moment, Kit decided that "nonplussed" was an excellent word. He looked up at Beth, whose lips were going to withstand serious damage if she did not stop biting them. Her eyes gleamed. "Your father," she whispered.

"Ah." He looked back down at Mattie, who stared at him with the sweetest, most innocent expression he had ever seen. "My father had—" He stopped, uncertain how blunt to be. The girl could not be more than five or six. He tried again. "My father had an accident while hunting."

Beth gasped but hid the reaction quickly.

Mattie took the answer in stride. "Not a horse? Or a baby?"

"No."

She bounced again, shifting positions. "Mr. Mead goes hunting sometimes. He brought back a deer last week. They are much bigger than I thought. It's in the larder doing . . . something. I forgot what Aunt Daphne said. But we should eat some soon. She said the meat is tasty. Are you a papa?"

"Um . . ."

A stark cry sounded from across the hall. All three fell silent a moment, then Mattie whispered. "They say Mary is having a baby now."

Beth stroked her hair. "She is."

"Sounds awful. That's how Mummy sounded. It was awful too. But now Mummy is dead. Will Mary . . . I don't know—" The girl's face crumpled, and fat tears rolled from her eyes.

"My darling," Beth said, her words gentle. "The duke should rest." She pulled on the girl's arm, and Mattie went to her, climbing up Beth's body and draping limply around her waist and shoulders like a fur stole. The child's body shook as she buried her face in Beth's neck.

Beth nodded over the girl's back, mouthing, *I will be back.*

Kit returned the nod and watched her leave, his chest unreasonably tight, yet it had nothing to do with his illness. His eyes burned, and he wiped them with the sheet as out of his confusion came one solid thought.

After this house, his life would never be the same again.

Tuesday, 13 September 1825
Timmons Manor
Half past seven in the evening

"DO YOU REALIZE how dangerous your proposal is?"

Beth nodded. After the cold buffet supper Cook had laid out for all the house's residents, and another two hours in Mattie's company, Beth's bloom of an idea had come into full flower. She sought Sophie out in her office, wanting to put it before her before Mary gave birth, a process that was still ongoing in the Tulip Room. "I do. And I know everyone may not agree. But I have considered what I want, what he wants, and what could be the best solution for all of us. It *is* a possible path that could resolve most of the issues."

"And if Mary does not agree?"

"All I ask is that we present the idea to both of them."

"You believe he would be willing to tackle such an arduous task?"

"I think he would do anything to preserve his family."

"And you, what of your own sacrifice?"

Beth paused. This was the one she had thought hardest about. "I—I think it will work."

"Where is Mattie now?"

"In bed in the Lily Room. No one has thought to move her bed into the nursery. I cannot see her sleeping in the room where her mother died." The undertaker had come and gone, transporting Charlotte's body to Shipton. Beth had kept Mattie with her in the stables and kitchen until she knew they had left."

Sophie's eyes watered again. "Quite right. We should have thought"—she took off her spectacles and rubbed her eyes. "One death, one life soon to come."

"It is a wonder any of you have coherent thought."

Sophie sniffed. "Even so." She swallowed and replaced her spectacles. "I will discuss this with Daphne. Please do not say anything to anyone else until I have done so."

"Of course. It is why I came to you first."

"We will wait until after the baby is born."

"Agreed."

Daphne appeared in the doorway, a blood-smeared apron over her clothes and her sleeves rolled back to the elbows. "It is time!" she announced and vanished again, her footsteps bounding away.

Sophie shot to her feet, racing from the room as Beth followed. Halfway up the steps, she glanced over her shoulder. "Stay with Kirkstone. Close the door."

They split paths at the top of the staircase and Beth ran into the Rose Room, shutting the door.

Kit pushed up in the bed. "What's wrong?"

Beth swallowed. "I think it's time for Mary's child."

He glanced over her shoulder at the door. "I should—"

She put her hands out. "No. They will let us know when it over."

An ear-shattering scream wrenched the air. Without thinking, Beth lunged forward and wrapped her arms around Kit. He hesitated but slowly closed his arms around her, pulling her tight against his chest. "I want to help," he whispered.

"I do too, but we cannot."

His grip on her tightened, and Beth felt the warmth of his body eke through every muscle. She settled her head against his shoulder and pressed against him as another cry rang out. She ached for Mary, for the pain she must be feeling, but nothing felt as natural, as instinctual as clinging to this man. His breath quickened against her neck, turning ragged when the loudest cry of them all echoed through the walls.

Then . . . silence. Interminable silence.

Gradually, Beth released him, raising her head. He did likewise, his voice breathy. "Do you think—"

The soft mewling of a new baby reached them, and they both gasped for breaths. Beth pushed off the bed and rushed to the door, jerking it open.

Daphne stood on the other side, her clothes even more soaked with blood than before. "You have a niece," she announced to Kit, her eyes bright. "Mary is fine. Sitting up and holding her." She turned and went back into the Tulip Room, shutting the door.

Beth faced Kit again. His mouth hung open. He sat up. "I must see her." He swung his legs off the bed, letting the covers fall back. "I must."

He should not. Beth knew he should not.

She also knew he had to.

"Let me help you. You will need breeches."

He blinked. "Breeches."

"Those things with which you cover legs and loins."

He glanced down where the sheet had fallen away, and his cheeks reddened, although his smile grew. "Ah. Those things."

Beth felt her own cheeks heat as she went to the dressing room and opened one of his travel packs. Searching until she found the needed garment, she brought it to him, then turned her back as he slipped them on.

Beth swallowed, her mouth dry. He was indeed a most well-formed man.

"I am covered."

She turned. "Stand slowly. Lean on me. Step carefully."

He did, and together they made their way to the door. She had expected him to put more weight against her, but as they walked, she realized he needed her more for balance than support. She knocked once on the Tulip Room door, then opened it.

Every woman in the room stopped, staring at them. Daphne's expression turned stern. "You should not—"

"Kit!" Mary's cry from the bed held both relief and love. Propped against the headboard, she cradled an infant in one arm. With the other, she reached out for her brother. "Kit!"

Daphne relented and stepped back, as did Sophie and Ruth as Kit hobbled to the bed, releasing Beth and clinging to the foot posts for balance. "Mary!" His choked word broke as he eased down on the bed next to her, cupping her face in one hand. His eyes brimmed as he touched her baby with one finger.

"I was so worried," she whispered.

His eyes widened. "You?" He looked down at the child again. "You had a baby! I could hear you—" His voice cracked again.

"I thought you would die."

"Not until I saw you again. And this!" He wiped his eyes.

"She is beautiful."

Both fell silent a moment, gazing at the child, then Mary stroked his arm. "Do not kill him."

Kit's head snapped up. "What?"

Mary's soft smile widened. "Because I know you want to."

He paused, letting out a long breath. "I do. I most dearly want to."

His sister shook her head. "It would be beneath you."

"It would most certainly not—"

"You are the better man. You did not abandon me."

"Never."

"Precisely."

Kit fell silent again.

"Brother. You will find a way. I know it."

Beth looked at Sophie, arching one eyebrow. Sophie shook her head and mouthed, *Not yet.*

Daphne looked one from woman to another, her scowl becoming a look of curiosity. Sophie shook her head again. *Later.*

Kit placed a gentle hand on the baby's head. "You wish to keep her."

It was not a question, and Beth watched Mary's eyes glow as she squeezed her brother's arm.

He sighed. "Very well. I will not kill him. But we will need to wait on any other decisions for the moment."

Mary's face creased. "Brother, please—"

Beth looked at Sophie, her eyes pleading. Finally, Sophie let out an annoyed growl, obviously resigned to this. She stepped forward. "Kirkstone."

He looked over at her, and Sophie looked from him to Mary to Daphne, then finally to Beth, her eyes lingering on her as she spoke. "Beth has put a proposal to me that could work for everyone involved. I wanted to wait until I could discuss it with each of you, but clearly a delay may not be the best idea where Mary is concerned."

All eyes turned toward Beth then, and she swallowed hard.

A dangerous proposal indeed.

CHAPTER THIRTEEN

Tuesday, 13 September 1825
Timmons Manor
Half past eight in the evening

KIT WATCHED AS Beth seemed to struggle to find her words. Apparently, she was not completely prepared for this announcement either. But she licked her lips and went on.

"I tried to devise a solution to address what everyone seemed to want." She focused on Kit. "You wish to salvage your family and Mary's reputation." She looked at Sophie and Daphne. "You wished to have the duke out from under your roof, and you will need to find a home for Charlotte's children." Beth focused on Mary. "I do not know you well, but I suspected you would want to keep your child but not marry her father."

Mary bristled, stiffening beside him in the bed. "I do not." She looked at Kit. "Surely you did not think I would marry him—"

He held up one hand. "It would be the obvious solution, but no—"

"He abandoned me. Lied to me. And to you! I do not wish you to kill him, but I also never want to see him again!"

The babe in her arms stirred and mewed. The midwife was at her side immediately. "Let me hold her."

Mary relented and eased the child into the midwife's arms.

Sophie stepped into the midwife's place as the woman moved away. "Mary, let Beth continue."

They all looked at her again. Beth took another deep inhale. "What I propose will not be simple or easy for any of us. It will require some sacrifices." She paused and Sophie nodded at her.

"I propose that we spread the tale that the duke and I were—inappropriate—with each other earlier in the year, before he left London to find Mary and before I was connected to Aldermaston. When I came here it was not to escape my brother's scandal but my own—I was with child—and I knew this was close to the duke's home estate. When his grace discovered this he sought me out here and carried me back to Kirkstone. We married before the child was born, and Mary came to help me with the child, despite risks to her own reputation. She had not fled the Kirkstone estate as had been thought but had been staying with friends. When we return to Kirkstone, I will help her prepare for her first season in London, along with the duchess, with no one the wiser." She paused for a breath and went on. "I also propose that his grace accept Charlotte's children as his wards. Kirkstone Abbey would be an excellent place for them. Her son could stay in Litton until he no longer needs a wet nurse, then be brought there."

Daphne's face was a stoic mask, but she asked the question Kit felt too stunned to voice.

"You would marry him?"

Beth nodded. "If he is willing."

Willing? Kit felt as if he would jump from his skin at any moment. It was an insane, impossible, courageous, dangerous plan.

Starting with her marrying him. Lady Elizabeth Ashton. The woman who had just felt incredibly soft, strong—and natural—in his arms. The very woman he had sought to marry earlier that year.

He looked at his sister. Mary's face gyrated through a dozen emotions, and she finally whispered. "Would I still be her mother?"

Beth nodded. "In private. In public and to the rest of the world, she would legally be our first child, since we married before her birth."

Mary's brows knitted. "But how—"

"I suspect you both know a vicar who would be willing to provide an appropriate date on a wedding license."

Kit choked back a snort of laughter.

"Indeed." Daphne's sour word held a touch of humor.

One thought did prick at Kit's mind. "What about your family?"

She tilted her head to one side, peering at him. "They preferred you to Aldermaston from the beginning. You have been vetted and approved by four of the most demanding men in the beau monde. Robert once suggested that Aldermaston was far too weak for me. That I could 'eat him alive.' He had no such qualms about you. It would please them to think I came here for you."

"You know this is mad." Daphne crossed her arms. "Completely mad."

Beth nodded. "Yes. But also completely doable if we dedicate ourselves to it. It will not be easy, and there are a dozen ways it could go awry."

It was also brilliant. Kit squeezed his sister's hand. "What do you think?"

Mary looked from him to Beth again, her eyes moist. "I could still have a season in London."

Beth nodded. "Unsullied. Your mother is above reproach and will present you to the queen. Your brother and I will absorb the cuts."

Sophie cleared her throat. "You are giving up your own season. You could still have another two or three years on the Marriage Mart."

Beth shook her head. "I have discovered that after four days in this house and four hours with Mattie that I no longer care as much about having a London season." She looked at Kit and his heart clutched. "Some things are more important."

"So how do you propose we proceed?" asked Daphne.

Beth's eyes remained on him, and every muscle in his body tightened, even the parts recently covered, as she smiled.

She spoke evenly. "I suggest the duke send for his largest family carriage. It will take several days for a message to arrive and the carriage to travel down. As soon as Mary can travel, we will pack the six of us—Mary and her daughter, Kendall, Mattie, Kit, and me—and prepare to return to Kirkstone Abbey, where we will arrange for the marriage. When Charlotte's son is ready, we will send for him. We will inform our families in confidence now, but as we settle, we will spread the tale through loosely sealed letters sent to family and friends in London. It will not take long."

"That is truth." Sophie touched Mary's shoulder. "You are certain?"

Mary hesitated, and for a moment Kit wondered if she had changed her mind. Then . . .

"I think this will work."

Sophie straightened her shoulders and addressed him. "Then let us get you back to your room. Mary needs to rest. We all need to rest. Tomorrow we have work to do."

Tuesday, 13 September 1825
Timmons Manor Library
Ten in the evening

BETH STARED AT the quill, rolling it back and forth between two fingers, waiting for the words to come—but they did not. Her mind had gone annoyingly blank.

Over the afternoon and evening of flurried activity following the death, birth, and her own announcement, Beth had slowly come to realize that she had not just stepped into an unfathomable mire.

She had opened Pandora's box.

After Sophie had ushered everyone but the midwife out of Mary's bedchamber, Kit had gone silent, retreating to his room with hers and Daphne's help. He had barely glanced at her as he had settled back into bed and had asked Daphne—not Beth—for aid with preparing the messages to his mother. Beth had retreated from the bedchamber at that point, heading downstairs to the manor library to begin her own missives. None of them would be taken to the mail drop at The Queen's Arms for a few days, so if the proper words did not come right away, perhaps a good night's sleep would help.

And, indeed, even after considering a dozen different ways to present the plan to her parents, Beth's pages remained blank.

"They will come." The soft but firm voice from the doorway roused Beth from her stupor. "The words. What you are about to say is not an easy message to convey." Daphne strolled across the room and sat in a wingback near the escritoire. "I remember that all too well."

Beth pushed the foolscap back into its cubbyhole and capped the ink, returning the quill to its box. "You wrote such a letter?"

Daphne nodded. "To inform my parents I intended to stay here with Sophie, and not marry the priggish earl they had chosen for me. Ten years or so ago, just after the war. After Waterloo. I had spent most of the war in Greece with an aunt, which is where I met Sophie. She had been on the one holiday she had taken in years. We became immediate friends, and she invited me here. I had been avoiding the Marriage Mart for several years by then, so I accepted the invitation without reserve. She had already begun the work you see around us, and I knew this is where I belonged." She paused and studied a fingernail. "But it took me almost a month to find the words to tell my parents."

"Did they accept your decision?"

Daphne chewed her lower lip, her gaze distant. "After a fashion. After a few explosions and declarations of ruination and despair." She looked up at Beth. "I eventually struck a bargain—I would never again set foot in London and they would disown me, as if I never existed."

"That does not sound like much of a bargain."

Daphne gave a wry grin. "But it allowed me to stay here." She shrugged one shoulder. "I did go back once, when my mother died two years ago. I was surprised my brother even told me—even more surprised at how they welcomed me. But I did not attempt to stay, nor did they ask. My brother did give me money—part of my mother's income, according to him—which was generous."

"Have you seen them since?"

Daphne shook her head. "No. Nor do I expect to. My brother—the duke—has heirs now. I am the long-estranged, eccentric aunt they tell bedtime stories about, I suppose. A warning about what happens when decent girls go astray."

Even in her numbness, Beth understood. "So your struggle to write meant nothing in the end."

Daphne's smile widened. "I knew you were a clever one." She stood. "Put it plainly and do not hesitate or pull punches. From what I read about your mother in the gossip columns, she is not one to coddle anyone, especially not her own children."

"This is true."

Daphne turned to leave, then paused, looking back at her. "Would you be willing to do this if he were not a duke?"

Beth considered the question. "I am doing it because I know him, and I did care for him, even if I did not accept his suit. I do not think I would be comfortable marrying a stranger, duke or no."

Daphne seemed to accept the answer and nodded. "However, if it turns out that he is a miserable husband, send me a missive. My aunt," she grinned broadly, "still lives in Greece and is always in need of good company."

Beth chuckled. "I will." Daphne left, and Beth stared at the writing materials a few more minutes. No. Trying any longer tonight was useless. She stood and headed back to the Lily Room, where she found Mattie curled into a fetal position in the middle of the bed.

Beth watched the girl sleep a few moments, as exhaustion drained every inch of her own body. Despite her initial claims to Sophie and Daphne, more than four hours with this child had demonstrated to Beth that she did not know nearly as much about children as she thought. Mattie's mind had been insatiable, from questions about her mother's death to why butterflies did not move in a straight line. Giggles about a sudden birdsong would shift to sobs without a blink, and fifteen minutes of relentless questions would end with long stares at the sky and soft whispers aimed at Charlotte, who "was now with God and all the other angels like her."

The peace that now eased all tension from the child's face also soothed Beth's mind. The coming days would be difficult, but as Beth rang for Kendall, one comforting thought settled in her mind.

When all the trials and ills had fled from Pandora's box, one small flicker had remained behind.

Hope.

Wednesday, 14 September 1825
Timmons Manor
Half past one in the morning

KIT STARED AT the canopy over the bed, hands behind his head. He had thought sleep would come easily tonight, as his coughing had abated somewhat. After the frenzy of the afternoon, he had been left almost entirely alone, except for the abrupt arrival of the same scowl-faced woman with a tray of tea and victuals, leaving him to feel completely assured that cooks should not ever leave their kitchens and mingle with other folk.

To his relief, Meg had been the one to retrieve the tray later, leaving behind the pungent aroma of spiced chicken, bread, and stewed vegetables. He had eaten little but felt more of his strength returning. She returned briefly to refresh the water for his tisane, stir the fire and add coals, and leave a new camphor poultice, all of which should have eased him into slumber. But Kit had listened to a clock somewhere chime midnight, then one, the night slipping away while he could not rid his mind of one image, one moment from the afternoon, which recurred in his mind until he thought madness might descend.

Beth had been in his room after her grand pronouncement, helping Daphne. But she had given him shy, sideways glances, her cheeks pink, as if she were suddenly awkward and uncertain in his presence. He had asked Daphne for help with his messages, since he thought she would know more about where foolscap and ink would be kept than Beth. But when he had done so, Beth had looked startled, leaving his bedchamber soon after.

Why would she be so suddenly shy with him when she had boldly suggested they marry as a solution to this entire unexpected and awkward situation?

Had he said or done something to put her off? He had spoken little in Mary's bedchamber, and only a few in his own, except for the question to Daphne.

The wind outside shifted, and a shutter somewhere rattled against a wall. Kit could feel in his bones the brewing of a storm, although moonlight yet gleamed through the two windows in the room, casting long gray and white shadings across his bed and the floors nearby. Shadows from scudding clouds occasionally broke up those patterns, and the entire night began to reflect his own tumultuous mood.

Moonlight felt odd in this chamber not his own. It had been dark as pitch until tonight, the thick curtains pulled tight and clamped to keep out all light. But earlier today, someone had opened them to allow in the sun, a pleasant change. Who . . . had Beth done that?

Beth.

Kit whispered her name.

He had never known she went by that name within her family. Their encounters in the spring and early summer—balls, soirees, and his afternoon calls on her—had been formal and strictly chaperoned. Although she had tugged at his heart even then, nothing had gripped him like this. After all, she had been *Lady Elizabeth*, diamond of the *ton*. She had shimmered and glittered when she walked and danced among her peers, her laughter bright and her hand highly desired. She had been kind, confident, and clever, ever aware of the *ton's* eyes on her, including his own—until she had declined his offer to court her. Like a wisp, a summer butterfly, she had whirled around his life for a brief time, a flit of beauty on the wind. Then she was gone. Out of reach, even for a duke.

Unattainable.

Kit suddenly understood why Sophie insisted that all staying in this house use their Christian names. It equalized them, removed all barriers, almost necessary in a situation like this. Although Sophie—Lady Sophia Timmons—clearly ran the house, the protocol of the beau monde had no place when providing comfort and security to desperate women and helping them give birth in safety and sanctuary.

Surrounded by such women, Beth's *ton* façade had crumbled. Lady Elizabeth had melded into Beth, still clever and beautiful but with a kindness that had overwhelmed her sense of propriety. Would she be able to return to the persona of Lady Elizabeth, darling of the beau monde? Would she want to?

Did *he* want her to, now that she would be his?

Kit felt a weight on his chest that far exceeded that of the poultice.

He was a duke. She would be his duchess. As ranking members of the aristocracy, they would have obligations, of course, some of which they would have no choices about. But that world—that precise world of arbitrary manners and protocol seemed exceptionally far away. And the Beth he had met here, the lovely, gentle girl in a scarf and muslin gown, had done more than help heal his body.

She had won his heart.

But she had also sacrificed herself in the process. As they re-entered Society, would she resent him? Resent what he and his sister had thrust upon her?

Kit closed his eyes, that weight threatening to crush him as he realized that he could still lose her to the world she had loved so much.

"Kit?" A soft word, like the whisper of the wind.

His eyes flew open, and he tried to push up, looking around. Had he imagined—

"Are you awake?"

No. Not his imagination. But he had not heard the door—he had only barely heard her call his name. He shoved up in his bed, and the poultice hit the floor with a quiet thump. He swallowed hard. "I am."

Beth appeared to glide across the room, an ethereal presence in her dressing gown, her long silken curls draped over her shoulders and breasts. She picked up the poultice and placed it on the chair near his bed. "I could not sleep."

He cleared his throat. "I thought you would be exhausted."

"I am, but my thoughts will not hush."

Do I dare . . . He held out his hand to her. "Sit with me?"

Her eyes widened, gray in the silvery light, but after a moment, she nodded. He scooted over toward the middle of the bed, and she clambered on. He raised his arm, and she curled against him, her body warm and supple against his chest, a feeling as natural as their earlier embrace. He tucked the bed's covers over her, then wrapped her in a gentle hug. She sighed, leaning her head on his shoulder.

"My mother," she whispered, "would be mortified."

His gut tightened. "But are you?"

She shook her head and buried her fingers in the cloth of his shirt. "I should be, I suppose. This is all so sudden, and the solution is practicable as well as practical, and should be just the usual kind of business of arranging a Society marriage—one done for the convenience and expedience of all parties . . ."

She sounded as if she were trying to convince herself of the wisdom of her own idea. "But . . ."

She paused. "When it occurred to me that this was a possible solution, it did not feel practical." She peered up at him. "It felt . . ."

"Natural."

Beth nodded. "As if it were meant to be. As if this was why all of us have come to be in this place at this time." Her fingers twisted tighter into his shirt, and Kit's breath caught. "As if choosing Aldermaston had been a colossal mistake and the universe had conspired to fix it. That all along I was meant to come here for you." Her cheeks colored and she looked down again. "I suppose that sounds preposterous—girlish and stupid and selfish."

"I have never known you to say or do anything preposterous or stupid or selfish"—he shrugged one shoulder—"other than choosing Aldermaston over me in the first place."

Beth grinned and let out a slight giggle, definitely a girlish sound, reminding Kit of exactly how young this poised and clever woman truly was.

He stroked her cheek tilting her head up so he could focus on her eyes. "Are you certain you want to follow this path? If you went back to London now, the power of your family could pull you through any remaining scandal. No one is going to stare down the Duchess of Kennet for long. Once she recovers, I know without a doubt she would wipe the floors of ballrooms from London to Edinburgh with anyone who tried."

Beth snickered, the image obviously amusing her. "I did not realize you had met my mother."

"More often than you might think. And I am an observant man."

She stilled, her eyes narrowing a bit. "You called on my mother?"

"And your father. And your brothers. You knew they had vetted me. Do you think they did so without meeting with me?"

Her eyebrows arched. "I did."

Kit smiled and touched her cheek again. "They knew what you could offer me. They wanted to see what I could offer you." He let out a long breath. "You know this is a plan born of madness. You do not have to do this. You are a diamond. Worthy of a prince. You could return and be the center of London Society again. Are you convinced you do not want that?"

Beth turned her gaze out the window, but her stare was distant, at someplace far beyond the clouds. "My mother always told me that one moment, one instant, can change your life forever. I thought she meant not to get caught out with some rake, but after her apoplexy, I realized she had a much larger warning in mind. An accident, a loss of attention for even a moment, the wrong choice, the wrong path"—she took a shuddering breath—"and your world changes forever." She turned her face to his again. "Over the past few days, I have come to see that my moment happened when you collapsed on Sophie's floor. I did not see it at the time"—she released his shirt to stroke his cheek—"but from that second, you have become my path."

Kit could barely breathe, his words choked. "You know there is no going back for our kind. You know that. If we marry, you are mine forever."

"I could want nothing more." She cupped his cheek with her palm. "I want nothing more."

But she *would* want more—Kit knew this to the depths of his soul—and sooner than she realized it. More than he could give her. He should let her go, release her from this insane plan, set this summer butterfly back on her wandering flight. He should—

Kit's lips brushed hers, a bare whisper of a kiss. Her eyes widened at first as he paused, then they slipped closed as he kissed her again, pressing more firmly, then pulling at her lower lip.

Beth whimpered, her body relaxing in his arms as he deepened the kiss, exploring the lush warmth of her mouth. Every muscle in his body tightened, and his desire for this woman sent a stark arousal into his loins. His cock hardened, even as his mind reminded him he barely had the wherewithal to eat, much less treat Beth in his bed the way she deserved.

In the distance, that clock that had counted his earlier hours away chimed twice.

Kit eased out of the kiss, brushing Beth's hair away from her face and touching each of her eyelids with his lips. Her eyes opened slowly, her expression gentle and dreamy. He smiled. "Soon, I will treat you as the queen you are. But tonight we must both sleep."

She nodded, and Kit expected her to leave his bed, returning to her room. Instead she nestled deeper into the covers and tighter against his side, resting her head on his chest and wrapping one arm around him.

The instantaneous effect on his body made his breath catch and his mind riveted with the thought that if she stayed in his bed, he would surely be dead by morning. His instinct to rouse her and insist she leave warred with the pure joy he felt from having Beth against him. He pressed his head back against the pillow and took several deep breaths. He would be fine. He would be—

Beth sighed.

Kit looked down at her. Her face, like her body, had relaxed, and he had never seen such an unencumbered expression of peace. Her beauty encompassed every part of her—mind, body, and soul—making her the most radiant woman he had ever known.

His future lay in her, and he would not deny her this. Or, he doubted, anything in the months to come. No matter what.

After watching Beth a bit longer—the soft evenness of her breath, the gentle flutter of her dark lashes against her cheeks, the sweet pink in her cheeks—Kit closed his eyes. And slept.

PART TWO
Kirkstone Abbey

Chapter Fourteen

Friday, 23 September 1825
Kirkstone Pass
Half past two in the afternoon

"See? It casts a shadow like a steeple. Like a church. And 'kirk' is the Scottish word for 'church.' So it's the kirkstone."

Beth grinned as Mattie squinted, peering at Kit as if he had gone mad. She could not blame the child. It seemed rather farfetched to her as well. But she had grown up with her brother Michael seeing shapes in odd things, like clouds and tree bark, so she had long ago accepted this kind of imaginative visioning. She placed her hand on Mattie's shoulder. "Sometimes you simply have to accept people at their word."

"Were they drunk?" Mattie asked.

Now Kit looked confused. "Who?"

Mattie pointed at the huge stone currently under discussion. "The people who said that it looked like a church. Mummy used to say that when people were drunk, they saw all sorts of things that weren't there."

Beth choked on her laugh, coughing into her hand.

Kit scowled at both of them. "Clearly we must work on your imagination. It has obviously been stunted."

Mattie crossed her arms. "I don't know what that means."

Beth guided Mattie back to the waiting carriage. "I will explain later." She glanced over her shoulder at Kit, whose cheeks had reddened somewhat, possibly from the afternoon sun.

Or maybe not.

Their roadside stop had resulted from a morning of endless questioning on this last day of their travel. As their carriage had headed up what felt like an endless mountain, Mattie had merely inquired as to why he was the Duke of Kirkstone, and what was a kirkstone, and how did he become a duke, and why his family name was not Kirkstone but Caudale yet everyone called him Kirkstone, and why were titles so peculiar anyway.

Her curiosity never ceased.

Kit, deciding a history lesson would answer her questions, had instructed the carriage driver to stop at the landmark stone that had given much of the area its name. As their entourage— the ducal carriage, a wagon loaded with trunks, and Kit's horse— waited on the nearby road, Kit had led the way to the stone, beaming with pride at its history.

Mattie had been less enthused. Even though they had only been on the road for three days—such an entourage did not move with any sort of speed—Mattie had been a sullen traveler. Still caught in a miasma of grief, especially in the evenings, she had often broken down into a tearful mess, clinging to Beth and begging for her mother.

Kit had been sorely affected by these fits, often pacing the room, his eyes wet, and Beth wondered how much he still missed his father, especially as his life was about to shift dramatically one more time.

Not that the coming changes would be easy on any of them.

The footman—sent by the duchess, along with the coachman and the carriage—helped Beth and Mattie back into the carriage, and they settled against the back seat cushions, Mattie closest to the window. Kendall and Mary sat on the seat opposite her, and both had been remarkably silent on this final leg. Through the open door, she could see Kit pacing back and forth near the stone, a sign of the tension that had seized him the last few days. He dreaded arriving at Kirkstone Abbey almost as much as she did. As she supposed they all did. And for good reason.

His mother, still the Duchess of Kirkstone, had not taken the news of her son's upcoming nuptials with any sort of grace.

Daphne had been right—the words had come to both of them, and they had sent cautiously worded letters to Kirkstone Abbey by hired messenger and to London by Royal Mail Coach— which turned out to be a much faster delivery service than Beth had realized. Responses to both had come by special messenger two days before they were to leave.

Beth's letter from the Duke and Duchess of Kennet had been typical of her parents—full of questions and reassurances. After all, they had already met Kit and knew his character.

Kit's missive from his mother had thrown him into a rage that had sent everyone, even Mary, fleeing from his bedchamber. Only after Sophie had confronted him behind a locked door had he calmed enough to speak coherently. They had drafted a second letter and sent the messenger off to the north.

Beth still had no idea what either had said, but she knew in her heart her reception at Kirkstone Abbey would not be a welcoming one. Still . . . they had little choice, and Kit seemed completely determined at this point to proceed with their plan.

Her plan.

Mary shifted as her daughter stirred restlessly in her arms. "What is he doing?"

"Pacing."

Mary shook her head. "That is our reward for allowing him to get well. He has always paced, especially when something is bothering him."

"Do you know what was in your mother's letters to him?"

Mary sighed. "No, but I suspect it was phrased with my mother's usual tact and kindness." She peered at Beth from under long, dark lashes. "You should know that my mother can be . . .

blunt. She is all cream and honey when she is out in Society. At home, her bent toward vinegar and salt reappears. It is one of the reasons I knew I had to leave, once I discovered the extent of my mistake." She smiled down at her infant, love beaming in her eyes. "Which was no mistake." She kissed the child's forehead and settled her with a slight rocking motion.

Outside, Kit gave instructions to the coachman, then the carriage lurched as he pulled up into it, the footman closing the door behind him. He dropped into the seat, hunched into the far corner, and crossed his arms, staring out the window. Beth glanced at Mary, who shook her head. All of them remained silent as the carriage continued through the pass and over one of the highest peaks in northern England.

Mattie stared out the window, eyes wide as she looked up at the fells, their sharp slopes covered in grass and heather, with stubby trees showing the signs of autumn. As before the road—soft and lumpy from the first rains of autumn—caused the carriage to rock and buck. Beth held onto Mattie with one arm and the frame of the window with the other. As the carriage, which had been climbing steadily since they had left their inn that morning, leveled out then began a slow descent, Mattie let out a small gasp. "Is that it?"

Beth peered over the girl's head and felt her own breath catch.

"It is." Kit leaned a bit closer to Beth. "Welcome to Kirkstone Abbey."

"Why is it called an abbey?"

Kit stroked Mattie's hair. "Because it used to be one." When Mary cleared her throat, he went on. "Or rather it is built on what used to be one. Do you know what an abbey is?"

"Aunt Sophie says that it's where nuns and monks lived a long time ago until a bully of a king tossed them out and tore down their homes. She said nuns and monks were like vicars but better."

"Sophie would explain it that way," Kit muttered.

Mary smiled, her voice low as she spoke over her daughter's head. "About two hundred years ago, our ancestors acquired the land and built the house around what was left of the old abbey. You can still see some of the arches and walls. I will show them to you once we get everyone settled."

"It's big! Much bigger than Aunt Sophie's house."

"Fifteen bedchambers, as well as all kinds of other rooms and servants' quarters."

"You have a cook too?"

"Yes." Kit smiled.

"Will she let me have biscuits?"

"Biscuits are for teatime."

"Are there ponies?"

"Yes." Kit glanced at Beth. "And sheep and cows and dogs."

Mattie looked away from the window. "Like Boru?"

"There are not many dogs like Boru. But I think you will like the ones we have."

Beth pulled Mattie onto her lap, scooting closer to the window for a better look. Even from this distance the vista that lay before them enchanted her. Built into the side of the fell, the gray stone house seemed to reach for the sky even as it stretched its wings across the slopes. Past the main house, outbuildings extended beyond the fell, spreading deep into the rolling fields surrounding the estate, fields marked by the grids of stone walls and anchored by at least five stone barns.

As the carriage banked around a curve to the left, Beth could see that the house faced a low, broad lake bordered by tree lines and more fields. On the other side of the estate, the road forked in three different directions, and she could see the roofs and tendrils of smoke from two separate villages.

"Do the villages support the estate or the other way around?" Beth asked.

Kit's low voice spoke near her ear. "Both." He pointed to the village on the right. "That village is primarily shepherds, weavers, and carders. They help the tenants tend our sheep and then they turn the wool into textiles, which we sell and share the profits with them. The other village, Patterdale, has few shops. It is mostly houses. Beyond Patterdale is Glenridding. More shops, more people. Their butchers buy our cows, and we buy back the beef we need. They also have a small industrial kiln for pottery." He grinned at Beth and touched her arm. "And a dressmaker, who I understand is quite talented."

Beth returned his smile. They had grown increasingly more comfortable with each other over the past ten days, which had reassured her that her plan might work out. As Kit had healed— he continued to cough now and then but his strength had mostly returned—he had become more affectionate with her. While remaining proper, especially in the company of others, he had touched her more often. But she had not returned to his bed, and there had been no other kisses.

For which Beth had been grateful. Even the thought of that kiss fogged her mind and left her speech muddled. They had too much to do, to achieve. She had needed a clear head.

No matter how much she craved another kiss.

His breath on her cheek reminded her of that, and her gaze met his. "I should make her acquaintance."

"I will be honored to accompany you for the introduction."

Mary cleared her throat. "I dare you to look at her like that when Mother is in the room."

Kit's eyes glittered as he leaned back and faced his sister. "Challenge accepted . . . although not today."

Mary chuckled. "I will be surprised if we all survive today."

They fell silent again as the carriage reached the bottom of the rise, the villages disappearing behind tall stands of trees. The road ran between the estate and the lake, mirroring the edge with its curves. Finally, the carriage slowed, then shifted to the right, leaving the main road and pulling hard up a short slope onto a broad graveled area in front of the house. The wagon continued on, following the drive around to the back of the house.

Beth felt the footman dismount and waited until he opened

the door on her side. She gripped Mattie's waist to keep her from leaping from the carriage, whispering, "Wait. The duke must exit first, then let the footman help you down."

"Why?"

"Because that's how it is done."

Kit exited smoothly, stepping aside. Outside, the footman waited, his eyes bright.

"Put out your hand."

The girl did, and the footman moved to take it, aiding her descent. As her feet settled on the gravel, Mattie looked up at Beth, her eyes taking in every move as Beth let the footman help her out of the carriage. As Beth took her hand, Mattie leaned closer. "That was not as much fun."

Beth grinned and squeezed her hand. "I promise that one day you will be grateful for it." Mattie looked doubtful as they stood to the side, waiting as Mary, then Kendall, emerged.

Two narrow steps led to the simple but elegant front entrance to the estate house, which consisted of beveled wooden doors with polished scrollwork and bronze knockers. Kit offered Beth his arm, and as she took it, both doors opened to reveal a tall, broad man in a black and white livery, neatly appointed with silver buttons and gray braid on the shoulders and sleeve cuffs. He moved out onto the top step, followed by a woman dressed in all black. From the cluster of keys at her waist, Beth figured her for the housekeeper.

Kit nodded to both of them. "Pollard. Mrs. Marshall."

Pollard snapped his heels together and straightened his shoulders.

"Welcome back, Your Grace."

"It is certainly good to be back." Kit took a deep breath. "Pollard, Mrs. Marshall, this is Lady Elizabeth Ashton, my betrothed. Lady Elizabeth, this is Pollard, our butler, and Mrs. Marshall, our housekeeper."

Pollard, his lined face impassive, bowed. "My lady."

Mrs. Marshall bowed her head and dropped a quick curtsy.

Beth repeated their names and nodded her acknowledgment of the introductions as Kit went on.

"And this is Mattie. Who will become my ward. Did my mother inform you of the situation?"

"She did, Your Grace, and she is anxious to see you."

"I have no doubt."

The butler stepped out of the doorway, and Kit led the way into the entrance hall. Beth heard the carriage drive away and glanced behind her to see Mrs. Marshall address Kendall in a low voice. The two women turned and headed toward the side of the house in the same direction as the carriage.

"Where are they going?" Mattie asked.

Beth bent slightly to whisper. "Servants do not enter by the front door. Mrs. Marshall is escorting Kendall to the servants' entrance."

"That seems silly."

"And try to remember that little girls should not ask so many questions when there are a lot of people around."

Mattie scowled but remained quiet.

The party paused in the entrance hall and Beth tried not to gawk. While not as fine as the one at Ashton Park, the country estate of Beth's family, it nonetheless had clearly been decorated to impress. A polished granite floor was covered by a deep burgundy carpet that muffled both footsteps and voice. Twin carved tables stood on either side, their deep red wood and marble inlays gleaming and their oriental vases flourishing with fresh-cut flowers. The artworks on the walls looked as if they might have been painted by Constable, and soaring above them were framed coats of arms bracketed by shields and crossed swords. At the far end of the hall, a curving cantilevered staircase seemed to float up to the first floor, its balustrades thick as a man's arms and carved with the same intricate pattern as the front door.

Near the foot of the stairs a woman waited, dressed all in white, with a blue apron and headscarf. Pollard turned to her and she came forward. "Your Grace, Lady Mary, Lady Elizabeth, this is Mrs. Staunton. She has been hired to care for the children."

Mary and Beth looked at each other. "I do not think—" Mary began.

"She is experienced, with extraordinary skills. She has five children of her own and has worked for two other noble houses before as a nurse and a governess."

The woman stepped a bit closer. She had pleasant, soft features and brown hair streaked with silver.

Mattie wrapped both arms around Beth's legs. "No."

Mary turned to Kit. "I do not see why—"

He shook his head. "We must talk to Mother. And they cannot go in there. You know that."

With a sigh, Mary shifted her daughter's sleeping form to Mrs. Staunton. Beth watched as the woman cautiously and competently settled the infant in the crook of her arm. "I will take good care of her, my lady." Her voice, velvety soft, seemed to comfort the child, who smacked her lips, her small hands clutching the closest bit of fabric.

Beth peeled Mattie's arms away from her legs and squatted next to her. "We talked about this."

"I didn't like it then either."

"Mattie—"

"I want to go back to Aunt Sophie's."

"We cannot—"

"Mattie, are you hungry?"

Mattie's eyes snapped toward Mrs. Staunton. She bit her lower lip.

Mrs. Staunton took a tentative step closer. "It is so late in the day, I knew you would be ready for tea. I have biscuits and cake and jam and clotted cream."

Mattie looked back at Beth. "She is trying to trick me."

Beth squeezed the girl's hands. "She is trying to take care of you. Feeding you is part of that."

"She will tell me there are toys next."

"You do not have to play with them. But you do need to go with her."

Mattie glanced up at Mrs. Staunton, who now held out her hand. "You have a playroom?"

Mrs. Staunton nodded. "A large one."

"Kit said there were dogs."

Mrs. Staunton frowned. "Kit?"

Kit cleared his throat. "That would be me. You, um, may have to work on that."

"Indeed." Pollard sniffed.

Gingerly, Mattie took the nurse's hand. "But there are dogs."

"Yes. But we will see them later."

With a last glance at Beth, Mattie accompanied Mrs. Staunton and they disappeared down a corridor to the right of the stairs.

"That went smoother than I expected," muttered Kit.

Pollard cleared his throat. "Her Grace is in the receiving room. May I take your coats?"

Kit straightened his shoulders. "Yes. Right." He slipped off his topcoat, as the ladies removed their cloaks. He looked at Mary, then Beth. "Into the lion's den?"

"Lead on, Daniel," Mary said.

Kit offered Beth his arm again and guided her past the staircase and down a corridor to the left of the stairs. They passed two open doors—the rooms appeared to be a man's study and a library—then paused at a closed door. Taking a deep breath, Kit opened it and ushered the women inside.

Two steps into the room, Beth froze, her breath lodged in her chest as her eyes went up. And up. Her heart thudded, but not at the sight of the Duchess of Kirkstone, who sat in the middle of a settee, her skirts spread and occupying most of the cushions. Instead, Beth felt spellbound by the room-filling presence of the Duke of Kennet.

Her father.

CHAPTER FIFTEEN

Friday, 23 September 1825
Kirkstone Abbey
Four in the afternoon

KIT HEARD BETH'S gasp and felt her grip on his arm tighten. He understood. He too stared at the man who often dominated any room he occupied, simply by his physical presence. Philip Ashton, the Duke of Kennet, stood six-five, with shoulders as broad as many doors, and his graying blond hair looking like a golden crown. His thick woolen travel kit—plain but finely sewn—made the man seem larger and more intimidating, and Kit understood why even many of the rowdies in Parliament hushed when he stood to speak. Kennet made his mother's receiving room feel cramped and tiny.

"Papa." The soft word sounded as if it had come from Mattie. Beth put one foot forward, stopping when the duke gave a slight shake of his head. And a wink.

"Well! I am glad you are as shocked as we have been over the past two weeks." Kit's mother shifted on her settee, her scowling deepening as she huffed. "It is about time you two were brought up short. I am hoping His Grace will be able to talk sense into you, since I apparently cannot. This mad plan of yours is beyond the pale. I will not have it, any of it. You have brought disgrace on this house."

Kit tensed, determined to hold his tongue as well as his manners. "Lady Elizabeth, may I present my mother, Catherine, Duchess of Kirkstone. Mother, Lady Elizabeth Ashton."

Beth executed a precise curtsy at his mother, her hand tight as a vice on his arm, her lips a thin line.

His mother huffed.

Beside him, Mary moved a bare inch, just enough to draw her mother's attention.

"And you!" The duchess pointed at her daughter. "I will deal with you soon enough. Your behavior is outrageous, horrifying, and if you think—" She broke off and pointed at a settee on the other side of a low table from her own. "Sit!"

Kit grabbed his sister's arm. "Not yet," he said, fighting to keep his voice calm as he faced his mother. As he had so often in the past. "I think, Mother, you have forgotten who is now in charge of this household. I am the duke."

She stiffened. "How dare you—"

"And I suspect His Grace is here not to talk sense but to discuss a marriage contract. Because I am going to marry Lady Elizabeth—"

"She has trapped you!"

"And we are going to pursue this plan, which is primarily aimed at saving *Mary's* reputation. Or would you prefer your daughter sacrifice herself on the tines of your indignation, when you could instead escort her to London next year and have a successful season for both of you?"

The cloying silence in the room annoyed Kit almost as much as the fury that still flashed in his mother's eyes.

After a moment, Kennet put a fist to his mouth, coughing politely. "Your Grace"—Kit could feel the duke's bass voice clear to his bones—"perhaps you and I should adjourn to your study to continue this conversation."

Kit felt grateful, knowing that not even his mother would contradict Kennet. He nodded. "I believe that to be a wise plan."

He eased his arm away from Beth, who looked up, pure panic coloring her eyes. "Mary," he whispered, "will help," and motioned for Kennet to follow him. The duke picked up a small leather case that had been resting at his feet and did so.

The two entered Kit's study and he closed the door. Suddenly at a loss, he was not sure whether to sit behind his desk or next to the small fireplace. The study, the most masculine room in the house, still reminded him of his father with its scents of tobacco, leather, whisky—and a high note of the horses his father had loved so much. How would his father have handled—"Would you care for a whisky?"

"I would. Thank you." Kennet chose one of the cozy leather wingbacks near the fire and set the case on the floor next to the chair.

Kit poured the beverages and sat in the wingback opposite, setting the glasses on a table between them. "I realize my mother must have—"

Kennet gave a dismissive wave. "She has been perfectly kind to me since I arrived this morning, as she sees us as allies instead of adversaries. She will have to forgive me later when she realizes this is not the case."

"If you do not mind me asking, how did you get here so quickly?"

Kennet smiled and reached for his glass. "My youngest son trades and breeds horses and owns several conveyances that are significantly faster than a lumbering and heavily loaded carriage. I brought only the bare minimum of luggage, and I left the day after we received Lady Elizabeth's letter. Having met your mother on numerous occasions in the past, I suspected you might need support in your quest."

The relief Kit felt must have shown on his face, as Kennet chuckled. "As I thought."

"Your word will carry a great deal of weight with her."

"I am a little concerned that we left Lady Elizabeth and Lady Mary alone with her."

Kit took a sip of the whisky, relishing the burning heat of it in his throat. "Mary has stood her own ground with Mother for many years. And your daughter"—Kit paused, peering into his glass—"is remarkable. Her strength is beyond anything I would have expected in a lady of her status."

"She has three older brothers who never coddled her." The pride in Kennet's voice was reflected in his eyes. "And she never backed down from them either. She even persuaded Robert to teach her to box."

"Box!"

"Apparently, she has a wicked right cross." He took another deep breath. "All of which made her decision to travel to Timmons Manor quite the surprise for us. We thought she would want to face the scandal head on, not run from it."

"I do not believe she was in retreat." Kit swirled the amber liquid. "She said that since the scandal brought an end to her season—and the end of her relationship with Aldermaston—that she felt bored and aimless. She wanted to do something besides read and stitch all day."

Kennet studied him. "She did? Interesting." He paused, then set the whisky aside and focused on Kit. "You should know something about my daughter. While she does not lie, she will often obfuscate. She will banter and complain and stalk about, without ever admitting the true nature of her feelings. And the truth is that when Aldermaston set her aside, it terrified her, but not for the reasons you might think. She chose him because she believed it would be the best match for the family."

"So she told me."

"When he responded as he did to the scandal, she realized he was not the man she believed him to be. She thought him to be like her brothers. Or like me. It never occurred to her that she could make such a poor choice, and she became convinced she could never make a 'right' choice. Ever. She wanted to come to Timmons Manor to avoid having to choose. It was not the scandal that ended her season. It was Lady Elizabeth herself."

Kit stared at him. "Are you saying that she did not come for a visit? She came to stay?"

Kennet nodded. "She did not intend to return to London."

"That was rather . . . rash."

The duke grinned and picked up his glass again, saluting Kit with it. "We thought she might change her mind after a few weeks of a Yorkshire winter but decided to let her fear run its course. She is still young."

Kit took a deep breath. "Sometimes I forget this was her first season. She seems much older at times."

"Again, her older brothers had a hand in that. Thomas was eleven when she was born and left for Eton not long after. He came home on holidays and enchanted her with wild tales and adventures. It took a supreme effort from her governess to keep her in petticoats and pinafores." Kennet paused, took another sip of whisky, then set it down and reached inside his coat. "Did she show you what she wrote to us?"

"No."

"We thought not." Kennet stood as he pulled from his pocket several folded pieces of foolscap. "But I think you should hear this." He moved next to the fireplace, facing Kit. "She explained what had happened, and what she hoped was about to happen, then added this.

"'I realize how unexpected and abrupt this all seems, but I feel strongly it is something I must do. I have been shaken by the unfortunate choice I made earlier—I have lost faith in my ability to see a man's character as clearly as I thought I could. Yes, I should have listened to you—and Thomas and Robert and Michael—but they have been so besotted as of late, I knew they could not understand my desire to make a wise match without regard to emotions. I do feel as if the fates, or God, or however you would describe it, have presented me with a second chance for that wise choice. Kirkstone is strong—even within his illness— both in his physical nature and his character. His dedication to his family—to the point of sacrificing himself—speaks to my mind and heart in a way I did not think possible. I liked him before. Now I admire him. I want to see if those feelings are well founded.'"

Kennet paused. "Do you understand why I am sharing this?"

Kit shifted, his gaze drawn by the dancing flames in the fireplace. His chest had tightened, listening to the words—*she admires me!*—but the undertone carried a troubling hesitation. He looked up at the duke. "She is testing me."

Kennet nodded. "And herself."

Kit closed his eyes. "And I left her alone with my mother."

The duke chuckled, folded the letter, and returned it to his coat pocket. He sat and took a bracing swig of whisky. "You will both have trials by fire over the next few days. There is no need to coddle her."

"Sink or swim."

Nodding, Kennet reached for the case on the floor. "Let us discuss business before I wax too maudlin to be thorough." He hesitated. "Give her something special."

Kit's eyebrows arched. "Such as?"

"That will be up to you. It could be anything from a pony to a small piece of jewelry. But it must have a special meaning to you. You will need to draw her into a sweeter intimacy than just what will be found in your bed."

Kit stared at the man, his face heating, and Kennet laughed. "Three brothers. Older brothers with a nosy younger sister. Thomas had been through three mistresses and Robert two by the time she was out of leading strings, and when they were not around, she prowled through everything they owned. She may not be fully aware of what happens between a man and a woman, but she is not completely ignorant either. My sweet daughter is innocent but not unknowing."

He opened the case and withdrew a sheath of papers. "My solicitor had drafted a marriage contract when Aldermaston was still involved, and he made some adjustments once we received that letter." He extended the papers. "Take a day or so to review them. I do not intend to stay long, but I did want to give the horses at least two days' rest before starting back. But the weather will turn before too many more days have passed." He stood and so did Kit. "Now I am going to invite my daughter to take a walk."

❊❊❊

BETH HAD WATCHED the two men leave the room with a dread made up partly of fear and partly of anger at being left alone with this . . . woman.

Then the door closed, and she heard a sniff. "Cowardly lumps."

She turned toward to the duchess. "I . . . I beg your pardon."

The woman nodded at the door, her dark eyes narrow. "Men. Cowards, the lot of them. They would rather flee to their whisky and tobacco than deal with an angry woman."

Mary dropped down onto the opposing settee. "Well, you *are* in a fine tether. Any man in his right mind would bolt."

The duchess huffed at her daughter, then peered up at Beth. "Well, sit down, girl. No use in gawking at the door. That will not bring him back in here."

Beth looked around the room. Now that her father had gone, she realized the space was larger than she first thought. It held not only the two settees and the table but also an escritoire and chair in a corner, a reading area with two armchairs and a sofa near a broad window overlooking a garden, and matching wingbacks between the settees and the door. The blue and cream décor gave it a light airy feel, and one chandelier—anchored by a broad plaster medallion in the ceiling—added to the overall elegance of the room. An elegance mirrored in the duchess, whose erect posture formed the perfect frame for her black silk gown—she still wore the colors of mourning, but the black and purple feathers in her tightly coiffed hair lent a bit of unexpected lightness to her appearance.

Beth eased down on one of the wingbacks, perching on the edge, her back to the door. "This"—she swallowed hard—"this is a lovely room."

Another huff. "Thank you, but I do not think this is the time and place for chit-chat. The men will be back shortly, so we must make plans."

Beth blinked. "I do not . . . how long has my father been here?"

The duchess fluffed her skirts again, extracting from the folds a tiny creature that Beth first thought was a mouse. It squeaked.

"Is that—"

"Oh, good heavens," Mary said. "Has Bronwyn had another litter?" She looked at Beth, her lips a thin line. "One of my mother's hounds. The bitch is always whelping a litter."

"You are not one who should criticize," the duchess replied, cuddling the pup in the crook of her arm.

Mary bristled. "I beg your pardon!"

The duchess sniffed. "Beg all you like, but you are the one who has whelped a bastard, bringing all this down on our heads. You are fortunate your brother has decided to martyr himself on this woman's dastardly sword instead of forcing you out into the streets where you belong."

"My brother is hardly a saint!"

"No, but he almost died trying to save you." The duchess looked down at the pup, stroking it tenderly.

Mary looked at Beth. "Did you tell—"

Beth shook her head. "I did not—"

The duchess rolled her eyes, looking up at the ceiling. "Are all young people so blindered?" She looked back at Mary. "For pity's sake, Lady Sophia wrote to me. She wanted to let me know some details she felt certain that Kit either did not know or would hesitate to tell me. She is the one who encouraged me to hire Mrs. Staunton for the children and told me what that poor child went through before her mother's death, which I doubt either of you know." She looked from Mary to Beth. "Do you?"

As they both shook their heads, the duchess focused on Beth. "So you agreed to bring a child into a stranger's household without knowing anything about her background?"

Beth felt stymied. "I—She is—Her mother died, and I knew it would be difficult for Sophie to keep her. She seemed lost—"

"Of course she seemed lost! The child has not had a home since the day she was born! Her mother"—she scowled at her daughter—"was like you. Too easy to believe the lies of men, but unlike you, she found herself on the street. That child has been a beggar and a thief, and do not be surprised if you discover some of our silver missing!"

The pup whimpered. The duchess took a deep breath and stroked it.

Beth felt adrift, although one of the duchess' previous statements stuck in her mind. "I did not trap him."

Still focused on the pup, the duchess gave her a sideways glance. "I know that. Kit has not been trapped by a girl since he was seven and climbed a tree to get Mary an apple."

"Which I did not ask him to do."

"No, but you sat on the ground and laughed when he could not get down, instead of going for help."

"His fault for climbing the tree."

The duchess glanced at Beth. "She did not ask him for it, no. All she did was talk for half an hour about how luscious and delicious and ripe those apples were. She held out the temptation instead of asking for it directly."

Beth closed her eyes as understanding swept over her. "You think I lured him with the plan's results."

The duchess faced Beth directly. "Did you not? Did he not throw those results up at me not ten minutes ago? Mary's salvation, which was why he was at Timmons Manor to begin with?"

Mary gave a little gasp, and her mother looked at her. "Do you just now see that he would do anything for you? Anything?"

The duchess turned back to Beth. "Results are very pretty. Shiny. And men are always drawn to lovely, shiny things. It is why so many prefer mistresses to wives. And when those things are no longer so lovely or shiny"—she glowered at Mary—"such as heavily laden with child, they turn away, in search of a different lovely and shiny creation."

Beth felt as if she were choking, her throat dry, her words lodged on her tongue.

The duchess placed the pup on the cushion beside her and draped a part of her skirt over it, then turned to Beth. "Your plan is an ambitious one. It will take work. What will you do when he tires of you? Tires of the work? And what if you tire of him? Of the child? This is a hard country, harsh and cruel. Will you leave him for the warmth of your family in London?"

Family. The word broke the dam. Beth straightened. "No. Because Kit will be my family. And Mattie, and Mary, and her child." She swallowed. "And you. My home will be here, and I will not give up on my family. Family is what makes the work worth it, all the struggles. Family is how you survive all the struggles, all the scandals, all that life brings your way, good or bad. That is exactly what I sought in London and did not find, and it is what I saw in Kit, when he arrived at Timmons Manor. He was there because of family. So was I, in ways I did not understand at the time.

"Kit warned me you could be blunt, but so is my own mother, and so am I. So you may not like me, and you may try to make life difficult, but Kit and I have agreed on this course of action together. I will marry him and you will be my family. And I will fight for you just as he does. Because that is what family does."

The duchess stared at her, dark eyes slowly gleaming as she looked up and over Beth's shoulder. "Quite a speech, would you not say?"

Beth's breath caught and she stood and turned. Kit and her father stood in the doorway. "I—I did not—" She stopped, unsure of what to say.

Her father's eyes shone, and one corner of his mouth jerked. He nodded but remained silent.

Kit, on the other hand, looked as if he had turned to stone, and he looked from her to Mary, then to his mother, and his eyes narrowed. "Your Grace"—his low baritone resonated in the room—"would you please escort your daughter for a stroll? I wish to speak with my mother."

"Of course." Kennet held out his hand toward Beth. "Please join me, Lady Elizabeth."

Beth almost shook her head. She did not wish to leave, but some good sense seemed to have remained in her brain and the shake became a nod. She crossed to her father, her eyes on Kit, whose stillness unnerved her.

"Kit?"

He blinked but otherwise did not acknowledge her.

"Beth." Her father's soft urge pulled her along and she went to him, taking his hand. As they moved into the hall, the duke folded her hand into the crook of his elbow and led her back out the front entrance, both silent as they walked. Some rain had fallen during the last few days of their journey and the temperatures had dropped, but autumn had not yet set in with all its glory of colors and heavy downfalls of rain. The late afternoon sun hit Beth and she paused, closed her eyes, and turned her face up toward the rays.

"You used to do that when you were a little girl."

Beth smiled and opened her eyes, looking up at her father's face. "Am I not still a little girl?"

His deep blue eyes sparkled. "To me, you always will be."

"Hm." She resumed walking, as did he, and they followed a gravel path around the side of the house. "I was not certain you ever saw us as children. You were so strict about protocol, especially where I was concerned, Robert sometimes wondered why you even employed a governess for me."

"Because it was my way of protecting you. Protocol and

propriety not only teaches young women how they should act, it teaches them how men should act. And to be alert when a man is not proper with them."

Beth watched her own footsteps. "Aldermaston was always proper."

"I have no doubt. The man's father could give starch a run for its money."

"Kirkstone as well." She paused. "In London."

Her father remained silent a few moments, then he whispered, "The duchess is not the only one Lady Sophia wrote."

Beth stopped, her eyes widening as she looked up at him again. "What did she tell you?"

His gentle smile reassured her. "To be precise, she wrote Rose, giving her permission to share what she felt necessary. We know he arrived at Timmons Manor ill and close to death. That you provided unwavering nursing care for him. That their household is not exactly a model of propriety." He tilted his head. "I also have noticed you are both struggling to remain formal with each other today."

Beth felt a sharp heat in her face that had nothing to do with the sun. "We did not . . . we were not . . ." She took a deep breath, but her father held up his hand.

"I do not think you need to explain further. You are saying there would be no need for me to call him out."

"Absolutely not!"

Kennet laughed. "I think that is as much as your father needs to know."

They strolled again, and the path forked—to the right lay the rear of the house and several outbuildings. To the left, the path entered a plush garden and split in three directions. In the garden, their steps slowed, and Beth inhaled, relishing the rich scents of the fall blooms.

"You know why I came?"

She squeezed his arm. "For the marriage contracts."

Kennet shook his head. "That could have been handled by

messenger. I came because your mother was worried."

"That I would make the same mistake twice?"

He smiled. "No. That you were doing this only because *you* were afraid of making a second mistake. That you were making a desperate choice instead of one of your own free will."

"Mostly, I wanted to help."

"So the tendencies of Rose and Lady Sophia have infected you as well? Who, precisely, did you think you were helping?"

Beth fell silent, realizing that "Mary" sounded quite insufficient. Less than a month ago, she did not even know the woman existed.

Her father pointed to a bench beneath a small yew. They sat, and Beth folded her hands in her lap. "Does Mother still think I am trying to run away from what I did?"

Kennet studied her for a moment. "For how many years have you been claiming that you would prefer a safe, wise match to a love match, even asking us to help you do that?"

"Always. Is that not the way marriages of the *ton* are supposed to be conducted? Two people make a connection that will help their families? How often have I heard that Society marriages are more about lineage and connection than love?"

He shrugged. "Always."

"So is that not what I was supposed to do?"

"And what else did your mother always tell you?"

Beth looked out over the various beds of the garden. Like the ones at Timmons Manor, these flourished with varieties in an array of colors. In the light breeze of the afternoon, the blooms stirred, the rustling of leaves in the trees surrounding the grounds like a peaceful whisper.

"Beth?"

She took a deep breath. "She said to consider a match with my head first, then my heart. That both worked together. One without the other was a path to disappointment."

"And Aldermaston?"

Beth did not want to admit it, but she did. "He was a choice of my head."

"And your heart?"

"Thought he was fine. Appropriate. We seemed suited. That should have been enough."

"When seas were calm, it was. But you are an Ashton. Even when seas appear calm . . ."

"There is a maelstrom waiting over the horizon." Beth realized one of her fingernails had split, and for a second wondered when that had happened. "Papa?"

"Yes?"

"Do you still like him? Kirkstone."

"I do. I especially like the way he took control from his mother earlier. I have known her for years as well, and she can be domineering. But the previous duke had a similar personality to his son, and an excellent vision for this area. Has he mentioned the mills in Manchester?"

Beth stiffened. "What mills?"

Kennet chuckled. "This has all happened quickly. You have a lot to learn about each other. The Kirkstone estate includes a wool mill in Manchester, purchased to help the farmers and shepherds in the county. The previous duke was in negotiations to purchase another when he died. I suspect your young duke will continue those when the time comes, if he hasn't already." He reached for her hand. "You are about to discover, my sweet girl, that a marriage is more than what passes between a woman and man before and after the wedding. It is a lifelong partnership. While I think you knew that"—he tapped the side of her head, then pointed at her heart—"the understanding of what it truly means has only barely begun. But the question you should ask yourself now, before this becomes a permanent situation, is whether you are thinking with your heart or your head—or both?"

Footsteps on the gravel path drew their attention, and they looked up to see Kit approaching, his posture rigid and his face flushed. He bowed. "Lady Elizabeth. Your Grace. My mother"—

he took a deep breath—"Would you please join us for tea?" He cleared his throat. "My mother has suggested that afterward we could all use a rest before changing for supper, which will be served promptly at eight."

Her father stood but he motioned for Beth to wait. "If you will give me a few moments, I would prefer to change now. These travel clothes are a bit grimy, and I would like to don something fresher before partaking of any refreshment. Would you escort Lady Elizabeth back inside?"

Kit blinked, startled, then nodded. "Of course." He watched Kennet leave, then gazed down at Beth. "I apologize if my mother—"

Beth reached for his hand. "Sit a moment?"

He hesitated, then nodded and joined her on the bench. She turned to face him. "What I said earlier . . . I was sincere. I consider you my family now. And whatever happens with your mother, please know that I will stand with you. I know that ever since you arrived at Timmons Manor, everything has been swirled up"—she gave a quick smile—"in a maelstrom. And that we have had little time to plan or even understand how this may play out. But I did not make the suggestion lightly. I believe we can be an exceptional match. And I trust you."

Kit studied her for a few seconds, then his entire body seemed to collapse, his shoulders bowing. He closed his eyes. "My God, Beth. You cannot know how much this means—"

Beth slid her arms around him, leaning against him. With a sigh, he drew her closer pressing his head against hers. They remained silent, and Beth let his warmth, the strength of his body flow through hers.

When he spoke again, the words held a quiet tenderness, a wisp of breath against her temple. "Your father did not need to change clothes, did he?"

She grinned. "No. I have seen him take tea after a mud-drenched gallop over the fields."

"Wise man."

"He is that."

Kit eased out of her arms. "Something for me to aspire to."

"Something I suspect you are already traveling toward." She peered up at him. "You own a wool mill?"

His eyebrows arched. "Exactly how much investigating did your father do?"

"According to my brothers, my father knows everything that transpires in London and counties far beyond."

"Hm. No wonder Parliament listens to him."

"They would not dare do otherwise."

He tilted his head and smiled at her. "Shall we go in?"

"I suppose we must."

They stood and she took his arm but stopped as he hesitated. "Kit?"

After a moment, he straightened again. "Could we speak later tonight? After supper?"

"I do not see why not."

"I am sure that while your father is here, Mother will want to maintain the tradition of having the men discuss business over port while the women go through. Meet me here after?"

Beth nodded.

"And . . ." He stopped, swallowing.

"And?"

"Until we speak, please do not let anything my mother says burden you too greatly."

The concern in his eyes enchanted her, and she smiled. "Do not worry too much on my account. On my eleventh birthday, my brother Robert convinced me that I should join my parents for supper. That all young women moved from eating with the children to dining with the adults once they became eleven. I did not even have a maid at that age. But I believed him. I put on my finest dress and presented myself with a flourish in the drawing room, where they had gathered with their guests before the evening meal. The prime minister and his wife. Who, I might add, were exceptionally good sports about the whole incident.

But I had never seen my father so pale or my mother so red."

Kit snickered. "And Robert?"

"He hid until he could flee back to Eton. I have not believed the word of any one person since. Especially not my brothers, and not even two of them. They conspire." She cupped his cheek with her palm. "I am much more resilient than some people seem to believe."

Kit traced two fingers along the side of her neck, sending a sweet but unexpected shiver down her spine. "Oh, I do believe that." He stepped away and offered her his arm. "Shall we present a united front?"

"Let's."

CHAPTER SIXTEEN

Friday, 23 September 1825
Kirkstone Abbey
Half past ten in the evening

KIT PACED BACK and forth on the gravel path near the bench, trying to calm his uneasiness over what he was about to do, to take this step in his relationship with Beth.

He felt like a coward. Despite their growing affection for each other, he and Beth had kept details of their marriage strictly businesslike. She seemed comfortable with that, and his own emotions had been so scattered, referring to the wedding in precise and efficient terms had kept him grounded.

But she deserved more.

The scream of a fox in the nearby woods caused Kit to jump, cursing under his breath. The sounds of the night—insects, birds, the rustle of nocturnal hunters—should have eased his nerves. Instead, they crowded into his mind, making him even more jumpy. He stopped pacing and looked out over the countryside, taking a deep, and hopefully calming, breath. This vista had always been a solace to him, one he had sought out often during his father's last weeks. On the far side of the road, light from the gibbous moon glimmered on the expanse of the Broad Water, the shallow lake used by the local flocks and fields, and illuminated the countryside with bright silvery beams. A moist chill hung in the air—a clear sign of a coming autumn storm—penetrating Kit's evening coat and breeches.

Kit went over his mental list of items he wished to discuss with Beth one more time. Tonight, over port, he had asked Kennet for his blessing on the marriage and to stay as a witness to it. The duke had seemed startled but pleased, and he had agreed. Kit hoped Beth would be pleased as well, to have at least one member of her family at her wedding.

Yet one more thing this plan had forced her to sacrifice—a Society wedding. Such an event had long been a bone of contention between his mother and Mary—his mother had dreamed of a major event; Mary had never desired such a thing. Thus Kit's decision to use it as ammunition in his earlier argument with the duchess.

He had used it again in their second discussion, after he had asked the Ashtons to leave. She had not been so pleasant about it this time, but she had agreed that Beth seemed to be an appropriate choice, and she would give the girl a chance. When he had asked for his final item on tonight's list, however, the duchess had exploded, and both he and Mary had to prevail on her. "An 'act of faith,'" Mary had called it, for which he would be forever grateful.

Kit slid his hand into his coat pocket, fingers caressing the slender box. "A leap of faith for all of us," he muttered.

Beth had sacrificed so much, all with the goal of salvaging his sister's future, a woman Beth barely knew. The time had come for him to acknowledge that in more than words. More than with concise details in a marriage contract.

He heard her footsteps on the gravel and turned, his breath catching.

Lady Elizabeth Ashton glowed in the shimmering moonlight, her hair a soft silver, its pearl and ruby pins glittering like starlight. She had donned a light, silver-blue cloak, which flowed in gentle waves from her shoulders, and she wore white kid gloves. Her eyes sparkled as she gazed up at him, her head tilting back as she approached.

The words burst from him in a harsh whisper. "My God, you are so beautiful!"

Her eyes widened, as did her smile. "I believe you have seen me before, sir."

His cheeks warmed. "Of course. I mean . . ."

"But I thank you."

Gracious. As always. He held out his hand. "Please, sit with me."

She took his hand and settled on the bench, a slow, feminine descent. So proper, reminding him that they were taking liberties that would never have been allowed in London—and making him grateful they were so far away from Society at this moment. He took a deep breath as he sat beside her. "Thank you for meeting me."

She squeezed his hand. "I think we are beyond the usual formalities."

Kit finally smiled. "Old habits can be comfortable."

Beth shifted slightly to face him more fully. "Why are you uncomfortable?"

Kit looked away, hoping the reflection off the lake would soothe him but it helped little. "I still cannot quite believe your willingness to do something so sacrificial for someone you barely know." He faced her, the words rushing out with the hope he could get them said without faltering. "I know your idea first came to mind as a way to provide a solution for Mary, but you could have returned to London and found the triumph any woman could possibly want. While I do believe this path will benefit you, as you have claimed, it is not the only one you could have taken, with similar results. But you are giving up any possibility of another life. And I continually expected you to realize that. To leave. If you want to do so, I will not hold you to any promise otherwise. Your father is here. He could escort you home. If you wish."

Her smile faded as her face paled. "Do you wish me to leave?"

Kit shot to his feet. "No!" He stepped away, looking back and forth, fighting for the right words. "You have brought something to our lives—my life—I could only have dreamed of. You are everything I have wanted in a wife. But I do not want the years to pass and have you resent me for taking you away from"—he gestured southward, but the words failed, and he scrubbed his palm across his mouth.

Beth stood and reached for his hand, pulling it down and pressing it against her stomach. "Why," she whispered, "would I want to leave a man with whom I have fallen in love for the empty promises of a world of shadows?"

Kit froze, the pressure in his chest worse than any of his days of illness. His eyes burned, as did his lungs.

Her gentle smile returned. "You must breathe, my darling."

He sucked in a lungful of air as he dropped back to the bench. Beth joined him, cupping his cheek, waiting. He eventually found his voice. "You love me?"

"More than I thought I could any man."

He blurted out, "Then you do not mind if I asked for your father's blessing?" Well, that had not come out exactly as he had planned.

Beth blinked a few times. "You asked for my father's blessing?"

He nodded. "And for him to stay and witness our marriage. I thought . . . I thought that might please you."

"And he agreed?"

"He did. To both."

Her eyes glistened. "For me."

"Considering what you have given up, I cannot think of—"

Beth kissed him. A gentle soft press of her lips to his, but it stopped his words. "I do not consider what I am doing a sacrifice. It very much feels as if I have finally found the right path for my life, the direction I should have taken weeks ago. Do I want to return to London someday? Of course I do. At your side. This marriage may have come about because of necessity, but it is not one of sacrifice." She kissed him again. "In truth, you will probably discover that I am not that generous."

As he gazed at her, tears slid down her cheeks, and he brushed them away. "Why are you crying?"

"You do realize that women cry when they are happy."

He kissed the corner of her eye, tasting the salt on her cheek. "That seems unfortunate." He slipped his arms around her, pulling her close. She leaned her head on his shoulder with a quiet sigh, and Kit felt the tension leave his body. He gripped her even tighter as she wrapped her cloak about his shoulders, her warmth easing through him. "So our scandalous ways continue."

"Your mother would be mortified."

"My mother remains in a state of mortification. It is her natural demeanor."

"It will certainly make mealtimes intriguing."

Kit chuckled, then eased away from her. "I actually look forward to that. She and I have battled for years, and Mary and my father always refused to engage."

"Ah, well, my brothers will tell you that engaging in a heated conversation is not something I have been shy about."

He smiled, then took a deep breath and reached into his coat, pulling out the slim wooden case that had been pressing against his ribs. "Beth, I do not have a betrothal ring for you—"

"I do not need—"

"Nor a wedding band, as of yet."

"Kit, I—"

"But I want you to have this." He held out the case. "My betrothal gift to you."

She looked from his face to the box. "I . . ." Her eyes met his again. "Why?"

"This was my grandmother's. And her husband's mother's. It has passed from mother to the bride of the oldest son for several generations. It came to my mother when she married. Now it should go to you. My promise to you. You will always be my wife, always be my family."

Beth's hands trembled as she took it, opening it slowly. And she gasped. "Kit, it's beautiful!"

Moonlight glinted off the silver and blue cameo bracelet lying against the black velvet lining. "It's blue jasper in a silver and platinum setting. The silhouettes are mother-of-pearl. I think it was made in Venice, but the true origin has been lost over the years."

"It's priceless! Kit, I cannot—"

His hands closed over hers. "You can. You will. It will be too large on you, but I want you to have it. To wear it." He lifted the bracelet from the case. "Let me put it on you."

Beth shook her head, pulling away. "No." Tears flowed down her face, glistening in the moonlight. "When we are married. Instead of the ring, you should put it on me then."

That felt right—perfect. He nodded and returned the bracelet to its case, closing it, and tucking it back into his coat. He cupped her face in his hands. "Tell me these are tears of happiness."

"Most definitely."

Kit kissed her then, a deep and lingering exploration of her mouth, which sent a fiery spear of desire and longing through him, a craving he had not felt in a long time. One hand slid around her shoulders, the other to her waist as he pulled her hard against him. Beth whimpered as her arms encircled his shoulders, the fingers of one hand entwining in his hair. Kit felt the soft mounds of her breasts against his chest, and with a sudden jerk, he pulled her into his lap.

The action broke their kiss, and Beth yelped, then giggled as she settled against him, leaning her head on his shoulder. With a sigh, she whispered, "Now I understand."

"Understand what?" He brushed a kiss against her temple as he caressed her hip and thigh with long, tender strokes. Beneath her, every muscle had tightened, his arousal hard as it pushed up against her buttocks, and his mind locked on an image of her in his bed, writhing warm and eager beneath him.

"Whenever my parents think they are alone, my mother sits

in his lap. I have seen them several times, and I thought it odd, that only children sit in laps. One time, in his study, they were both reading. Just sitting there." She raised up and looked down at him, her hands pressed against his chest. "I did not realize . . ." As her voice faded, she reached up to push a lock of hair off his forehead. "We should probably go inside."

Kit felt as if he were on fire, and her words barely penetrated his thoughts. "Why?"

"Because I do not want to." She brushed her lips against his forehead. "Because I know," she whispered, "that you do not want to either." She wiggled her hips slightly, grinding against his arousal.

Kit hissed, the movement more painful against his cock than he had expected. Beth bit her lower lip, but her eyes gleamed.

Her father had been right. "You wicked woman."

Beth giggled. "Brothers do not always realize when they are being overheard."

Kit pushed one arm under her knees and the other behind her shoulders and stood. Beth yelped and clung to him, her surprise vanishing into a flurry of giggles.

"I could easily toss you into the lake."

She kissed his jaw, just beneath his ear. "But you will not." Her hands clutched his coat, her fingertips pressing into his muscles.

The feel of her body held so tightly against him made Kit dizzy with need, but he realized he had not quite gained back as much of his strength as he had thought. "No." He let her legs slip down his body until she found her balance.

Yet even released, Beth still pressed against him. "I do not want to let you go." Her quiet words held a deep affection, and Kit closed his eyes as he held her.

"I will see the vicar tomorrow."

"You think he will agree to our scheme."

"I think he will understand that evil actions often result in unforeseen consequences. That his best interest will be in making amends for what he did to my sister."

"He will deny it. As he already has."

"I can be unexpectedly persuasive."

"Take my father with you."

Kit paused, a bit of apprehension tightening his chest. "Do you believe I cannot accomplish this on my own?"

"This vicar was your father's man, was he not?"

"Yes, and dependent on this estate for his livelihood."

"Yet he has already lied to you. He is older. He most likely will not have the respect for you that he did for your father, even if you have earned it." She looked away from him a moment. "I have seen this at work. With my brothers. With my own efforts. People who revere—or fear—my father often think they can lie to his children with impunity. Until we proved otherwise."

Kit saw the sadness in her eyes. "Is this about your brothers? Or Aldermaston?"

Beth's eyes flashed a brief moment, then the sorrow returned. "Perhaps both."

He cupped her face with one hand. "Beth, your value to me has less to do with who your family is than what they are to you. Do you have any idea what it means that the Duke of Kennet came to his daughter at a time when his wife is recovering and his sons are struggling? It is phenomenal, and it speaks more about your family than you can possibly imagine."

She reached up, her fingers tracing through his hair. "I do love you."

"Then let us deal with this situation one scandal at a time."

Beth nodded, and he held her, feeling her head against his chest, her hand on his waistcoat, until the chill of the evening made them both shiver.

BETH LAY IN her bed, staring at the canopy overhead until the moon disappeared behind the gathering storm clouds. The fire in the grate had dwindled to mere embers, and the last bits of reddish light in the bedchamber cast dim shadows over the mahogany furnishings and down-filled covers and mattress. The bedchamber, as small as the one at Timmons Manor but much more luxurious with its appointments, felt like a cozy refuge on what would become a stormy night.

The weather, however, more reflected Beth's thoughts than her surroundings. Every moment of that evening with Kit glided through her thoughts, tumbling over each other. She now knew without a doubt that he wanted her—as his wife, in his bed—in a way that went far beyond what his mother continually referred to as "this mad scheme."

The duchess simply did not believe that Beth cared for her son—and she would not for some time to come. But she would put doubts aside for the sake of both her children. And duchesses kept secrets better than any government spy. No, the ability of Kit's mother to keep silent troubled Beth far less than the rest of their plan because it depended on strangers to cooperate. The vicar. The wet nurse caring for Charlotte's baby. The staff here at Kirkstone Abbey. Mattie.

Mattie was a darling girl, clever and curious. But like most children, she could blurt out honest statements without concern for social necessities. Which meant she could not yet be trusted to keep the true parentage of Mary's child a secret. Yet some of the information Mattie had said about Charlotte might be a path to convincing Mattie that keeping such a secret had great value. And if the duchess were correct, Mattie had lived part of her life depending on stealth and quickness. That too could be ammunition.

Perhaps the christening would help. Mary had not yet named her daughter. She had not wanted any name that reminded her of the vicar—nor had she chosen a family name. Her relationship with her mother made that name choice unlikely, but she might be persuaded, if it helped continue the façade they were building.

The vicar worried Beth the most, even along those lines, as part of the plan involved him christening and registering the child as belonging to Beth and Kit. How far would his own guilt—and fear of Kit—carry him before he said something he should not?

A soft tap on her bedchamber door drew her attention, and Beth sat up as the door opened. The Duchess of Kirkstone stepped into the room, her dressing gown as black as her afternoon's dress had been, as well as the one she had worn at supper. Her dark hair, with its bright glints of silver, hung in a braid down her back. She closed the door, standing beside it, but said nothing.

Beth took a deep breath. "Your Grace."

More silence.

"Is there something you wish of me?"

After a few more moments, the duchess crossed to the bench at the foot of the bed. She sat, but twisted to face Beth. "Mary tells me that earlier this year, my son courted you while he was in London. Is this correct?"

"It is."

"Why did you not choose him then?"

"Because I was foolish."

Apparently not the answer the duchess was expecting. She stilled, but her eyes widened. "How so?"

"I approached the match as a merger of companies. I wanted to choose a husband whose family would be good partners with mine. I chose a man with whom I was a friend, but whose family would extend my father's investments. While they needed my dowry as an influx of liquidity for their estate, many of their holdings would dovetail with the businesses already under my father's purview."

"My god, girl, you sound like a businessman, not a bride!"

Beth chewed her lower lip. "I was trying to be just that."

"So you declined my son's interests in you because his estate did not—what did you call it—'dovetail' with your father's?"

"I—" Beth stopped, not wanting to admit the rest. But she felt she had to. "That. And I . . . I liked him too much. I did not want to make a match based on emotions." She paused. "I also did not really want to move to so far north. Ashton Park, our own country estate, is less than two days' travel from London. I was afraid I would miss the city, and if there were no business reason for the match . . ."

The duchess' mouth twisted. "And four days in Yorkshire changed your mind?"

Beth shook her head. "No. Four days caring for your son did. And weeks of seeing what a scandal was doing to my family and my place in Society. I knew people could be fickle—I did not realize that I could be so foolish as to choose one of the most fickle of all. While my first choice saw our match as one good for the families and for our mutual estates, he obviously did not see that as a foundation to face obstacles such as a scandal. And that he would surrender to his father's wishes and not his own—" Beth stopped, realizing she still felt a deep-seated anger toward Aldermaston for his actions—and his weaknesses.

The duchess studied her, again unmoving, for several moments. "Do you continue to doubt your wisdom?"

"I did in the beginning. I was afraid that"—Beth took a deep breath—"I was letting my heart lead me astray. But I saw him with Mary, saw what he went through to find her—"

"Do you love him?"

"Yes. I do." When the duchess did not respond, Beth asked, "Did you love your husband?"

She shook her head. "Not in the beginning. But, then, I had only met him twice before the banns were read. My parents arranged the match"—a brief smile flitted over her face—"for the wisdom of it. A merger of families. I had no say. And, like you, the prospect of living in Yorkshire did not fill me with excitement. My family is from southern Wales, where the climate is . . . somewhat different. But we grew to respect each other, and I learned to love this country. It can be harsh but also beautiful. I love it more than I did my husband, but we were caring with each other. I miss him."

"You are still in mourning."

The duchess nodded. "I could move to half-mourning, I suppose, but I wish to wait a while longer."

"My understanding is that there are minimum periods for mourning—not maximum ones."

"True. And I do prefer purple to black. I will give it some consideration." She stood. "Two more things. One is that tomorrow, your things will be moved into the duchess's bedchamber. It adjoins my son's through a dual dressing room suite. I vacated the chamber when he moved into the duke's bedchamber after his father's death. The duchess's side has been empty since. I have accepted that the two of you are determined to marry, so there is no reason to continue the façade that you will not. Second, you may call me Catherine in private, if you wish. If we are to be allies in this resurrection of Mary's reputation, I suspect it will be somewhat easier if we are more comfortable with each other." She pointed at Beth. "But understand, I still do not like this plan. It is too much subterfuge for my tastes. You realize how much could go wrong?"

"I do."

Catherine let out a long sigh. "Very well. Do you have a riding habit?"

Beth's mind skipped. "I beg your pardon?"

"I do not stutter, girl. Do you have a riding habit?"

"Um, yes, Daphne loaned—yes, I do."

"Good. Don it first thing. While the men are off to see that bloody vicar, you and I will tour the estate." She gave another quick smile. "And you must meet my dogs."

"I will be ready at breakfast."

"Good. Perhaps now that we have some things decided, we can both get some sleep."

"Yes, Your Gr—Catherine."

Catherine gave a quick nod, then strode from the room.

Allies. Beth sighed. "Well, it is better than enemies."

Chapter Seventeen

Saturday, 24 September 1825
The Vicar's Cottage, Patterdale
Half past ten in the morning

KIT FOUGHT THE urge to kill the man. He thought he had put that desire behind him in light of the "mad scheme," but looking at the vicar now, knowing all too well what he had done to Mary—and trying without success to rid himself of the image of his innocent sister in the man's bed—the need to strangle him barehanded flooded back over Kit.

He had once been a handsome man—this vicar of many years—and Kit remembered him from his childhood. Now everything about the man seemed to . . . *sag.* Jowls, ears, belly, eyelids, shoulders, arms. Even the bags under his eyes seemed to sway down toward his jawline. He could not possibly be much older than Kennet, but the contrast between the two staggered Kit's imagination.

"You . . . you . . . cannot . . . *ask* this of me!"

Kennet stood abruptly, crossing his arms and moving behind the armchair from which he had risen. The vicar, timorous and stuttering, had led the two men into his office, where he sat behind his desk and Kit and Kennet had taken up the two cabriolet chairs in front of it. The office, with its bookcases, low ceiling, and simple furnishings, was serviceable but small.

When Kennet stood, his presence filled the room to the point of stuffiness. The vicar looked up at the duke, his voice breaking even further. "I cannot—"

Kit leaned forward. "Is this where you did it?"

The vicar paused. "Did—"

"Is this where you seduced my sister? I know this is where you lied to me about it. And before you think of lying again, I suggest you consider that mass of red hair on your head, those freckles on your face and arms, and whether they might show up in a child of your loins."

The vicar seemed to collapse. "What you ask . . ."

Kennet cleared his throat. "We are not asking. Your tasks are simple. You marry the Duke of Kirkstone to Lady Elizabeth Ashton. One marriage of many you will perform this year. Only you enter it into the register for last month. You will set up a christening for a child, their child, and you will enter that into the village registry as well. Afterwards, you will write your superiors and express your wish to retire from your position. Tomorrow, you will tell your parishioners the same."

"I cannot support my—"

Kit slapped the desk, silencing him. "You will go live with your son in Manchester. I will provide a stipend for expenses. And you will sign a document avowing to your silence in this matter, or I will present Mary and the child you sired to your superior with a formal writ of complaint."

"But—" Spittle dropped from the corner of his mouth.

Kennet pulled two folded pieces of foolscap from his coat and dropped them on the desk. He pointed at one. "This is a special license, brought from London and authorized by the archbishop for the purpose of this marriage, and using the date you will put in your registry. You will marry them and sign this. The other is the agreement for silence. We will be back Monday at this same time for the wedding and the signed documents. We will arrange for the christening then."

Kit hid his own shock as the vicar looked at the pages as if they were vipers, continuing to sputter. "How . . . how . . . did you manage—"

"I am the Duke of Kennet!" His bass roar reverberated off the walls, and the vicar jerked back in his chair. "And you forget yourself, sir! These are *not requests!*" His voice dropped an octave, into the muted bass pipe sound of a massive organ. "You have two dukes of the realm in your office. You challenge us at your own peril. Do you understand?"

The vicar wiped his mouth with one hand. "Yes, Your Grace."

"Excellent." Kennet looked at Kit. "Let us go, so he can make his arrangements." They left without being shown out, walking in silence back to their horses. As both turned toward Kirkstone Abbey, they waited until they were out of hearing of any other person.

Kit glanced at the duke. "You came up here with a special license."

The corner of Kennet's mouth jerked. "I believe in being prepared for all obstacles. In my experience, clergymen can be quite stubborn, especially if they have stepped somewhere they should not have."

"And the agreement for silence?"

"One of many I brought. Enough for anyone involved in this. There are financial as well as social penalties involved."

"I think I have a lot to learn about being a duke."

Kennet chuckled. "You will. One of them is always look ahead and prepare for any situation. The other is not to use rank as leverage except in extreme cases. This man thought he got away with seducing a duke's sister and lying about it. It made him feel powerful. He needed to see that was an illusion."

Kit nodded, understanding why his own father had expressed both respect for and fear of the Duke of Kennet. After riding in silence for almost a mile, Kennet glanced around. No one was near, but he still lowered his voice.

"Kit?"

"Yes, sir?"

"Mary's child has red hair and freckles?"

Kit grinned. "No. But I do not believe I said she did."

Kennet laughed, a broad sound from deep inside. "My boy, you may not have as much to learn as you may think."

THE DUCHESS OF Kirkstone laughed, a sound that so surprised Beth that she almost tumbled from her horse. She pivoted in her saddle to see Catherine atop her own horse, watching three of her hounds roughhousing, growling and tumbling over each other around the horse's legs. Seven more dogs milled about, watching and barking their excitement, tails wagging furiously. Despite the flurry of activity around their legs, both of their Highland ponies stood placidly, their long manes and tales stirring in the light morning breeze.

The laugh was, however, Catherine's first show of emotion that morning. She had demonstrated little interest in meeting Beth's gaze, always looking elsewhere as they finished the morning meal and made their way past several outbuildings to the stables—the largest structure on the property other than the main house. The number of horses housed within surprised Beth, given the smaller size of the estate—more than even gathered at Ashton Park. Two empty stalls reminded her of the current errand of the two dukes, but the remaining mounts ranged from alert and eager Arabians moving about in their stalls to placid and thick workhorses to the smaller but firmly built Dales and Highland ponies, mounts well-suited for the varying terrain surrounding the estate. The groom seemed pleased by Beth's compliments and admiration for the animals, while Catherine strode resolutely down the center aisle of the main stable and out the other side, where two side-saddled mounts already stood waiting for them.

The duchess had chosen a bay-colored Highland pony for Beth, and Beth had stood back to wait as a groom gathered the reins and steadied a mounting block with one foot. Catherine mounted her own pony, a gray Highland of similar build, with ease, moving out of the stable yard gate and letting the dogs gather about as they waited for Beth to mount. Her laughter at the dogs' cavorting had come as Beth guided her horse toward the gate, settling onto its broad back.

Catherine looked around and saw Beth's look of curiosity. "These three are litter mates. They pummel their siblings and no other dog would dare interfere."

"Sounds like my brothers."

The duchess smiled slightly, then bent and tapped one of the hounds with her riding crop. He looked up at her, woofed, and went to join the rest of the pack, as did its siblings.

"Are we going hunting?"

Catherine straightened in her saddle, gazing out over the property. "Not at all. They will run with us today, but it will mainly be for the fun of it. I run with them a lot. Sometimes they catch something, but usually not. They know the difference between a hunt and a pleasant outing—more and different horses and people as well as the horns. Have you ever ridden a Highland pony before?"

"I rode a Dales pony at Timmons Manor."

"Similar. These ponies are taller but more sure-footed for where we are going, but they do have a tendency to balk. So be on your guard for that. Richard keeps thoroughbreds for the hunt."

"Richard?"

Catherine paused, squinting, her lips pursed. "Ah. The duke. I forget that you have picked up Mary's abominable habit of calling him Kit."

"That is what he asked me to call him."

"So he did not protest Sophia Timmons's lack of propriety as much as he pretends." Catherine stroked her horse's neck.

"I did not think—"

"Richard Christian Caudale. Formally Richard, Eighth Duke of Kirkstone."

"So why Kit?"

Catherine paused, glancing at her. "It is what my mother-in-law called her husband. He was also Christian, and Richard grew up hearing it from her. They were exceptionally close."

"Kit and his grandmother."

The duchess gazed down at her dogs. "Has he shown you the bracelet?"

"It is remarkable. And beautiful."

"Did he tell you it has passed from mother to the heir for his bride across several generations?"

"He did. I also know you were reluctant to surrender it."

Catherine looked up at her again, a bemused smile on her face, although her gaze remained on some distant point. "He thinks he knows why, but he does not. It is not because of you. Richard's grandmother has been dead for more than a decade, and I am still envious of his relationship with her."

"My oldest brother, Thomas, had a relationship like that with our grandfather, who died when Thomas was only ten. I never knew the man—he died before I was born—but my mother always said his death changed Thomas."

Catherine's mouth tightened. "Richard was sixteen. Away at school. He missed an entire year because he would not leave here, as if the rest of us would die at any moment."

"His family is everything to him."

Catherine finally looked at Beth. "So you are aware, this is what you are marrying into. He takes nothing about his family lightly."

"Neither do I."

The dogs around the duchess began to tumble and dance around each other again, barking and leaping. Catherine made a clicking noise with her tongue, which calmed them a bit. "We should go. They are impatient to run."

"Which one is Bronwyn?"

Surprise brightened Catherine's face, her eyes shining for the first time. "You remember?"

"I do not see a duchess cuddling a newborn pup every day."

Catherine looked back toward a building on the far side of the stable. "She is in the kennels with her litter. She will not run until they are weaned. She had tried to reject the little one I had, but I have persuaded her otherwise." She looked out over the pack again. "At least for now. If she pushes him aside again, we will bring him into the kitchens and feed him there." She paused. "Do you think Mattie would like such a task?"

Exhilaration shot through Beth. "She would be overjoyed!"

Catherine waved the crop at her. "Let us not bring it up yet. It would be better if Bronwyn nursed him. But we shall see." She clucked her tongue at the dogs. "Follow me. We will start slow, but we have steep slopes to climb. I will try to explain as we go." She gathered her reins and urged her pony into a walk. "Hie! Hie!"

The dogs responded, bounding out in front of them, as Beth settled in her saddle and touched her pony's withers with her crop. The pony fell in beside the duchess and they moved from behind the stables out across the grounds of Kirkstone Abbey.

The house and its immediate outbuildings had been nestled into a terrace-like area a few hundred yards up the side of a great fell. The road across the pass lay at the base of the fell, and from the road westward lay the lake Kit called the Broad Water and a forested dale beyond. The terrace, ancient enough that Beth could not tell if it were a natural formation of the fell or had been carved into by human workers, extended for several miles in every direction, as if it had once been the roadbed itself. At both ends, it sloped down and rejoined the current road.

When they had ridden almost a mile north, Catherine halted, and pointed back toward the estate with her crop. "From here you can see the remaining walls of the original abbey." She pointed to walls and the two towers of the house, aged granite structures clearly more ancient than the rest of the manor house. "There is a painting in the library of the abbey as it was in the fourteenth century, before the dissolution of the monasteries in the fifteenth. Purely the painter's imagination but quite a magnificent vision of it. King Henry's men did their best to destroy it. The land and the remaining ruins, along with a yearly income, were then granted to some favorite of the king."

"The first duke of Kirkstone?"

Catherine nodded. "I forget most of the details. A tiny territory but the family has been proud of it."

"It is beautiful." Beth meant it. The area seemed to combine the lush beauty of the rolling dales with the stark wonder of the tumultuous fells. Green fields seemed to ebb and flow among small lakes, thick copses of oaks and yews, and steep slopes of mountain grasses. Black-faced sheep dotted the land between fences, with occasional squares of late summer crops.

"Ah, you say that now, but the snows come early this far north and stay until late in the spring. It can be a harsh landscape if you are not prepared."

Beth looked back at her. "Were you?"

"Hardly. But I found my way. So will you." She shifted in her saddle. "I have made an appointment with our dressmaker, Mrs. Weston, in Glenridding. Wednesday. I wish you and Mary to go and began picking fabrics and patterns for her gowns next season. I have heard she has received the latest publications regarding the upcoming fashions."

"So soon?"

"Remember. Harsh winters. And many things will have to be ordered and shipped. We do not wish to wait too late." She clucked her tongue and set her horse and dogs in motion again, and Beth followed.

Yet something nagged at her about this entire conversation, but Beth could not quite pin down the details. For someone who had been so angry about their plans and so resistant to the change, the duchess seemed almost too chipper, too . . . gleeful. Too . . .

Aldermaston's face flashed into her memory. Not the sad expression on his face as he had ended their relationship, but the one prior to that, when he had tried to reassure her the scandal that had descended on her family meant nothing to him. He had said the words—but his face had been motionless, his gaze distant. They had danced but he had looked beyond her, his expression so remote he could have been dead.

And Beth suddenly knew.

For whatever reason, the duchess had said the right words. But her expressions did not agree with what emerged from her mouth. And like Aldermaston, she was not to be trusted.

CHAPTER EIGHTEEN

Saturday, 24 September 1825
Kirkstone Abbey
Half past three in the afternoon

KIT STARED AT his mother, confusion clouding his mind and warring with his anger. "You put her on the bay pony." He paced back and forth before the fireplace in the receiving room, clenching his fists at his side. "Why? You know better! Did you *want* her to get hurt?"

His mother had centered herself on a settee again, far too calm for Kit's liking. "I wanted her to see the estate. To see what she is in for."

"There are other horses!"

"Well, she did not get hurt, did she?"

"She is bloodied!"

"But not broken."

"Her only riding habit is ruined! Why would you do this?"

His mother flared. "If she cannot handle one animal prone to balking, she is not an adequate rider, is she? And she needs to be to handle this estate."

"Prone to balking? Are you mad? It bucked her right over its head. She could have been killed!"

"Well, she was not. She is merely muddy. She should not

have tried to jump him over that stream."

"Muddy *and* bloody. Her father and her maid will not let me in to see her. And how many jumps had she taken before?"

His mother's lips pursed.

Kit growled. "How many?"

She huffed. "Five."

"How many streams?"

His mother crossed her arms.

Kit did not relent. "How many streams?"

The word barely made it past her lips. "Three."

"So she should have avoided that stream because . . ."

"I warned her he could balk at any time. To be prepared."

"Balk. Not buck. He did not balk. He launched her into the air like a bloody cannonball!"

"And she landed without injury."

Kit finally stopped pacing, glaring at her. "A sprained wrist and a bloody face is not without injury."

"As I said, nothing is broken."

"You are a callous fool."

His mother shot to her feet. "You will *not* talk to me that way. You bring these strangers into my house without warning, disrupting our lives, and declaring yourself to be the almighty duke when you have done nothing, *nothing* to live up to that title. You have spent almost year wandering about, playing the poor grieving son, lounging in Parliament, as if you had no responsibility to this estate, to this house, to me! And you want me to bend under like some untrained child. *I will not have it!*"

"So you try to get her killed? You think *that* earns respect?"

"At least I am trying to defend my family. Not open it up to the entire world."

"Defend it? By killing the woman I love?"

His mother's head snapped back. "Love. The two of you. Children. Declaring love as if neither of you had a lick of sense. She even abandoned whatever good sense she had about making a decent Society match for this madness."

"You are angry because you had no say in it."

Her eyes seemed to blaze at him. "Of course I am! I asked you not to go to London, to wait for the mourning for your father to pass. But you went anyway, leaving Mary and me alone. Why do you think she turned to the vicar for solace instead of her brother?"

"You will not blame me for that!"

"Why not? You blame yourself for it! If you had not, we would not be in the situation at all."

"If. If. If. You both need to have a whisky and shut it."

Kit jerked at Mary's voice, which sounded before the door to the receiving room opened fully. She stepped inside and closed the door. "The door may be closed but both of you can be heard down the corridor and into the entrance hall. I heard everything after you called Mother a fool, and I had to shoo away three maids just to come in."

The duchess dropped back to the settee, and Mary waited, motioning for Kit to take the other one. After stewing a moment, he did, scrubbing across his mouth with one hand, still trying to rein in his fury.

Mary stood near the end of the low table addressing them both. "Kennet let me see her. She is bruised and upset but otherwise managing." She put a palm to her cheek. "She has a scrape that runs up the side of her face, so she will be quite lovely for the wedding on Monday."

Their mother snarled. "There should not be a wed—"

"Just hush, Mother," Mary said. "You did not manage to kill her, so there will be a wedding."

"I did not want—"

"You wanted to stop the wedding." Mary pushed down beside her mother on the settee, forcing the duchess to edge over. "We all know what you wanted. You thought if she were injured sufficiently, she would not go through with it. You are clearly overlooking the fact that even if he has to carry her bodily to the chapel, there will be a wedding." Mary turned on Kit. "And you and I both know we should never have left the two of them alone. Beth does not know our mother, but we do."

"She is an innocent," Kit muttered.

"Bah!"

Mary glared at her mother. "The girl has had a few disappointments in life but by and large has been protected. Even though at Timmons Manor she saw what happens to women who abandon their wariness—yes, including me—she still believes people are basically decent." She looked at Kit. "And I do not know about you, but I find that charming. I would rather not see that destroyed."

Mary faced her mother again. "For the first time in my life, I have a chance at a friendship. A real friendship. And you are on a mission to ruin it."

"She is a naïve dolt."

"No. She is not. She is clever and beautiful and good." She straightened on the settee, addressing them both. "And I have a suggestion." When neither of them responded, she continued. "If you think Kennet will leave her here after this, you have badly mistaken his ability to protect his own family. I propose a slight alteration to the 'mad scheme.' After the wedding and the christening"—she focused on her mother—"and after we visit the dressmaker so that she can start on next spring's gowns, Kit and Beth accompany Kennet back to London. There the two of them can establish our town house as their residence as a married couple, and Kit can close up his duties as duke for the year. In December they will close the house and we will join them as well as the Kennet clan at Ashton Park for their Christmas ball. People begin arriving for it in early December. After Twelfth Night, we return here until Kit is needed for the next session of Parliament." She glowered at her mother. "And you will refrain from trying to get Beth killed."

The duchess huffed. "I was not trying—"

"Just hush."

"What about those awful children?"

"They are not awful, and they will stay here with us. One of them, after all, is your grandchild." Mary looked at Kit. "Well?"

Kit stood and went to stare into the fire. Although he saw the sense in it—he could hardly stand guard over Beth day and night here—it felt as if it were a compromise that would put Beth back into the very world she had fled from.

Mary came to stand beside him, resting her hand on his back. "Beth would, of course, have to agree to it. But she is as determined to be with you as you are with her."

"Do you think they will let me see her?"

"Not alone, but yes. Kennet was much calmer when I left."

"I'm surprised the walls are still standing."

"He was rather . . . bullish."

Kit straightened and turned to his mother. "You stay here."

"Of course, I will stay here. It is time for tea."

Kit froze, a snarl forming on his face, and Mary grasped his arm. "Stop. Go to Beth."

He stalked toward the door. "You should be grateful you have a daughter." He slammed the door behind him. Several almost closed doors shut quickly as he headed for the staircase. At the top of the stairs, he stopped in front of the bedchamber next to his. The servants had concluded Beth's move while she and his mother had been riding, so the injured Beth had been ensconced in a new bed when she had returned. He knocked and waited.

Kennet jerked open the door, glaring at him.

Kit swallowed. "May I come in?"

Kennet remained a statue. A frosty, glowering statue.

"Papa?" The soft, gentle voice from inside the bedchamber felt like a warm cataract flowing over him. "Let him enter."

Kennet stepped aside, holding the door open, remaining silent and stone-faced.

Kit eased into a bedchamber he had visited many times over the years. But the familiar furnishings looked oddly new, drenched as they were in the afternoon sun—all the curtains had been thrown back—and draped not in his mother's pervasive mourning black but in shades of peach, blue, red, and gold. Clearly her maid had not finished unpacking before Beth returned. Her ripped and muddy riding habit lay in a pile near the dressing room door. But as he sought for Beth among the piles of pillows on the bed, he could not see her. There was a soft laugh from the corner behind him.

"I am here, silly."

He spun, spotting her at the escritoire, his breath leaving in a gasp as he saw her red, swollen, and scratched face. Instantly, he dropped to his knees beside her, clutching her hands. She winced, and he released her as if she aflame. "Did I hurt you?"

Beth's expression gentled, and she cupped his cheek with her hand. "No. But I am exceedingly sore. Sudden movements are uncomfortable."

Her face horrified him. He reached toward it but stopped before touching it. "I am appalled that my mother—"

"She did warn me."

"But not that he could . . . she knew—"

"Stop. What is done is done. But we must decide what we are to do next."

"My daughter did not deserve this."

Kit rose to his feet and faced Kennet. "No, sir. She did not. I apologize. I should not have left her alone with my mother."

"Where was your sister?"

"Feeding her child."

Beth pushed to her feet, and both men lunged to help her. She held up her hands. "Stop it. Both of you. I am bruised, not broken. I can walk by my—"

"Your face definitely looks broken," Kit blurted out.

She looked askance at him, then at her father. "Is he like this in Parliament?"

Kennet's expression finally softened from stone to plaster. "We have only had one session together, but . . . yes."

Beth took Kit's hand and tugged him toward the bench at the foot of the bed. She eased down, bracing against the footboard of the bed, and urged him to sit beside her. "Do you wish to postpone the wedding?"

Kit shook his head. "Absolutely not, if you are well enough."

"This is hardly the first time I have been tossed from a horse. I will be sorer tomorrow, but by Monday I will be better, and some of the swelling"—she gestured at her face—"will be gone. I have refused to look in the mirror, since my appearance made both Kendall and my father turn white. But if you are willing to marry a monster—"

"You are not a monster."

"I can bear it."

"But are *you* still willing to marry *me*, after what my mother has done?"

Beth looked down at her hands, an action that made Kit want to drop to his knees and beg, and her voice turned hoarse. "Why does she resent me?"

"She resents the way this happened. That it was brought to her doorstep. It was more than she was prepared to accept. A marriage. Her daughter's seduction, two children, soon to be three. It has upended her life, and she had no say or control. That is my fault. But I did not realize she would put you in danger in an attempt to stop the wedding."

She looked up at him. "For Mary's sake, we cannot postpone."

"No. But Mary has suggested that I take you away from here. That we return to London with your father and establish our residence there. We then go to the Christmas ball at Ashton Park and return here after Twelfth Night. Mary and my mother will join us as Ashton Park. The idea would be to weave Mother into this new family arrangement more slowly. It alters what we had originally planned, but not by much."

Beth looked up at her father. "What do you think?"

Kennet crossed his arms. "Since I do not plan to leave you here without hiring a bodyguard, it is a feasible alternative."

She took a deep breath. "But it puts me back into the heart of the scandal."

Kennet took a step closer. "As a bride. As the bride of a duke. The rest of the details about how and why can come later. For now, they will be no one's business and by the time the children come around next season, the scandal mongers will no longer be interested."

A mischievous light came into her eyes as she looked back at Kit. "Or is this a ploy merely to be alone with me?"

Her father coughed.

Kit stood, his face hot. "Um. I probably should not answer that."

"Indeed." Kennet's bass resonated.

Beth laughed. "Now. Will you both leave? I *would* like to rest. I'm going to ring for Kendall, then try to sleep."

As her father arched one eyebrow, she pointed to the dressing room door. "Until we are married, Kendall will sleep in there. There is a cot already prepared. And the bedchamber door will be locked. I will be perfectly safe."

Kennet still looked doubtful but waited near the door.

Kit knelt in front of her and tenderly lifted one hand to kiss it. "Until tomorrow." Then he stood and joined her father in the hall.

As the door closed, Kennet once again turned to stone. "Do not let anything else happen to her."

"I will not."

After a moment, Kennet let out a long breath. "I know this was not your fault. You could not have foreseen it. But I approve of this idea of returning to London. Both of you can benefit from being away from your families."

"I hope so."

"I will give you this much. If Aldermaston had the persever-ance and strength you have shown in dealing with your mother, he might still have Beth on his arm."

"Then I have never been so grateful the man is a bloody coward."

Kennet's mouth twisted. "Indeed."

"Would you like to join my mother for tea? She was about to send for it as I came upstairs. It would have only recently arrived."

"Is Beth aware of the twists in your sense of humor?"

"I believe so, sir."

"Hm."

"Tea?"

"You would like to see your mother's face when I walk in."

"Without a doubt."

Kennet held one arm wide. "Shall we go?"

BETH SETTLED INTO one of the most comfortable beds she had ever slept in with a deep sigh of relief. The down-filled mattress cradled her sore body, although she still winced with almost every move. Her bedchamber smelled strongly of liniment— which Kendall had massaged on her legs and arms—and chamomile tea—which Cook had sent up with a tray of cold meat, bread, and cheese. Beth had eaten little, but she had high hopes that the tea would ease her into sleep. The liniment had helped with the soreness, but she knew from previous spills that tomorrow would be worse.

Kendall had not drawn the curtains at the end of the day—by Beth's request—and the light from the almost full moon danced over the furnishings of her new bedchamber, broken occasionally by thick scudding clouds. The autumn weather here seemed to be so much more dramatic than it did in London, and Beth found it fascinating. Her father blamed it on the closeness to the Scottish border, with long dales and myriad lakes broken up by the higher mountains. Whatever the reason, it had captured her imagination as she had ridden over the country—until her pony had taken umbrage to jumping that last stream.

Beth tried to push away the memory of the ground rushing toward her as she fell, but she realized it would probably show up in nightmares for years to come. She gingerly touched the side of her face, which Kendall had tended to with the utmost care, murmuring repeatedly about scarring and villainous mothers-in-law. Beth had held her tongue, letting her maid ramble. Beth had been Kendall's sole charge for several years, and Beth knew she took what had happened to heart as dearly as her father and Kit did.

Kit. His expression when he had seen her at the escritoire had broken her heart.

Her father had been angry, affronted . . . and afraid. He had held her for a long time, whispering soothing noises as she had cried, almost as if she were still a small child. His muscles had been tense, and Beth knew he had wanted to rage at someone— knowing all too well he could not. Beth did not dare allow Kit entry when her father still desired to injure anyone connected with the incident. But, as always, his temper cooled, given enough time. She had pretended to be much less injured than she felt, in hopes of encouraging that, but she felt certain her father had seen past any pretense.

Kit, however, had looked completely devastated. Less an-gry—Mary had said he was taking that emotion out on their mother—than wounded. That together he and Mary had devised a way to move past this comforted Beth to her very core. Just as her parents had always done—as her whole family did—Kit and Mary preferred to find solutions rather than dwell on the obstacles.

Beth closed her eyes. She wanted Kit now more than ever. Her mind drifted, her desire moving beyond the need for a simple hug to a craving to hold him in her bed, to feel the touch of his fingers on her skin, his breath against her cheek. To feel him caress the most intimate parts of her body, her breasts, the soft skin between her thighs.

Pushing back the covers, Beth rolled out of bed, holding to

the table next to the bed for balance. Every muscle ached, pulling against the soreness. "This is idiocy," she muttered as she took a few tentative steps. The aches eased a bit as she moved, although her back protested as she reached for her dressing gown. She abandoned it, instead, moving toward the dressing room door in only her night rail. She paused to light a candle on the mantel, then reached for the door handle. As she entered, Kendall stirred on her cot, and Beth paused, waiting to see if her maid would awaken. When she did not, Beth padded slowly, holding to the various rows of shelves in the room, toward the door on the far side of the room.

A low counter marked the division of the two main sections of the dressing room—the duchess's on one side and the duke's on the other—and Beth paused, taking in the neat stacks of clothes and cravats, the rows of boots and slippers on the duke's side. A man's dress form stood in one corner of the main section, along with a platform for ironing. Beth knew that Kit had a valet—he must have!—but she had met few of the servants here beyond Pollard and Mrs. Marshall. A valet would be needed for this kind of care and organization.

Beth inhaled deeply. This area smelled like Kit, a lingering scent of sandalwood and mint, with a musk she had known from no other person.

She closed her eyes as her entire body seemed to respond to the aroma, deepening her desire to be with him. After a moment, she opened them again and moved toward the door into his bedchamber.

She opened it quietly, slipped inside, and paused as she closed it again. The candle flickered with the change of air but steadied itself. Like her own bedchamber, this one was much larger than the first she had stayed in, a companion to the duchess' chamber in layout and furnishings. But unlike hers—which held the styling of a woman in mourning—this one spoke of a highly masculine presence, with its heavier furniture and stark décor. The posts of his bed had to be as thick as a man's leg and their simple design held none of the scrollwork or carvings of hers. The leather upholstery of the wingback and ottoman near the fireplace glistened in the last flames of the evening. A companion table held a stack of four books. The escritoire in the corner—of the same heavy mahogany as the bed—had to be at least twice the size of hers.

In the fireplace, two of the coal embers cracked and collapsed in on themselves, and Kit, who was a mound of dark covers in the bed, stirred and shifted positions, rolling to face her. Beth held her breath, but he slept on, his eyes closed, his sable brown lashes resting on his cheeks. His blond hair stuck up and out, like a badly trimmed hedge, but his face had relaxed in sleep, peaceful as a child's, despite the stubble of his unshaven face.

As Beth watched him, her chest tightened with need even as her heart seemed to soar. How had she gotten to this place in such a short time—this place of love, of need. Less than three months ago, another man had walked her through Hyde Park, paid regular calls, and danced the required dances at any number of balls. He had been a comfortable and congenial companion. While she had also danced with Kit and accepted afternoon calls from him, he had been too wild, too unsettled—too passionate— for her. While she had been attracted to him, emotions had seemed too far-fetched a reason for a match.

But she had never felt for Aldermaston what she did now for this man. This urgent draw to him, this need to be next to him—a desire that had pulled her from her bed, sore muscles and scraped face included. She wanted to touch him, even as her mind warred with her, urging caution. *Go back to your room!*

"It is significantly warmer in the bed than out of it."

Beth's breath caught. "I—I—I did not mean to wake you."

Kit opened his eyes. "I believe it was the fire."

Those coals. She glanced toward the fireplace.

"Once they die down, it will be quite chilly in here. Not good for your soreness." He peeled the covers back. "Come to bed."

She glanced back at the dressing room door. "I should

not . . ."

"I will only hold you."

Beth stepped closer, the movement making her candle flicker. "It is improper."

"As it is after midnight, this is your wedding eve. I doubt anyone—even my mother—will protest. And it is hardly the first time you have seen me in my nightshirt."

She grinned, which made her face ache, but she ignored it. She swallowed, then set the candle on the bedside table and snuffed the flame. She sat on the edge of the bed.

"How are you most comfortable?"

"On my left side, I think."

He scooted toward the center of the bed and opened his arms. Smiling—and occasionally wincing—Beth eased in beside him until she was pressed against him, halfway on the bed and halfway draped over his torso. She settled against him, and Kit pulled the covers up and over them both. He wrapped his arms around her and snuggled her into place. Beth rested her head on his chest, startled at how quickly the heat of his body permeated her muscles, easing the tension from them.

"I think this will help," she whispered.

He kissed her forehead. "I hope so." He paused then asked, "Why do you smell like my horse?"

Beth laughed, then moaned. "Do not do that. Do not make me laugh."

"Not my intention."

She tilted her head to meet his gaze. "Kendall borrowed liniment from your groom. She insisted it would help."

"Has it?"

"It has, actually. A little stingy at first, but it has soothed some of the soreness. Sorry if I stink."

He nuzzled his nose against her hairline, kissing the feathery edge of it. "I happen to like the way my horse smells. And if it helps, it will be worth it."

She relaxed her head against him again. "I know women are

supposed to smell like flowers and exotic perfumes, but it is not always possible."

"Exotic perfumes make me sneeze."

"I will take note to avoid them then."

"Beth."

"Hm." The warmth of his embrace had a lulling effect on Beth's mind.

"Why are you in here?"

She hesitated, not wanting to admit it, but he deserved the truth and she was far too sleepy to concoct some ridiculous excuse. "Because I wanted to be with you. To touch you. I am finding it increasingly harder to be away from you. Even if I am not in a condition to do more, I wanted to feel you against me."

He remained silent long enough that sleep began to cloud her thoughts. Between the warmth and the soft comfort of being in his arms, her senses drifted away. But she did hear the one word he said before sleep overtook her.

"Good." His hold around her tightened. "Good."

CHAPTER NINETEEN

Monday, 26 September 1825
Kirkstone Abbey
Half past ten in the morning

KIT PACED, AS he had most of the morning. First in his bedchamber, until his valet Colby threatened to seek another position. Then in the dining room after breakfast, now in the receiving room. His muscles were so tense every nerve seemed to tingle, and even the smallest sound from outside the room made him jerk in anticipation.

His mother, who had once again centered herself on a settee, watched him with undisguised disdain. "Perhaps she had changed her mind about this after all."

"Mother . . ." Mary's word held a warning tone. She had made a nest in the corner of the opposing settee, closest to the fire. Her feet rested on a small footstool, and a warm quilted blanket was tucked about her lap and buttocks. A basket of needlework sat beside her, and she worked with a dedicated rhythm on what appeared to be a pair of tiny socks.

Catherine huffed. "It is not too late to hope she has come to her senses."

Kit stared at her, fighting every response that flitted through his mind.

That his mother might be, in truth, correct, did not help. He had not seen Beth since she had left his bed early Sunday morning with a feathery kiss and a light stroke of her fingers on his chest. He hoped she had no idea how much sleep he had lost, fighting his own desire and the ongoing arousal it created. Eventually he had become so sleepy that his cock stopped hardening, but his night had been uncomfortable to the point of painful.

Yet he would not have had it otherwise. As she slept in his arms, he watched her, overwhelmed that she felt safe enough with him to lie in his bed, knowing he would not demand more. He wanted her, yes, desperately, but he would not ask it of her when she needed rest, healing . . . and protection. And in those early hours before dawn, Kit knew he would protect this woman with his life, if necessary.

In a very short time, Lady Elizabeth Ashton had become the center of his universe.

And he would have it no other way.

Unless she desired it . . .

A thought that chilled him to the bone.

Kit stopped pacing and leaned on the mantelpiece, staring into the fire. He had knocked on her bedchamber door yesterday, but her maid had refused him entry. Instead, he had heard enough cries of pain, yelps, and thumps from her bedchamber that he had retreated to the stables, unable to stand the sounds of her in pain. A long ride had cleared his mind, and the sounds had silenced by the time he had returned. Later, he saw the servants removing a bathtub from her chamber and a light meal tray brought in.

He thought she might be better, but sleep had not come easily to him last night—and Beth had not returned to his bed.

He should go to her, see if she were lingering because of doubts, because of—

A rustle of activity outside the door drew his attention. Whispers of "Oh, my lady!" and "Lady Elizabeth!" echoed up and down the corridor. Kit straightened, turned toward the door, and waited, resisting the urge to jerk it open.

Slowly it did open, easing back as the Duke of Kennet stepped into the room, handsome and tall in a formal kit of a black frock coat, silver waistcoat, and white buckskin breeches. He paused and held out his hand toward the hallway. An arm extended to take his hand, slender and bare except for the silver-colored silk glove covering the hand, and Lady Elizabeth Ashton stepped into the room.

Kit's breath caught, his chest tightening.

Despite the red and purple scrape on her cheek, she was glimmering and resplendent, wearing a royal blue, silver, and white gown he remembered from a ball earlier in the year. It had been altered slightly—it was missing its long white sleeves and had gained a white gauze overlay of the royal blue skirt—but it left him as breathless now as it had when he first saw it, with its neckline trimmed in silver ribbons and short puffed sleeves. Royal blue at the shoulder and accented with white ruffles, the sleeves were cinched around the upper arms. Beneath the white gauze overlay, a wide band around the hem of the royal blue skirt featured embroidered cross-hatchings in a lighter blue. The simple chignon that had corralled her golden hair held glints of sapphire pins, a constellation of blue wreathing her head. She wore a simple silver necklace that he recognized as Mary's, but the descending pendant drew attention to the pale and flawless mounds of her décolletage.

Kit's mouth went dry.

Kennet cleared his throat.

Beth giggled, hiding the sound behind her hand.

Catherine huffed. "Oh, for pity's sake."

Beth sobered, but her eyes still gleamed. "I am afraid it's from earlier in the season, but there was no time . . ." Her voice trailed off as she took a step into the room, with a slight limp.

Kit moved to her side, taking her other hand. "Are you in pain?"

Her smile, gentle and sweet, warmed his heart. "Not as much

as you might think. Kendall worked something of a miracle on me yesterday." She leaned a bit closer and whisper. "I should be more floral today."

Kit grinned. "A refreshing change." He could not stop gazing at her.

Through the open door of the room, his mother's favorite hound trotted in, jumping onto the settee and settling down by the duchess. She put an affectionate hand on the dog's neck, even as she huffed at Kit. "Go on then. Get this done so we can get it behind us."

Kit looked up at Kennet, who nodded. "Your carriage is waiting."

Offering his arm, Kit pulled Beth as close as he dared as they walked to the front door and out of the house. They remained mostly silent as they rode the jostling road toward Patterdale, with Kit watching Beth's every expression for hints of pain or doubt. As he helped her out in front of the small village church, she whispered, "If you do not look at something *other* than me, you will no doubt trip and wind up looking *like* me."

"I could never be as lovely."

With a wry grin, Kennet muttered, "I will see to the vicar. You two wait in the chapel."

They did, with Beth gazing up at the arches and stained glass of the ancient stone structure, wonder in her eyes. "This is truly beautiful." She held out her hand toward the colored rays of sun that illuminated the interior, casting ghostly versions of the window's artwork on the stone floor. "Even the dust motes are lovely, dancing in the light."

Kit looked around at the stonework and statues as familiar to him as Kirkstone Abbey itself. "I grew up with this place. It is like my home."

She squeezed his arm. "Then I am glad we are marrying here instead of London."

"No regrets about a Society wedding?"

"None."

After a few moments, Kennet joined them, although his face looked slightly thunderous.

"Papa?"

His lips thinned and whitened as he pressed them together. "The vicar will be with us shortly. I had to . . . rouse him."

Kit did not want to envision what that entailed, especially given the expression on Kennet's face. "Drunk?"

A single nod. "Almost incoherent. His housekeeper is brewing coffee."

Kit grimaced, then turned to Beth. "You should sit." He looked around. Only a few of the benches from the previous day's service remained. With no permanent seating in the chapel, most of the local families brought their own—and took them home afterward. He and Kennet moved one of the remaining ones closer to the altar and helped Beth sit. She winced less than she had on Saturday, but the stiffness of her movements reminded him that the physical consummation of their relationship would have to wait a bit longer. But knowing that tonight he could freely and without subterfuge take her into his bed lifted his spirits and encouraged him toward the next steps.

She squeezed his hand and looked from him to her father. "When do you plan to leave?"

Kennet sat, shifted his weight, and glanced once more toward the door of the rectory. "The child will be christened tomorrow, and I understand that you and Mary plan to visit the dressmaker on Wednesday, if you are able."

"I will be."

"Then we will plan to leave Friday morning. My groom will leave today in my smaller carriage, taking as much of the baggage as it can hold. He will let the inns and homes along the way know we will be following, and he will notify the servants at the Kirkstone town home that the duke is on his way back to London—with his new duchess." He sat beside her, favoring his right leg, which he stretched out once he sat. He lifted Beth's hand and kissed the back of it. "You must visit your mother as soon as you are settled."

Her eyes brightened. "Of course. I miss her." She gestured at his leg. "Are you in pain?"

He chuckled under his breath. "You and Michael. You both worry too much. I am not ill or injured, my dear. Merely old. The older one becomes, the more random things ache without warning and for no apparent reason."

As Beth gave her father's arm a gentle squeeze, the door of the chapel slammed open and the vicar stumbled in, his face red and blotchy. He braced himself against the doorframe to steady his balance, glared at Kennet, then Kit. Kit stiffened, a sudden wariness clenching his gut. Kennet too stood, pulling himself to his full height.

The vicar took a deep breath—and belched. The sound echoed off the stone walls.

"My God," Beth muttered.

The vicar made a show of straightening himself—his shoulders, his posture, his clothes, and his hair, then took lumbering steps toward them. He threw a hand out toward Beth. "This her?"

Beth pushed gingerly to her feet. "I am the bride. Lady Elizabeth Ashton."

"Hmph. You ever been to a wedding?" He put a hand to his stomach and belched again.

Kit grimaced, but Beth turned regal, her back straight, head high, and chin down. "I have, sir. My brother Thomas married in July."

"Fine. You two, stand over there, face each other." He pointed toward the altar. As they took their positions, he cleared his throat. "You will stand, you will listen, and you will repeat when asked. Understood?"

They both nodded and clasped hands. He glowered at Kennet. "You can stand anywhere." As the duke took up a position behind the couple, the vicar cleared his throat and began the ceremony, reciting from memory. As they repeated their vows, the animosity from the vicar faded from Kit's mind as he gazed at Beth. Her beauty enchanted him, but even more so the tender affection in her gaze, and the flashes of memory that entranced his heart—the way she had cared for him in his illness, her sweetness toward Mattie, her resilience against his mother. Her eyes glistened as she spoke the bonding words, the declarations of fealty and love.

Then Kit pronounced his own vows, his words sounding choked and raw, even to his own ears. In the back of his mind, he saw Beth in the bedchamber at Timmons House, after Mary had given birth, describing a plan she thought would save them all from ruin—but especially his sister. She had cared less about her own future than that of a woman who was almost a stranger, for the sake of a family she barely knew. She had focused on Mary, her eyes filled with admiration and affection.

But she had not truly been looking at Mary. Her eyes had been directed lower, to the bundle in Mary's arms.

And in that moment, Kit realized that her desire had not been to salvage the reputations of his sister, his family, or even herself.

It had been for the child.

Mary's child. Who would no longer be seen by the world at large as a by-blow, a bastard child of a ruined girl and a reprobate cleric. Beth had done all of this for another woman's child.

Kit stuttered, stumbling over the words he was meant to repeat. He stammered, unable to recall them, staring at her.

"Kirkstone," prompted Kennet.

"It was for her child!" he blurted out. "Bloody, hell, Beth, this was all for *her* child!"

The chapel fell silent. The vicar and Kennet stared at him, but Beth merely smiled. Her hands tightened on his. "Yes. Then. But no longer. Now it is for you as well." Still smiling, she glanced at the vicar. "Could you please repeat that last bit? I believe the groom has lost his place."

The vicar stared at Beth a few moments, his eyes narrow, his mouth tight. "This was *your* plan?"

Beth hesitated, a look of confusion on her face, then Kennet cleared his throat and took a step closer. The vicar made a low harrumph in his throat, then repeated the previous words.

So did Kit as a flush of pure desire raced through his body, making his muscles tighten and his breath hitch. He did not think it possible to love anyone more than he did this woman in this moment. Whatever their vows, he knew he was bonded to her forever.

BETH WATCHED KIT'S face redden and his eyes brighten as he repeated the vows. His fingers clutched hers almost to the point of pain, yet the words flowed over her like a soft caress, this clear and unequivocal promise of unending love. Then the words paused, and he gave the vicar a look of puzzlement, then released her hands and began to fumble in his coat pocket, finally withdrawing the same slender case he had shown her in the garden. The bracelet.

"Kit?" she whispered.

He opened it and lifted out the blue jasper cameo bracelet, then handed the box to her father. "Hold out your arm."

She did, barely breathing as he circled her left arm with it and fastened it with trembling fingers. "I have no ring for you. Yet. But this has passed from mother to oldest son for more than eight generations. I can give you nothing more symbolic of enfolding you completely and forever into my family. I hope you will someday be able to give it to our son, on the occasion of his marriage."

Beth touched it with her right finger, as gingerly as if it were made from the most fragile of crystal. "It is so lovely."

The vicar made that odd harrumphing sound again, then "You may kiss the bride."

Beth stilled as Kit brushed his lips against her, a tender and almost chaste touch.

"Come on, then. Let us finish this." The vicar turned toward the door, stumbling as he did so, catching himself on the doorframe. They followed him, filled in the wedding lines, and watched as he signed the license. They left, with her father almost herding them back toward the carriage.

As Beth settled back against the cushions, she looked from Kit to her father. "Why was the vicar so odd?"

The two men looked at each other but remained silent, and a nudge of annoyance bloomed. "Papa. Tell me."

Kit took her hand in his. "The vicar has been a bit . . . reluctant to help us."

"Reluctant. Why? The man has to recognize it would be in his best interest, that this would help protect his own reputation."

Kit hesitated, then looked again at her father, who cleared his throat. "Beth, these things can be difficult when a man of the cloth is involved. He merely planned to deny anything had happened with Mary, that she blamed him for her own failing and that the father of her child was probably some farm lad. You saw the man. Would you believe a young woman like Mary could be drawn by someone like him?"

Annoyance became irritation. "Yes, I would, and so would other women. The only people who would see him as an unlikely match are men. You see a sodden old wretch because that is what he wants you to see. But you have not seen how many sodden old wretches among the nobility suddenly turn charming and witty when alone with a young woman. When their goal is seduction, they find all sorts of manners that will open doors. And legs. Spend a season with me on the dance floor, and you would well understand how he could lure a naïve young woman. Why do you think mothers and aunts and dragons of the *ton* circle ballrooms like lurking vultures? They know and they see." She crossed her arms. "So you had to bully him?"

Kit's face reddened again, and her father looked out the window.

"Well, make sure he records everything thing correctly to-morrow, or the mess left behind will be unredeemable."

Her father looked back at her, a soft smile on his face. "And when, Lady Elizabeth, did you become so mature?"

She smirked at him. "One can learn a great deal in a summer of scandal."

"Indeed."

When they arrived at Kirkstone Abbey, Catherine and Mary waited for them in the receiving room. The duchess still held court from the center of her settee, Bronwyn at her feet.

Kit looked her over. "Have you not moved since we left?"

Catherine scowled at him. "Of course, I have. Can you not tell I have changed my gown?" She stood up. "Since this wedding took place so late in the day, I have asked Cook to prepare an appropriate luncheon instead of a wedding breakfast."

Kit looked startled. "That was . . . gracious of you, Mother."

Beth stood beside him. "It was. Thank you, Catherine."

She huffed. "We all must eat. And now that the thing is done, there is no use pretending it can be undone."

"Does this mean you will stop trying to kill my wife?"

"I was most certainly not trying to kill her!"

Mary put a hand on Catherine's back. "Mother. Enough."

"Well, I was not."

Beth swallowed her laugh. "Mary, have you decided on a name?"

Her new sister-in-law seemed to glow. "Yes. If everyone agrees." She peered at her mother. "Yes?"

"I am listening."

"Catherine Aminta Elizabeth."

Silence. But Beth watched as tears glistened in Catherine's eyes and her father turned toward the fireplace and sniffed. Catherine's face softened and she caressed her daughter's cheek.

"Aminta?" asked Kit.

Beth squeezed his hand. "My grandmother. Papa's mother."

Mary's smiled gleamed. "I wanted a name that reflected both

families." Her voice dropped to a whisper. "So maybe there would be fewer questions about her parents."

"After tomorrow, there should be none at all," Kit said.

Mary reached a hand toward Beth, who took it. "And the next day we go to Glenridding to see Mrs. Weston. And hopefully everything will return to normal."

Pollard appeared in the doorway. "Your Grace, luncheon is served."

Catherine took a deep breath. "Let us go in, then." She raised one eyebrow at Kit. "And I promise not to attempt murder over the wedding cake."

CHAPTER TWENTY

Monday, 26 September 1825
Kirkstone Abbey
Half past eight in the evening

KIT CLOSED HIS book and replaced it on the stack and reached for the brandy sitting near the books. He had read the same page five times, all without grasping a single word. And the room around him, which had brought him such comfort over the past few months, plagued him now, as if its dark furnishings had become oppressive instead of soothing. Earlier, he had paced, changed nightshirts twice, and thought about ringing Colby to help him search for a different banyan, perhaps in his father's trunks in the attics. Kit had finally resorted to the book and a glass of brandy, which helped but not as much as he had hoped. His every nerve remained on edge.

And he was not sure why.

Well, yes, he knew *why*, but he also knew he should not be nervous. The woman was his wife. She apparently—although only God knew why—adored him. As he did her. He was also hardly an untried youth. He had been with other women—several, in fact. He knew how to cherish and caress a woman in his bed.

But unlike him, Beth *was* an innocent. Despite what they

were about to announce to the world, she had never been with a man in the most intimate of ways. He would be her first.

A fact that should unsettle any man.

Most of all, Kit did not want to hurt her—he feared that the most.

Stretching out his legs, he stared into the fire as the flames warmed him, thinking over the events of the afternoon. It had proceeded splendidly, beginning with the elaborate luncheon his mother had laid out, complete with a brandy-soaked wedding cake covered in white, sugary frosting. An extraordinary extravagance, and not one prepared quickly.

Apparently, seeing Beth tumble arse over teakettle had affected his mother more than she generally let on. Watching Beth struggle to recover, and witnessing Kit's response, had shaken her into a reluctant compliance. At least according to Mary. The duchess would remain grumpy about it, of course, but she was a lifelong curmudgeon. Light and sunny were never moods she embraced.

This afternoon, they even had relatively pleasant conversations, first in the receiving room, then he and Beth had walked into the garden again. He had been pleased to see she moved with more ease, less wincing. They had discussed plans for London, and Kit asked her where she would like to go on a honeymoon trip. Her answer—like so much about Lady Elizabeth Ashton—had startled him.

"India." She glanced around, as if searching for eavesdroppers. "Thomas brought a book on India from school, and I read it over and over. I have so dearly wanted to go."

"Then we will have to see if it can happen."

Beth had grinned like a schoolgirl and pushed up on her toes to kiss his cheek. She had developed an odd but charming habit of resting one hand on his waist, the other on his chest, a gesture both intimate and proper, chaste and enticing at the same time. He hoped she never stopped.

Then she had later whispered she would come to him tonight

at nine. To be his wife. That was how she had expressed it—"to be your wife"—but there was no mistaking what she meant. Afterward she had retreated to her bedchamber to rest and had taken the evening meal in her room. A room just on the other side of the dressing room. Her bedchamber . . . where she now prepared to come to him.

Dear God.

One of the coals in the fireplace popped, and Kit reached for another sip of the brandy. His father, who had taught him so much about being a duke, who had tried to explain what it meant to hold this position, had never prepared him for this moment.

But could any man ever truly prepare for such a time?

The tap came so faintly Kit almost did not hear it. He set the brandy down, almost sloshing it out of the glass, and went to open the door. Beth stood there, luminous in the light of the candles in the room and the one she held, like a medieval maiden ready to wander the moors. Her hair fell around her shoulders and down her back like a golden cascade. Her light blue linen night rail rested lightly on her arms and breasts, then hung loose and flowing around her body.

His words emerged on an airy rasp. "You are so beautiful!"

Beth smiled. "May I come in?"

"Oh!" Kit stepped back to usher her in. "You most certainly may."

She passed by him, and Kit realized the candle in her hand shuddered. He reached for it, pulling it gently from her hand. "Let me take that before you drop it."

She giggled, then covered her mouth. "It is so strange."

He set the candle on the bedside table. "What is?"

"Saturday night, when I came in here, I was not nervous at all. But now—"

"I am too."

Her eyes widened. "You are?"

Kit nodded and took her hands in his. Her fingers were chilled, and he pulled them closer to his chest. "I do not want to hurt you."

"I told you today that I am feeling much better. I do not think we need to wait."

He shook his head. "No. It's not that."

"Then . . . what?"

He hesitated, afraid that if he tried to explain, it would frighten her, but he glanced toward the bed, which had been turned down for the night. Then her smile turned gentle, her lips quivering. "Oh. That."

Kit pulled her closer, wrapping his arms around her and kissing her temple. "That."

Beth released a long breath and leaned against him, her body melding against his, her face pressed against his shoulder. "I trust you."

He tightened his hold on her. "You might want to wait until after before making that declaration."

She laughed softly, then leaned back to look into his face. "I meant completely. Not just with . . . that. When we first met, I liked you, but you always seemed to be . . . somewhere else. As if you did not really want to be where you were. I did not know if I could trust you. Now there is no question." Her words softened. "I admire you. I want you."

Kit's breath shuddered and every muscle tensed as he released her and cupped her face with both hands. Her skin, soft beneath his fingers, seemed to glow as he kissed her. As he explored her mouth, tasting the sweetness of her lips and tongue, Beth whimpered, her fingers clutching the cloth of his banyan, digging through to his shoulders. He pressed deeper, a heat surging through his loins and spreading across his body, as if seeking to burn through to his bones. His cock swelled, throbbing, and Kit let one hand drift down her back pressing her hips against his.

Kit eased away from her mouth, trailing a line of kisses and gentle nips down her jawline to the tender hollow of her neck. Whispering his name, Beth tugged at the collar of the banyan. He stepped away from her suddenly and shed the banyan and his nightshirt, and they fluttered to the floor in slowly deflating heaps. Beth's eyes shot wide, then a smile spread across her face. Following his gesture, she pulled her night rail up and over her head, tossing it onto the pile of his nightclothes.

Kit's world came to an abrupt halt as he stared at her. He had long admired her beauty, but this vision of loveliness seemed unreal, an idealized portrait of a woman from a classic artwork. Her body seemed perfectly proportioned, with long lines and taut muscles, a narrow waist, and hips that could lure a lover into obsession. Her hair, a bit wild now, flowed over her shoulders and curled around the firm mounds of her breasts, framing them in the golden candlelight. With their reddish pink areolae, tight buds, and pale skin, they were even more enticing than they had been in any gown, no matter what the décolletage. Free of stays and confining bodices, their allure enchanted him.

"You should breathe," Beth whispered, giving a slight giggle.

Kit gasped, then lunged for her, scooping her up in his arms. Beth yelped, clinging to him, then laughed as he carried her to the bed and lowered her onto the mound of pillows at the head. He stretched out beside her, propping on one elbow as his other hand stroked her body, his fingers tracing over her hips and stomach, then up over her breasts. He circled the tightening buds of her nipples with his fingertips, pinching each slightly.

Beth shivered then shifted, angling her body toward his as her hands played over his chest and neck. Her eyes glistened, brimming with tears, and one slid down the side of her face.

A spear of alarm shot through Kit and he stilled, then he kissed the tear away, its saltiness lingering on his tongue. "Why are you crying?"

"Happiness." She entwined her fingers into his hair. "Did you not know women cried when they were happy as well as sad?"

"A maneuver obviously meant to confuse and bewilder men."

She laughed again. "Kiss me again."

And he did.

BETH FELT AS if she were floating. Every touch of Kit's hands, of his body against hers made her more lightheaded than the one before. She closed her eyes as his mouth pressed her lips again, and she melted into the kiss, wanting to taste him as he had her, taking her cues from him with slow, firm thrusts of her tongue. Her desire for him, that deep-seated need that began as a smoldering heat between her legs, spread throughout her body, lifting her. She wanted more, *craved* more.

Her hands roamed over his chest and back, pulling him closer. He moaned deep in his throat and broke the kiss, turning his attention to her breasts. He shifted, taking one into his mouth, sucking on the nipple.

Arousal spiked through Beth, and she arched her back, her heels digging into the covers, a whimpered cry bursting from her. Kit took the sensitive bud between his teeth and tugged, worrying it gently, as Beth gasped for air. With his free hand, he pushed her thighs apart, his fingers toying with the light brown curls between her legs. She spread her legs, almost involuntarily, her back arching again when one finger traced up and down the slit of her sex, pressing between the tender folds.

Beth's fingers dug into the muscles of his shoulders. "Please!"

Kit raised his head, concern darkening his eyes. "Are you all right?"

Stupid man. "Yes! What are you doing to me?"

He grinned. "Cherishing you. Do you want me to stop?"

"No!" Her fingers trembled as they roamed over his skin. "But I want to"—she swallowed—"cherish you as well."

"Oh, my darling. You are. And more." He glanced down, and so did she.

Between them, his hardened cock stood at full attention, engorged and a deep red. She reached for it, curious as to how it felt. "May I?"

His eyes narrowed. "Carefully."

She hesitated. "I could hurt you?"

"Far too easily. It is not fragile but it is . . . tender."

Fascinated, Beth closed her hand around it. The softness of the skin surprised her as much as the hardness beneath it, like a fine velvet wrapped around a dress form. She caressed the tip with her thumb and Kit gasped, stilling her hand with his own.

"Does that hurt?"

He shook his head. "Hurt? No. But this evening will be far too short if you continue."

"Why?"

"After." He brought her hand to his mouth, sucking gently on one fingertip. "Lie back." He released her hand and pushed her shoulders back. As she settled back against the down pillows, Beth let out a long sigh beneath his kisses on her neck, shoulders, and breasts. His touch, firm but gentle, traced down her shoulders, across her nipples, and down the curves of her hips and thighs as he moved down in the bed.

As his body left the reach of her fingers, she clenched them into the covers and pushed up to look at him. "What are you doing?"

"Lie back. Close your eyes. Just focus on what you are feeling, not what I am doing."

Odd. And harder than she realized, as she desperately wanted to touch him, to feel his skin, his muscles beneath her hands. Her arms felt strangely empty, almost . . . bereft. "Kit . . ."

"Just feel. Close your eyes."

She did, a tinge of apprehension gripping her as he spread her legs, draping one over his shoulder. *What was he—oh!*

A stream of cool air raked over the curls of her sex as his fingers spread the lush folds. The effect sent a spire of heat through Beth's body, and she writhed. He shifted, anchoring her other thigh more firmly as the cool stream turned warm, the exploration deeper. The resulting wave of pleasure rolled over her and Beth moaned. She squeezed her eyes shut, allowing the unfamiliar sensation to overwhelm her.

The room spun, dizziness blending with the euphoria his touches created. The entire world floated as her fingers dug into the mattress. The firm gentleness of his hands became harder as she felt something enter the most intimate part of her body. She called his name, and he stilled, his movements ceasing.

"Does this hurt?"

She shook her head frantically, pushing up on her elbows, tears leaking from her eyes. "What are you doing?"

The touch inside her moved as he whispered. "Fingers." He lowered his head, and a sweet thrill rushed through her as he pushed his tongue among the folds.

"Ah!" Her head lolled back. "I did not think—"

"Do not think, my love. Just feel. Now close your eyes. You will be ready soon."

She raised her head again. "Ready?"

He smiled. "For me." And he wiggled his fingers again. "Surrender, darling."

Beth slumped back against the pillows. And she did, then, surrender to the ecstasy.

KIT RETURNED HIS attention to Beth's fragrant and lush core, adding a third finger to his exploration. She moaned again, her body's gyrations making him even harder than before. Whatever resistance he had expected from her had become, instead, an unyielding curiosity, and he had almost laughed as she asked over and over, "What are you doing?"

Someday soon, he would spend an entire afternoon explaining and exploring, letting her do the same for him, letting her satisfy that endless desire to *know* what was happening with her body. But for this evening, he simply wanted her to feel the pleasure that two people could bring to each other.

Beth had been pliant, willing, but her own desires seemed to have startled her. Yet her body had responded as he had hoped, and he could tell from the sweet and fragrant fluids that emerged from her swollen folds, from the tension in her muscles, from the way she had arched beneath him, that this had been pure desire for her.

He hoped that would continue.

She was ready.

Kit moved up over her, kissing her as he went, sucking lightly on each nipple as his knees pressed into the mattress between her legs. As he nipped the tender hollow at the base of her neck, he whispered, "It is time."

Beth locked her arms around his shoulders, pressed her cheek against his, and nodded. Bracing on one elbow, his other hand guided his cock to her entrance. He rubbed the tip up and down the slit a few times, then used his hand to spread her moisture over both of them. He pressed his cock against her, pushing the tip inside.

She tensed, and he paused. After a moment, he felt the muscles of her loins relax a bit, and she nodded. He entered farther, a few more inches, but he struggled now to stop. Inside, she was tight, but he did not meet the resistance he had expected. She nodded again, and with a deep groan, Kit pressed all the way in.

Beth cried out, arching against him, her fingernails digging into his back.

Kit fought for breath. "Are you in pain?"

She shook her head, clinging even tighter to him. "No. It is . . . unexpected."

He grinned and kissed her. She returned the kiss eagerly, as if hungry for his touch, and the spear of desire rocked him. He moved within her again, slow thrusts at first, then harder. Their kiss broke and Beth raised her hips to meet him.

All his thoughts vanished in a haze of lust and need, a craving that drove him to move faster, deeper against her. He watched her face as those blue eyes went from surprise to affection, from desire to need. A red blush moved up her chest and across her cheeks and her mouth parted. Within, he felt her muscles tighten around him, and as that tension began to roll through her, Beth gasped.

Kit shifted, altering the angle at which his cock thrust into her, and her body arched suddenly. Beth's cry mimicked his own as his loins jerked, his release coming deep inside her. Her arms fell away from him as he finished, dropping limply to each side, and Kit almost did the same, his energy drained. He eased out of her then stretched out on his side, gathering her against him, stroking her hair and back.

"Are you all right?"

She tilted her head to peer at him, then reached up and stroked his cheek before slipping her fingers into his hair. "I am . . . besotted." He laughed, but she brushed her lips against his. "Is it always that . . . glorious?"

His eyes widened. "Glorious?"

"Did you not think so?"

"I think you are."

She smiled and snuggled against him.

"Sometimes," he whispered. "It is even better."

She buried her face against his chest, muffling her words. "I will never survive."

Kit reached down to bring the covers up, which he smoothed over both of them, tucking them in. "You will. And you will thrive. We both will thrive."

"Then I hope it will last forever."

CHAPTER TWENTY-ONE

Wednesday, 28 September 1825
Glenridding
Half-past nine in the morning

BETH GRABBED THE edge of the seat in the rocking carriage to steady herself. Across from her Mary weaved in time with the sways and jolts caused by the hard and bumpy road as if she had been born to it. So did Kit beside her, although he looked oddly distracted. Next to Mary, Beth's father stared out the window, his gaze as distant as her husband's, although he also looked a bit green from the constant jerking.

Mary grinned at her. "You get used to it eventually. And this is better than when the October rain arrives. Then the mud becomes almost impassible over the fells. Much of winter here is spent holed up by the fire. When we do go out, it is on horseback. The ponies handle this much easier than the carriages."

"I feel as if my insides are being scrambled like a bowl of eggs."

Mary nodded. "No doubt. And you have done this three days in a row. You deserve a rest."

"Little chance of that. We leave Saturday." Beth glanced at Kit again, but he seemed to be paying no mind to the women's chatter, and she wondered if their trip yesterday still bothered him.

It had been the second stage of their plan. At ten yesterday morning, Lady Catherine Aminta Elizabeth Caudale had been christened at the chapel in Patterdale. The vicar, who had been in an even fouler mood than the day before, had performed the ceremony, then she and Mary had waited in the chapel with the baby—whose name had already been shortened to Mina. Mina, quite the sleeper, had taken serious umbrage to being awakened by a shot of cold water to her head, thus proving to all within hearing distance the many ways that stone walls can amplify sound.

The vicar had roared his displeasure and fled into the rectory hands over his ears, to be followed by two extremely angry dukes. When they had returned, her father had pronounced, "It is done," and the ride back to Kirkstone Abbey had been done in silence. Or, at least, with no talking. A ride over a rocky road in an aging carriage was anything but silent.

As was obvious now. Bouncing over what had to be yet another monstrous boulder in the road, the carriage careened around a turn. Beth braced herself against the corner as Mary grinned at her again. The rifle-fire rattle of a stone bridge shuddered through them, then the coachman drew to a stop and the carriage wobbled as it lost the weight of a footman.

Mary peered out. "Ah, civilization at last." The door opened, and the footman waited. Kit and her father exited first, then Mary scooted out and dropped to the ground, barely allowing the footman to aid her. Beth followed more cautiously, leaning heavily on the footman's arm, her first steps tentative. With a wide grin, Mary pointed to the shop behind them, a modest storefront with two narrow curtain-covered windows and a wooden door two steps down from the pavement. No name announced its business, and only a number—14—verified its location. "This is Mrs. Weston's."

Kit adjusted the chapeau on his head. "We will be at our solicitor's for about an hour, then we will wait at the Brothers

Inn." He looked at the coachman, then the footman. "The carriage will wait here for you. Send Edwards for us when you are finished here."

The footman gave a crisp nod.

Mary scowled. "I thought we would do a bit of shopping when we are—"

"No." Kit's curt tone startled Beth, and she frowned even though he softened his next words. "We—we should return as soon as possible. There is too much to do before Friday."

His sister sniffed. "Very well." She took Beth's arm and turned her toward number 14, leading her down the steps and through the door. "Wonder what bee got up in his bum," she muttered as a small bell over the door announced their arrival.

Beth snorted a laugh, covering her mouth with her hand. "I wish I knew. He was out of sorts all yesterday afternoon and went to bed far too early last night."

Mary froze, peering at her from beneath black lashes. "Are you saying he did not . . ."

Beth felt the blood rush into her cheeks. "Oh, he did! Just . . . slept quickly."

Mary grinned. "That might not be a problem. I hear that sometimes men just . . . are gone . . . after."

Beth leaned closer, her tone conspiratorial. "I probably would not say that so . . . loudly."

"Well, we do appear to be alone. Are we early?"

"Somewhat. I think." Beth looked around the shop. As with many modistes and dressmakers, the number 14 establishment had a small but neatly appointed salon to welcome guests, along with a waist-high counter for conducting business. A small table and four chairs occupied one side of the room, while the other featured a sitting area with a sofa and two wingbacks near a small fireplace. Behind the counter, a curtained arch led to other areas.

"Ladies! Welcome!"

A woman appeared from behind the curtains. She wore a russet silk day gown, and her gray and brown hair had been gathered into a puffy style that seemed to be slowly escaping from its pins and ribbons. She came from behind the counter and greeted Mary with a quick kiss on the cheek. "Lady Mary. It has been far too long."

"Mrs. Weston, this is my friend—and sister-in-law—Lady Elizabeth Ash"—Mary caught herself. "Elizabeth, the Duchess of Kirkstone."

Mrs. Weston curtsied. "Your Grace."

Beth blinked, looking from the dressmaker to Mary. "I—uh—"

Mary grinned. "Yes, that would be you, Beth." She looked at Mrs. Weston. "She is not yet used to the new title." She touched Beth's arm. "Your Grace, this is Mrs. Weston, our dressmaker."

Beth straightened. "A pleasure, Mrs. Weston. And Lady Mary is correct. It is an unfamiliar situation for me. But I hear you are quite the miracle worker."

Mrs. Weston blushed lightly. "I am appreciative of the compliments, Your Grace. I am not as talented as a London modiste, no doubt, but I do well with copying and adapting styles I have seen. And we had heard that the duke had brought home a bride. The entire parish has been riddled with the news, but you know how village people can carry on. I do believe the vicar has made quite the deal of it."

Beth stilled, a frisson of anxiety worming its way up her spine. "The vicar?"

Mrs. Weston clapped her hands together. "Oh, yes. He has been gadding about town the last couple of days, crowing about marrying you and that the timing is perfect, since the archbishop has called him to London for some special assignment."

Mary's eyes flashed in alarm. "He is leaving?"

"So he says."

When Mary turned to Beth, she shook her head, even as she spoke to Mrs. Weston. "I know the village will miss him, but I hope the new vicar will be more of a blessing."

Mrs. Weston turned somber. "Oh, I doubt we will miss him at all. Especially some of the younger—" She broke off and forced a smile back on her face. "Enough dawdling. Come, Lady Mary, let us select some fabric, look at the latest fashions, and make some decisions. And I will need to measure you. You have become quite the beautiful woman since I last saw you."

Mary gave a low laugh. "You mean a much *rounder* woman."

"Nonsense. All women are beautiful."

They followed her through the curtains into a larger room set up with three separate areas—a fitting platform with chairs, a long waist-high table covered with scissors, measuring tapes, pins, and thread. And an area with three dress forms in different sizes, one of which held a lovely red satin gown with gold lace trim and white embroidery. A young girl, no more than twelve, was placing pins around the hem. At the back of the room, an open door revealed what was obviously a dressing room, and another curtained arch led to what appeared to be a staircase and a small kitchen.

"Bitsy!" Mrs. Weston's call startled the girl, who snapped to attention. "Fetch those six bolts we talked about and bring them to the table. Then please put on the kettle for tea." She pointed at the worktable. "Did you put out the latest books?"

The girl nodded at the end of the table, where a stack of ladies' fashion publications waited, then she scurried through a door near the back of the room. Mrs. Weston walked to the end of the table and pulled one of the publications closer. "I marked several designs I think you will like. Shall we start?"

THE BROTHERS INN had been one of Kit's favorite pubs since his father had brought him for his first pint at fourteen. A stone structure of indeterminate age—not even the locals truly believed the claimed establishment date of 1506 over the door—it welcomed locals and strangers alike. Soldiers, farmers, MPs, sheriffs, even a prime minister or two had darkened the low front door that made everyone but the shortest lad duck to come in. The front room had a broad fireplace that heated patrons who clustered the ancient wooden benches, stools, and tables long ago darkened by age and infinite amounts of spilled ale and rum.

Kit inhaled deeply, relishing the blended scents of tobacco, baking bread, roasting lamb, and dark ale. Behind the bar, the proprietor, Jacob Edwards—his footman's father—raised a hand in greeting, which caused a number of the patrons to look around. Shouts of "His Majesty," "The Grand Duke," and catcalls about his marriage rebounded around the room, and Kit glanced at his new father-in-law.

Kennet had a wry grin on his face. "No protocol in your hometown pub, eh?"

"No leeway for the local nobility, that's certain."

"At least there's no guillotine in the town square."

"Yet."

Kennet laughed. "Let's have a pint."

Kit gestured at Jacob, and they took a table near the fireplace. The visit to the local solicitor had been brief, since it was primarily to inform him of the marriage and the changes that would be made to the estate and to Kit's will, once they reached London. The local man worked in tandem with the Kirkstone solicitors in London, acting as a liaison with the managers and stewards at the Abbey.

Yet Kit felt relieved to get that bit of business behind him and get to the pub where he could relax a few moments. As the proprietor set the ale down in front of them, Kit introduced the Duke of Kennet. Jacob bowed slightly. "Welcome, Your Grace. It be humble here, but we're proud of it. This is a right nice place to be."

Kennet nodded. "As you should be."

Jacob nodded over his shoulder. "Kirkstone, I knew you could stir up a row, but not that you could create a real ruckus, even before ya show up."

Kit's eyes narrowed. "What are you talking about?"

"The vicar. He was in here a bit ago, right proper into his cups, when someone came in talking about that big carriage ya just rode up in. He started screeching like a bloody barn owl and lit out like his bum were afire."

Kit looked at Kennet, who scowled and took a swig of ale. Kit turned back to Jacob. "What exactly was he screeching about?"

"Bloody fool been in here all morning bragging and swaging about that new position the archbishop's called him to. Saying he must've impressed someone along the way. Going on and on about getting to London and finally having a decent pay. Like every bloke in here don't know how good he's had it here. Then ya roll up and he brays about how we should be like the French and get rid of the arseholes—beg pardon—that run and ruin everything and have all the money. Like he's got need of a castle somewhere. Flies outta here, robes a-flappin'."

"Apparently," muttered Kennet, "the man does not like being in the same room with us."

"I'd say so, Your Grace." Jacob leaned a little closer. "But a-fore he left, he started screeching something about gettin' his own back." He looked from one man to the other. "Don't know what he meant but thought you should know."

Kit nodded, trying to stuff down the urge to go after the vicar for another session, such as they had yesterday at the rectory. "Thank you, Jacob." As the proprietor started to leave, Kit said, "And you should know that boy of yours is settling in to his new position with aplomb. Doing extremely well."

Jacob seemed to swell to twice his size. "We are right proud of him, Your Grace. Thank you for the leg up."

As Jacob strode away, Kit drank, then realized Kennet was staring at him. "Ah. Jacob's son is our new footman. The one with us today."

"Ah." Kennet turned his stein with one finger. "Interesting lie your vicar has concocted."

"Pride makes a fool out of the wisest of men, so I've heard."

"One of your father's proverbs?"

"My mother's actually. More of a stern warning than a prov-erb."

Kennet took a sip of ale, obviously to hide a smile. "Compli-cated woman."

"She is that."

After a pause, Kennet looked at the door. "What do you think he meant?"

"Uncertain. But if he wants to come at us in the town square, he seriously underestimates his chances."

Kennet shook his head. "I do not think it will be that direct. The man lies. He seduces. He is a conniver. Men such as that never attack from the front." Kennet glanced at Jacob, then the door. "When we get back, I think you should warn your staff to be on their guard."

CHAPTER TWENTY-TWO

Wednesday, 28 September 1825
Glenridding
Eleven in the morning

BETH COULD NOT help giggling a little as Mary stood on the fitting platform in only her stays and chemise. Mary kept making faces at her and fidgeting as Bitsy circled her, trying to take her measurements, reporting them in a soft, high voice to Mrs. Weston.

Their morning had been absolutely splendid, all of them exclaiming loves for a variety of gowns and expressing dismay for some of the predicted styles of 1826. Mary's rather bawdy sense of humor made more than a few appearances in this comfortable and confidential gathering of women, and Beth had forgotten how much she had adored visiting her modiste in London with her mother. It meant the company of women when there was not nearly as much sniping and backbiting as there was at a ball or soiree. No criticisms of whose gown was the most hideous. Congenial and warm.

"Lady Mary, for heaven's sake, please stand still." Mrs. Weston's frustration showed in her tone, and Bitsy seemed downright flustered.

"But it tickles!"

Beth bit her lip, trying to stop the giggles, and retreated to one of the chairs in the far corner behind Mary. Mary twisted to wag a finger at her, and Beth mouthed, *stand still.*

They fell into silence for a few moments, then the bell over the front door jangled. Mrs. Weston scowled. "I do not have another appointment," she muttered and moved toward the curtain arch. She peered through the split and stiffened, pushing her way through and holding the curtains closed behind her.

"Sir! You cannot come in here!"

"I will! These people ruined my life!"

The guttural shout sent a chill through Beth. On her platform, Mary froze, turning stark white. She stared at Beth. "The vicar!"

Beth jerked to her feet. "Bitsy!" When the girl looked her way, Beth pointed to the back of the shop. "There's a back door?"

The girl nodded.

"Go. Now. The Brothers Inn. Find Kirkstone. Go!"

With only a second's hesitation, Bitsy shot from the room. In the front, sounds of a scuffle including a deep grunt from the vicar and yelps of pain from Mrs. Weston. "You cannot go back there!"

Beth pointed at the dressing room. "Go. Get dressed. Block yourself in."

"I cannot leave—"

"He's not here for me. Go!"

With a mere second's hesitation, Mary fled to the dressing room and closed the door. Beth stood near the platform, wondering what to do next, when Mrs. Weston stumbled backwards into the workroom, followed by the vicar, whose red face and watery eyes explained how the man had spent his morning. The reek of rum preceded his every step. Mrs. Weston tried to stay on her feet, but he grabbed her by the arm and slung her sideways. She fell, hitting her head on the table, and lay still.

He turned toward Beth, his face a mask of fury. "Where is she?"

Beth stood stiff, her feet slightly apart, just as her brother had taught her. Being in a row, he had explained, is no time to be ladylike. "She is not here."

"Liar!" He took two steps toward her.

Beth stiffened, refusing to move. "This was my appointment, sir. She left to find her brother. And my father."

"Liar. I know she is still here. I've been watching. And your precious husband is getting drunk at the pub. I've been watching them too. Bastards." He took another step. "You have ruined my life!"

Beth held her ground. "There is a back door. She went out that way." She pointed toward the back arch. "Perhaps you can catch her."

His eyes narrowed, and spittle flew from his lips as he snarled at her. "You would betray a friend?" He coughed, then spit. "Of course you would. That is what you people do. Whatever benefits you."

"If you go after her, you will encounter my husband and my father. I hardly think that qualifies as a betrayal." Beth clinched her fists at her side. In the back of her mind, all the lessons her brother Robert had taught her, all the scenarios of protecting herself should she be accosted on the street, tumbled through like scenes in a play. Ruffians, he had insisted, hide in some unexpected corners.

Oh, Robert, you have no idea.

She glanced at the table. There lay two possible weapons. Scissors. A quill.

The vicar caught her glance, and he gave a harsh laugh. "Think you can stop me?"

"I am willing to try."

He moved toward her, putting his body between her and the table, bare inches away from her. "Useless. Like the rest of you. You could never reach them." He looked over his right shoulder at the table. "Now where is sh—"

Beth struck. The perfect right cross, her fist driving hard into his cheek and jowl, the sound of bone and flesh colliding.

Beth had forgotten how much it hurt. She screeched in anger and pain, but the blow spun him halfway around, and Beth leaped on his back, clawing her way upward, and wrapping her arms around his neck. The vicar bellowed, stumbling about, his arms flailing as he tried to reach her, clutching at her arms.

Suddenly both clawed at nothing but air. Beth screamed again, her arms windmilling and feet kicking, reaching for him, even as someone lifted her, pulling her away from the vicar. Male voices filled the air, and suddenly the room overflowed with men, shouting and pulling at the vicar.

"Lady Elizabeth!" Her father's bass shout split the air, and most of the other voices ceased.

Beth stared at him, her senses finally returning, her body quivering violently as she was lowered to the ground. She planted her feet and twisted to see who had grabbed her. Kit looked down at her, eyebrows arched. She swallowed, gasping for air. "He tried to—he tried—"

On the other side the room, the vicar shook off the hands holding him. "I did nothing of the kind. She and that other one. They ru—" He stopped, smearing a hand over his mouth, clearly recognizing what he was about to say in front of all the villagers who had spent the morning hearing about his new "position." "I did not. I . . . I only meant—"

"I suspect," her father announced, "this was a misunderstanding that is best forgotten by all involved." He looked down at two men tending to Mrs. Weston, who was slowly regaining consciousness. "You will see to her, Mr. Edwards?"

One of the men nodded. Her father turned his attention to the vicar. "Agreed?"

The man nodded, then turned and shoved his way through the crowd and out of the shop.

"Gentlemen, we appreciate your help. We are forever in your debt."

The crowd took the hint and began filing out of the room. The two men with Mrs. Weston helped her to a chair.

"She should see a doctor," Beth said, surprised that her voice was so calm. "She fell against the table and hit her head."

One of the two straightened. "I'll fetch him." And he was gone.

The door to the dressing room opened slowly, and Mary peered out, checking the room. "The arsehole is gone?"

Beth nodded. She looked up at Kit again. "You may let me go now."

"Not on your life." He looked over her head at her father. "So her brother taught her to box?"

Her father looked at her. "Yes. Apparently better than I thought."

Beth jerked away from Kit and turned on them both. "How much did you see?"

Kit motioned for Mary to join them, wrapping her in a hug before he answered. "We entered about the time the first punch landed. At least, I hope it was the first punch."

"The only punch."

"How is your hand?"

Beth stretched out her fingers, and a sharp pain raced up her arm. "Ah . . . not good. Hurts like the devil."

Kit released Mary and reached for Beth's hand, cradling it. "I think you should see that doctor as well."

Her father growled under his breath. "Then we must get you to London. I have had rather enough of the peace and quiet of the countryside."

Beth looked around the room. "Where's Bitsy?"

"Here." The quiet voice came from the back arch, and Beth beckoned the girl closer.

"You are one brave little girl, Miss Bitsy. You make sure you tell your parents I said so."

"Ain't got none."

"Oh?" Beth looked up at Kit, who pursed his lips and shook his head. Mary snickered.

"She lives with me." Mrs. Weston sat a bit straighter. "I was alone and so was she. Now we have each other."

"Thank God for that," Kit muttered. "I am just grateful you do not like cats."

Beth scowled. "Who says I do not like cats?"

Her father laughed and clapped Kit on the shoulder. "Let me tell you about Rufus."

EPILOGUE

Friday, 23 December 1825
Ashton Park, near the River Kennet
Nine in the evening

K IT STOOD AT the end of the reflecting pool, shivering in the chill of the evening. Ice and snow covered most of the pool, which stretched out several hundred yards from the front entrance of Ashton Park, but pockets of clear water reflected the moon, which shone huge and full in a star-laced sky. He tugged his topcoat a little tighter around his chest, crossing his arms for a bit more warmth, even though he had escaped the house in search of a little silence and cooler air. His quiet life at Kirkstone Abbey had left him unprepared for the swamp of guests and the heat of a country estate during an almost month-long house party. The fireplaces of every large room blazed every day and all through the night, and the crush of people in the public areas of the house overwhelmed his senses on an hourly basis. He and Beth shared her childhood bedchamber, but even that room felt close and overcrowded.

Kit longed for the silence of the fells and the winds that stirred heather and trees alike. But he knew now a great deal of time would pass before he would return to either.

He stared up at the massive country home, mulling over the

astonishing events of the past three months. The main house of the Ashton Park estate—easily four times the size of Kirkstone Abbey—gleamed brightly, a beacon of light in the late December night. Thousands of candles and oil and gas lamps illuminated every room, as the country house party, which had begun two weeks ago, culminated tonight in a massive ball, the highlight of the winter social season. No matter how deep the scandals the Kennet clan had been embroiled in the earlier part of the year, no member of London's Society elite wanted to miss this celebration of the Christmas holiday.

He and Beth had arrived at the beginning of the month, and even as he had explored the vast stretches of the estate, he had watched carriage after carriage arrive, depositing nobles, staff, and massive mountains of luggage into the house. A sign of the presence—and social and economic power—of the Duke and Duchess of Kennet.

Kit had been completely stunned by his recognition of that power. When the three of them had arrived in London at the end of September, Philip Ashton had taken him under his wing. For the next two months, Kit had joined Philip and his son Thomas—Beth's oldest brother and Philip's heir—on a whirlwind ride of meetings—solicitors, ambassadors, other nobles, merchants, shipping magnates, industrialists—and even the king, George IV. Kit had known that the duke's voice held sway in Parliament, but he had no idea that Phillip's expansion into the financial and business realms—a move begun by the previous duke—had resulted in what Kit referred to as the Kennet empire. By falling in love with Lady Elizabeth Ashton, Kit had married into one of the wealthiest and most powerful families in the country and had, without preparation, been thrust into the highest ranks of power.

How the world worked at those levels still astonished Kit. His own small duchy had survived on hard work, determination, and careful management of land and people. Changes had been few, and the estate still ran much as it had for the past three hundred years. Kennet's duchy, on the other hand, had tendrils that stretched across three continents, five major industries, and six estates. Ashton Park, the crown jewel, now hosted the premiere party of the year, but the business meetings never stopped. The previous morning Kit had met the head of a bank, another duke, and the chairman of a major conglomerate of shops. This afternoon, he had gathered in Philip's study with a member of the king's privy council, two representatives of the East India Company's Court of Directors, and an aide to a man with the lofty title of "governor-general of the presidency of Fort William in Bengal." All to make Kit an offer, the like of which he had never known existed three months ago. An offer that would ease him into a permanent position among the ranks of the kingmakers in the British Empire.

All because he had asked Philip Ashton about a budget for the honeymoon trip he and Beth had not yet been able to take.

The officials had expected him to accept immediately, to grasp an unprecedented opportunity with relish, and they were not pleased with the reason for his hesitation—that he wished to discuss it with his wife. But, as Philip Ashton had explained to them, Lady Elizabeth Ashton was not the usual aristocratic wife.

Indeed she was not. Not many of the Society women he had met would tend unfailingly to a half-dead, half-naked man while stripped down to a bare day gown, snuggle with that man to keep them both comforted, or use her brother-taught boxing skills to down a degenerate vicar.

Kit took a deep inhale of the cold night air. He had until noon tomorrow to decide. Which meant he had to talk to Beth tonight.

He had tried, but since he had left the meeting, his wife had been glued to her mother's side. Emalyn Ashton, still recovering from having a hemorrhagic apoplexy in July, had done quite well with her duties managing the house party, but Beth had become a guard dog to her mother since their arrival at Ashton Park, even rivaling her own father. And since the herald had announced the first guests to the ballroom tonight, Beth had stood less than three feet from the duchess.

But their lives were about to change in a most dramatic fashion. Again. And the wife he adored needed to be front and center of it. Kit straightened his shoulders and headed back into the fray that was Ashton Park.

BETH'S HEART SKIPPED a beat when she spotted Kit striding across the ballroom, skirting Christmas decorations and dodging dancers. Over the past three months, he had regained his full health, and had grown even more handsome—if that were possible. His friendship with her father and brothers had encouraged him, and his sense of honor and confidence had blossomed among other men—and in their bedchamber. When he came to her bed these days, his sense of control and his joy in their love took her breath away. She had never thought any man could make her swoon.

But her husband did.

She felt that familiar sense of dizziness as he crossed the room, his eyes focused on her.

"Oh, my! Ish he not a joy to shee?" Her mother's slurred words held a teasing pride as she looked up at Beth from her perch on the elaborately carved and deeply cushioned "throne" from which she observed the Christmas ball.

"Mother!" Beth's cheeks reddened.

The duchess chuckled. "Well, if such a man were coming to my bed every night, I might lose my good shenshe ash well."

On the other side of the throne, Beth's brother Michael turned scarlet and turned to study some of the Christmas decorations.

"You are incorrigible."

"Alwaysh." The duchess straightened as Kit approached. When he stopped and executed a precise bow to his hostess, Emalyn held out her hand.

Kit grasped the gloved fingers lightly and briefly. "Your Grace."

"Where have you been, Your Grashe? I expected to shee you danshing with my daughter all evening."

Small spots of red bloomed on each cheekbone. Kit glanced over his shoulder. "It is quite the crush this evening."

The duchess's eyes twinkled. "Perhapsh a walk then. Our gardens are lovely, even in the shnow."

"I did not wish to disturb—"

"Go." She waved her hand. "The both of you. She has lurked too long." Emalyn made a shooing motion with her right hand. "Michael will protect me from any drunken lords."

Beth did not need a second urging. She fell into step, taking Kit's elbow, as he led her toward the terrace doors. "Where have you been tonight? I haven't seen you since my father made off with you this morning."

"Outside."

They passed by a table loaded with sweets, a brandy-soaked cake, and ribbon-tied boughs of fir and rosemary. The scents made her stomach grumble. "Why?"

Kit snagged one of the sweets and passed it to her. "Hungry?"

She accepted it, smiling. "I have not eaten since tea."

"I thought not."

Beth nibbled on the tiny cake, which seemed to dissolve in her mouth, a blissful flavor on her tongue. "Answer me, please?"

"I have been thinking." Kit opened one of the glass doors leading to the terrace and escorted her outside. As he closed it, the night became a bit quieter.

Beth ate the rest of the cake, then brushed crumbs from her fingers. "About what?"

He led her to the far side of the terrace and stopped, facing her. The windows of the house cast his face in half-shadows that cut across his expression as his eyes turned serious. "I must ask you something."

A tinge of worry gripped her. "Does this have something to

do with all the meetings you and Papa have had?"

He nodded. "Your father is . . . an unusual man. A few weeks ago, I asked him if he could help me prepare a budget and arrangements for a honeymoon trip. The best companies to use. Hotels. That kind of thing."

That tinge of worry evaporated. "To where?"

He looked away from her a moment. "Your father—" He looked at her again. "Instead, he began involving me in dozens of meetings, including some with the East India Company."

Beth froze, not quite believing her ears. "The East India Company?"

He gave a single nod. "It is . . . complicated. But the end re-sult is that I have been offered a position—"

"A job? But aristocrats do not hold jobs."

"No. Not a job, not as you might think. An advisory position. It would be a type of council position with the governor-general of Fort—"

"India? India!" Beth bounced, grabbing both his arms. "Are you saying India?"

Kit's lips tightened, but his eyes gleamed in the stark shad-ows. "There would be an initial trip, then possibly an extended residency—"

Joy flooded Beth's ever fiber. "You are taking me to India!" The euphoria spread through her and seem to burst from her head. "You are not cozening me? This is not a prank?"

He shook his head, and now the smile he had been fighting broke through. "Not a prank. But are you certain? It is not an easy journey for a woman."

"I do not care. India! With you!" A thought hit her then, and she leaned back to look at him. "She knew, did she not? My mother knew."

Kit shrugged. "Your father did. He was there when they made the offer."

Beth nodded. "Then she knew, that devil woman." But she did not care. Beth wrapped her arms around him and pressed herself tightly against his chest. "India. With you."

After a moment's hesitation, Kit sighed and returned her embrace. "Are you most excited about India? Or India with me?"

She hugged him so firmly he grunted, and Beth almost laughed. "With you, silly man."

"Excellent. Because I am definitely not going without you."

Beth looked up at him, feeling as content as a princess whose dearest dreams had come true. "I never want to be anywhere without you. Not here. Not there. Ever. To the end of my days."

The End

About Abigail Bridges

Abigail Bridges wrote her first historical romance, titled *The Belle of the Ball*, when she was thirteen. It was, of course, horrid. But it firmly established her love of all things Regency, a mild obsession with Georgette Heyer, and a determination to become a writer. After a master's degree in English and years of being paid to write and edit other types of material, she has returned to her first love. She is busily binge-reading all her favorite authors, resuming her study of the history and culture of the Regency era, and plotting like a madwoman. She does all this in a small cottage near Birmingham, Alabama.

Twitter: @AbbyBridgesAuth
Instagram: @abigailbridgesauthor